THE CORAL ISLAND

THE
CORAL ISLAND

A Tale of the Pacific Ocean

by
R. M. BALLANTYNE

ABRIDGED

PRINTED IN · GREAT BRITAIN
DEAN & SON Ltd.
52/54 Southwark St. · LONDON SE1 1U.

MADE AND PRINTED IN GREAT BRITAIN BY PURNELL AND SONS LTD.,
PAULTON (AVON) AND LONDON.

SBN 603 03023 8

PREFACE

I was a boy when I went through the wonderful adventures herein set down. With the memory of my boyish feelings strong upon me, I present my book specially to boys, in the earnest hope that they may derive valuable information, much pleasure, great profit, and unbounded amusement from its pages.

One word more. If there is any boy or man who loves to be melancholy and morose, and who cannot enter with kindly sympathy into the regions of fun, let me seriously advise him to shut my book and put it away. It is not meant for him.

RALPH ROVER

Chapter 1

Roving has always been, and still is, my ruling passion, the joy of my heart, the very sunshine of my existence. In childhood, in boyhood, and in man's estate, I have been a rover; not a mere rambler among the woody glens and upon the hill-tops of my own native land, but an enthusiastic rover throughout the length and breadth of the wide, wide world.

It was a wild, black night of howling storm, the night in which I was born on the foaming bosom of the broad Atlantic Ocean. My father was a sea-captain; my grandfather was a sea-captain; my great-grandfather had been a marine. Nobody could tell positively what occupation *his* father had followed; but my dear mother used to assert that he had been a midshipman, whose grandfather, on the mother's side, had been an admiral in the royal navy. At any rate, we knew that, as far back as our family could be traced, it had been intimately connected with the great watery waste. Indeed, this was the case on both sides of the house; for my mother always went to sea with my father on his long voyages, until he retired from his life upon the water.

Thus it was, I suppose, that I came to inherit a roving disposition, and did not rest content until my father bound me apprentice to a coasting vessel, and let me go to sea.

For some years I was happy in visiting the sea-ports, and in coasting along the shores of my native land. My Christian name was Ralph, and my comrades added to this the name of Rover, in consequence of the passion which I always evinced for travelling. Rover was not my real name, but as I never received any other I came at last to answer to it as naturally as to my proper name; and as it is not a bad one, I see no good reason why I should not introduce myself to the reader as Ralph Rover. My shipmates were kind, good-natured fellows, and they and I got on very well together. They did, indeed, very frequently make game of and banter me, but not unkindly; and I overheard them sometimes saying that Ralph Rover was a "queer, old-fashioned fellow". This, I must confess, surprised me much, and I pondered the saying long, but could come at no satisfactory conclusion as to that wherein my old-fashionedness lay. It is true I was a quiet lad, and seldom spoke except when spoken to. Moreover, I never could understand the jokes of my companions even when they were explained to me: which dullness in apprehension occasioned me much grief; however, I tried to make up for it by

5

smiling and looking pleased when I observed that they were laughing at some witticism which I had failed to detect. I was also very fond of inquiring into the nature of things and their causes, and often fell into fits of abstraction while thus engaged in my mind. But in all this I saw nothing that did not seem to be exceedingly natural, and could by no means understand why my comrades should call me "an old-fashioned fellow".

Now, while engaged in the coasting trade, I fell in with many seamen who had travelled to almost every quarter of the globe; and I freely confess that my heart glowed ardently within me as they recounted their wild adventures in foreign lands—the dreadful storms they had weathered, the appalling dangers they had escaped, the wonderful creatures they had seen both on the land and in the sea, and the interesting lands and strange people they had visited. But of all the places of which they told me, none captivated and charmed my imagination so much as the Coral Islands of the Southern Seas. They told me of thousands of beautiful fertile islands that had been formed by a small creature called the coral insect, where summer reigned nearly all the year round; where the trees were laden with a constant harvest of luxuriant fruit; where the climate was almost perpetually delightful; yet where, strange to say, men were wild, bloodthirsty savages, excepting in those favoured isles to which the gospel of our Saviour had been conveyed. These exciting accounts had so great an effect upon my mind, that, when I reached the age of fifteen, I resolved to make a voyage to the South Seas.

I had no little difficulty at first in prevailing on my dear parents to let me go; but when I urged on my father that he would never have become a great captain had he remained in the coasting trade, he saw the truth of what I said, and gave his consent. My dear mother, seeing that my father had made up his mind, no longer offered opposition to my wishes. "But oh, Ralph," she said, on the day I bade her adieu, "come back soon to us, my dear boy, for we are getting old now, Ralph, and may not have many years to live."

I will not take up my reader's time with a minute account of all that occurred before I took my final leave of my dear parents. Suffice it to say that my father placed me under the charge of an old messmate of his own, a merchant captain, who was on the point of sailing to the South Seas in his own ship, the *Arrow*. My mother gave me her blessing and a small Bible; and her last request was, that I would never forget to read a chapter every day, and say my prayers; which I promised, with tears in my eyes, that I would certainly do.

Soon afterwards I went on board the *Arrow*, which was a fine large ship, and set sail for the islands of the Pacific Ocean.

Chapter 2

It was a bright, beautiful, warm day when our ship spread her canvas to the breeze, and sailed for the regions of the south. Oh, how my heart bounded with delight as I listened to the merry chorus of the sailors, while they hauled at the ropes and got in the anchor! The captain shouted; the men ran to obey; the noble ship bent over to the breeze, and the shore gradually faded from my view, while I stood looking on with a kind of feeling that the whole was a delightful dream.

The first thing that struck me as being different from anything I had yet seen during my short career on the sea, was the hoisting of the anchor on deck, and lashing it firmly down with ropes, as if we had now bid adieu to the land for ever, and would require its services no more.

"There, lass," cried a broad-shouldered jack-tar, giving the fluke of the anchor a hearty slap with his hand after the housing was completed—"there, lass, take a good nap now, for we shan't ask you to kiss the mud again for many a long day to come!"

And so it was. That anchor did not "kiss the mud" for many long days afterwards; and when at last it did, it was for the last time!

There were a number of boys in the ship, but two of them were my special favourites. Jack Martin was a tall, strapping, broad-shouldered youth of eighteen, with a handsome, good-humoured, firm face. He had had a good education, was clever and hearty and lion-like in his actions, but mild and quiet in disposition. Jack was a general favourite, and had a peculiar fondness for me. My other companion was Peterkin Gay. He was little, quick, funny, decidedly mischievous, and about fourteen years old. But Peterkin's mischief was almost always harmless, else he could not have been so much beloved as he was.

"Hallo, youngster!" cried Jack Martin, giving me a slap on the shoulder, the day I joined the ship, "come below, and I'll show you your berth. You and I are to be messmates and I think we shall be good friends."

Jack was right. He and I and Peterkin afterwards became the best and staunchest friends that ever tossed together on the stormy waves.

I shall say little about the first part of our voyage. We had the usual amount of rough weather and calm; also we saw many strange fish rolling in the sea, and I was greatly delighted one day by seeing a shoal of flying-fish dart out of the water and skim about a foot above the surface.

When we approached Cape Horn, at the southern extremity of America, the weather became very cold and stormy, and the sailors began to tell stories about the furious gales and the dangers of that terrible cape.

"Cape Horn," said one, "is the most horrible headland I ever doubled. I've sailed round it twice already, and both times the ship was a'most blow'd out o' the water."

"An' I've been round it once," said another, "an' that time the sails were split, and the ropes frozen in the blocks, so that they wouldn't work, and we wos all but lost."

"An' I've been round it five times," cried a third, "an' every time wos wuss than another, the gales was so treemendous!"

"And I've been round it no times at all," cried Peterkin, with an impudent wink of his eye, "an' *that* time I wos blow'd inside out!"

Nevertheless, we passed the dreaded cape without much rough weather' and, in the rourse of a few weeks afterwards, were sailing gently before a warm tropical breeze over the Pacific Ocean. Thus we proceeded on our voyage, sometimes bounding merrily before a fair breeze, at other times floating calmly on the glassy wave and fishing for the curious inhabitants of the deep—all of which, although the sailors thought little of them, were strange, and interesting, and very wonderful to me.

At last we came among the Coral Islands of the Pacific, and I shall never forget the delight with which I gazed—when we chanced to pass one—at the pure, white, dazzling shores, and the verdant palm trees, which looked bright and beautiful in the sunshine. And often did we three long to be landed on one, imagining that we should certainly find perfect happiness there! Our wish was granted sooner than we expected.

One night, soon after we entered the tropics, an awful storm burst upon our ship. The first squall of wind carried away two of our masts, and left only the foremast standing. Even this, however, was more than enough, for we did not dare to hoist a rag of sail on it. For five days the tempest raged in all its fury. Everything was swept off the decks except one small boat. The steersman was lashed to the wheel, lest he should be washed away, and we all gave ourselves up for lost. The captain said that he had no idea where we were, as we had been blown far out of our course; and we feared much that we might get among the dangerous coral reefs which are so numerous in the Pacific. At daybreak on the sixth morning of the gale we saw land ahead. It was an island encircled by a reef of coral on which the waves broke in fury. There was calm water within this reef, but we could only see one narrow opening into it. For this opening we steered, but ere we reached it a tremendous wave broke on our stern, tore the rudder completely off, and left us at the mercy of the winds and waves.

"It's all over with us now, lads!" said the captain to the men. "Get the boat ready to launch; we shall be on the rocks in less than half an hour."

The men obeyed in gloomy silence, for they felt that there was little hope of so small a boat living in such a sea.

"Come, boys," said Jack Martin, in a grave tone, to me and Peterkin, as we stood on the quarter-deck awaiting our fate—"come, boys; we three shall stick together. You see it is impossible that the little boat can reach the shore, crowded with men. It will be sure to upset, so I mean rather to trust myself to a large oar. I see through the telescope that the ship will strike at the tail of the reef, where the waves break into the quiet water inside; so, if we manage to cling to the oar till it is driven over the breakers, we may perhaps gain the shore. What say you; will you join me?"

We gladly agreed to follow Jack, for he inspired us with confidence, although I could perceive, by the sad tone of his voice, that he had little hope; and indeed, when I looked at the white waves that lashed the reef and boiled against the rocks as if in fury, I felt that there was but a step between us and death. My heart sank within me; but at that moment my thoughts turned to my beloved mother, and I remembered those words, which were among the last that she said to me: "Ralph, my dearest child, always remember in the hour of danger to look to your Lord and Saviour Jesus Christ. He alone is both able and willing to save your body and your soul." So I felt much comforted when I thought thereon.

The ship was now very near the rocks. The men were ready with the boat, and the captain beside them giving orders, when a tremendous wave came towards us. We three ran towards the bow to lay hold of our oar, and had barely reached it when the wave fell on the deck with a crash like thunder. At the same moment the ship struck, the foremast broke off close to the deck and went over the side, carrying the boat and men along with it. Our oar got entangled with the wreck, and Jack seized an axe to cut it free, but, owing to the motion of the ship, he missed the cordage and struck the axe deep into the oar. Another wave, however, washed it clear of the wreck. We all seized hold of it, and the next instant we were struggling in the wild sea. The last thing I saw was the boat whirling in the surf, and all the sailors tossed into the foaming waves. Then I became insensible.

Chapter 3

On recovering from my swoon, I found myself lying on a bank of soft grass, under the shelter of an overhanging rock, with Peterkin on his knees by my side tenderly bathing my temples with water, and endeavouring to stop the blood from a wound in my forehead.

"Speak to us, my dear Ralph," whispered Jack tenderly. "Are you better now?"

I smiled and looked up, saying, "Better! why, what do you mean, Jack? I'm quite well."

"Then what are you shamming for, and frightening us in this way?" said Peterkin, smiling through his tears; for the poor boy had been really under the impression that I was dying.

I now raised myself on my elbow, and putting my hand to my forehead, found that it had been cut pretty severely, and that I had lost a good deal of blood.

"Come, come, Ralph," said Jack, pressing me gently backward, "lie down, my boy; you're not right yet. Wet your lips with this water; it's cool and clear as crystal. I got it from a spring close at hand. There now, don't say a word, hold your tongue," said he, seeing me about to speak. "I'll tell you all about it, but you must not utter a syllable till you have rested well."

"Oh! don't stop him from speaking, Jack," said Peterkin, who, now that his fears for my safety were removed, busied himself in erecting a shelter of broken branches in order to protect me from the wind; which, however, was almost unnecessary, for the rock beside which I had been laid completely broke the force of the gale. "Let him speak, Jack; it's a comfort to hear that he's alive, after lying there stiff and white and sulky for a whole hour, just like an Egyptian mummy. Never saw such a fellow as you are, Ralph; always up to mischief. You've almost knocked out all my teeth and more than half choked me, and now you go shamming death. It's very wicked of you, indeed it is."

While Peterkin ran on in this style, my faculties became quite clear again, and I began to understand my position. "What do you mean by saying I half choked you, Peterkin?" said I.

"'What do I mean? Is English not your mother-tongue, or do you want me to repeat it in French, by way of making it clearer? Don't you remember——"

"I remember nothing," said I, interrupting him, "after we were thrown into the sea."

"Hush, Peterkin," said Jack; "you're exciting Ralph with your nonsense—I'll explain it to you. You recollect that after the ship struck, we three sprang over the bow into the sea; well, I noticed that the oar struck your head and gave you that cut on the brow, which nearly stunned you, so that you grasped Peterkin round the neck without knowing apparently what you were about. In doing so you pushed the telescope—which you clung to as if it had been your life—against Peterkin's mouth——"

"Pushed it against his mouth!" interrupted Peterkin; "say crammed it down his throat. Why, there's a distinct mark of the brass rim on the back of my gullet at this moment!"

"Well, well, be that as it may," continued Jack, "you clung to him, Ralph, till I feared you really would choke him; but I saw that he had a good hold of the oar, so I exerted myself to the utmost to push you towards the shore, which we luckily reached without much trouble, for the water inside the reef is quite calm."

"But the captain and crew, what of them?" I inquired anxiously.

Jack shook his head.

"Are they lost?"

"No, they are not lost, I hope, but I fear there is not much chance of their being saved. The ship struck at the very tail of the island on which we are cast. When the boat was tossed into the sea it fortunately did not upset, although it shipped a good deal of water, and all the men managed to scramble into it; but before they could get the oars out the gale carried them past the point and away to leeward of the island. After we landed I saw them endeavouring to pull towards us; but as they had only one pair of oars out of the eight that belong to the boat, and as the wind was blowing right in their teeth, they gradually lost ground. Then I saw them put about and hoist some sort of sail—a blanket, I fancy, for it was too small for the boat—and in half an hour they were out of sight."

"Poor fellows!" I murmured sorrowfully.

"But the more I think about it, I've better hope of them," continued Jack, in a more cheerful tone. "You see, Ralph, I've read a great deal about these South Sea Islands, and I know that in many places they are scattered about in thousands over the sea, so they're almost sure to fall in with one of them before long."

"I'm sure I hope so," said Peterkin earnestly. "But what has become of the wreck, Jack? I saw you clambering up the rocks there while I was watching Ralph. Did you say she had gone to pieces?"

"No, she has not gone to pieces, but she has gone to the bottom," replied Jack. "As I said before, she struck on the tail of the island and stove in her bow, but the next breaker swung her clear, and she floated away to leeward. The poor fellows in the boat made a hard struggle to reach her, but long before they came near her she filled and went down. It was after she foundered that I saw them trying to pull to the island."

There was a long silence after Jack ceased speaking, and I have no doubt that each was revolving in his mind our extraordinary position. For my part, I cannot say that my reflections were very agreeable. I knew that we were on an island, for Jack had said so, but whether it was inhabited or not I did not know. If it should be inhabited, I felt certain, from all I had heard of South Sea Islanders, that we should be roasted alive and eaten. If it should turn out to be uninhabited, I fancied that we should be starved to death. "Oh," thought I, "if the ship had only stuck on the rocks we might have done pretty well, for we could have obtained provisions from her, and tools to enable us to build a shelter; but now—alas! we are lost!" These last words I uttered aloud in my distress.

"Lost! Ralph?" exclaimed Jack, while a smile overspread his hearty countenance. "Saved, you should have said. Your cogitations seem to have taken a wrong road, and led you to a wrong conclusion."

"Do you know what conclusion *I* have come to?" said Peterkin. "I have made up my mind that it's capital—first rate—the best thing that ever happened to us, and the most splendid prospect that ever lay before three jolly young tars. We've got an island all to ourselves. We'll take possession in the name of the king; we'll go and enter the service of its black inhabitants. Of course we'll rise, naturally, to the top of affairs. White men always do in savage countries. You shall be king, Jack; Ralph, prime minister; and I shall be——"

"The court-jester," interrupted Jack.

"No," retorted Peterkin; "I'll have no title at all. I shall merely accept a highly responsible situation under government; for you see, Jack, I'm fond of having an enormous salary and nothing to do."

"But suppose there are no natives?"

"Then we'll build a charming villa, and plant a lovely garden round it, stuck all full of the most splendiferous tropical flowers, and we'll farm the land, plant, sow, reap, eat, sleep, and be merry."

"'But to be serious," said Jack, assuming a grave expression of countenance, which I observed always had the effect of checking Peterkin's disposition to make fun of everything, "we are really in rather an uncomfortable position. If this is a desert island, we shall have to live very much like the wild beasts, for we have not a tool of any kind, not even a knife."

"Yes, we have *that*," said Peterkin, fumbling in his trousers pocket, from which he drew forth a small penknife with only one blade, and that was broken.

"Well, that's better than nothing. But come," said Jack, rising; "we are wasting our time in *talking* instead of doing. You seem well enough to walk now, Ralph. Let us see what we have got in our pockets, and then let us climb some hill and ascertain what sort of island we have been cast upon, for, whether good or bad, it seems likely to be our home for some time to come."

Chapter 4

We now seated ourselves upon a rock, and began to examine into our personal property. When we reached the shore, after being wrecked, my companions had taken off part of their clothes and spread them out in the sun to dry; for although the gale was raging fiercely, there was not a single cloud in the bright sky. They had also stripped off most part of my wet clothes and spread them also on the rocks. Having resumed our garments, we now searched all our pockets with the utmost care, and laid their contents out on a flat stone before us; and now that our minds were fully alive to our condition, it was with no little anxiety that we turned our several pockets inside out, in order that nothing might escape us. When all was collected together, we found that our worldly goods consisted of the following articles:

First, A small penknife with a single blade broken off about the middle and very rusty, besides having two or three notches on its edge. (Peterkin said of this, with his usual pleasantry, that it would do for a saw as well as a knife, which was a great advantage.) Second, An old German-silver pencil-case without any lead in it. Third, A piece of whip-cord about six yards long. Fourth, A sailmaker's needle of a small size. Fifth, A ship's telescope, which I happened to have in my hand at the time the ship struck, and which I had clung to firmly all the time I was in the water. Indeed, it was with difficulty that Jack got it out of my grasp when I was lying insensible on the shore. I cannot understand why I kept such a firm hold of this telescope. They say that a drowning man will clutch at a straw. Perhaps it may have been some such feeling in me, for I did not know that it was in my hand at the time we were wrecked. However, we felt some pleasure in having it with us now, although we did not see that it could be much use to us, as the glass at the small end was broken to pieces. Our sixth article was a brass ring which Jack always wore on his little finger. I never understood why he wore it, for Jack was not vain of his appearance, and did not seem to care for ornaments of any kind. Peterkin said "it was in memory of the girl he left behind him!" But as he never spoke of this girl to either of us, I am inclined to think that Peterkin was either jesting or mistaken. In addition to these articles we had a little bit of tinder, and the clothes on our backs. These last were as follows.

Each of us had on a pair of stout canvas trousers, and a pair of sailor's thick shoes. Jack wore a red flannel shirt, a blue jacket, and a red Kilmarnock bonnet or night-cap, besides a pair of worsted socks, and a cotton pocket handkerchief, with sixteen portraits of Lord Nelson printed on it, and a union-jack in the middle. Peterkin had on a striped flannel shirt—which he wore outside his trousers, and belted round his waist, after the manner of a tunic—and a round black straw hat. He had no jacket, having thrown it off just before we were cast into the sea; but this was not of much consequence, as the climate of the island proved to be extremely mild—so much so, indeed, that Jack and I often preferred to go about without our jackets. Peterkin had also a pair of white cotton socks, and a blue handkerchief with white spots all over it. My own costume consisted of a blue flannel shirt, a blue jacket, a black cap, and a pair of worsted socks, besides the shoes and canvas trousers already mentioned. This was all we had, and besides these things we had nothing else; but when we thought of the danger from which we had escaped, and how much worse off we might have been had the ship struck on the reef during the night, we felt very thankful that we were possessed of so much, although, I must confess, we sometimes wished that we had had a little more.

While we were examining these things and talking about them, Jack suddenly started and exclaimed——

"The oar! We have forgotten the oar."

"What good will that do us?" said Peterkin; "there's wood enough on the island to make a thousand oars."

"Ay, lad," replied Jack; "but there's a bit of hoop iron at the end of it, and that may be of much use to us."

"Very true," said I, "let us go fetch it;" and with that we all three rose and hastened down to the beach. I still felt a little weak from loss of blood, so that my companions soon began to leave me behind; but Jack perceived this, and, with his usual considerate good nature, turned back to help me. This was now the first time that I had looked well about me since landing, as the spot where I had been laid was covered with thick bushes, which almost hid the country from our view. As we now emerged from among these and walked down the sandy beach together, I cast my eyes about and truly my heart glowed within me and my spirits rose at the beautiful prospect which I beheld on every side. The gale had suddenly died away, just as if it had blown furiously till it dashed our ship upon the rocks, and had nothing more to do after accomplishing that. The island on which we stood was hilly, and covered almost everywhere with the most beautiful and richly coloured trees, bushes, and shrubs, none of which I knew the names of at that time, except, indeed, the coco-nut palms, which I recognized at once from the many pictures that I had seen of them before I left home. A sandy beach of dazzling whiteness lined this bright green shore, and upon it there fell a gentle ripple of the sea. This last astonished me much, for I recollected that at home the sea used to fall in huge billows on the shore long after a storm had subsided. But on casting my glance out to sea the cause became apparent. About a mile distant from the shore I saw the great billows of the ocean rolling like a green wall, and falling with a long, loud roar upon a low coral reef, where they were dashed into white foam and flung up in clouds of spray. This spray sometimes flew exceedingly high, and every here and there a beautiful rainbow was formed for a moment among the falling drops. We afterwards found that this coral reef extended quite round the island, and formed a natural breakwater to it. Beyond this the sea rose and tossed violently from the effects of the storm; but between the reef and the shore it was as calm and as smooth as a pond.

My heart was filled with more delight than I can express at sight of so many glorious objects, and my thoughts turned suddenly to the contemplation of the Creator of them all. I mention this the more gladly, because at that time, I am ashamed to say, I very seldom thought of my Creator, although I was constantly surrounded by the most beautiful and wonderful of His works. I observed, from the expression of my companion's countenance, that he too derived much joy from the splendid scenery, which was all the more agreeable to us after our long voyage on the salt sea. There the breeze was fresh and cold, but here it was delightfully mild, and when a puff blew off the land, it came laden with the most exquisite perfume that can be imagined. While we thus gazed, we were startled by a loud "Huzza!" from Peterkin, and on looking towards the edge of the sea, we saw him capering and jumping about like a monkey, and ever and anon tugging with all his might at something that lay upon the shore.

"What an odd fellow he is, to be sure!" said Jack, taking me by the arm and hurrying forward; "come, let us hasten to see what it is."

"Here it is, boys, hurrah! Come along. Just what we want," cried Peterkin, still tugging as we drew near. "First rate; just the very ticket!"

On coming up we found that Peterkin was vainly endeavouring to pull the axe out of the oar, into which, it will be remembered, Jack struck it while endeavouring to cut away the cordage among which it had become entangled at the bow of the ship. Fortunately for us the axe had remained fast in the oar, and even now all Peterkin's strength could not draw it out of the cut.

"Ah! that is capital indeed," cried Jack, at the same time giving the axe a wrench that plucked it out of the tough wood. "How fortunate this is! It will be of more value to us than a hundred knives, and the edge is quite new and sharp."

"I'll answer for the toughness of the handle at any rate," cried Peterkin; "my arms are nearly pulled out of the sockets. But see here, our luck is great. There is iron on the blade." He pointed to a piece of hoop iron as he spoke, which had been nailed round the blade of the oar to prevent it from splitting.

This also was a fortunate discovery. Jack went down on his knees, and with the edge of the axe began carefully to force out the nails. But as they were firmly fixed in, and the operation blunted our axe, we carried the oar up with us to the place where we had left the rest of our things, intending to burn the wood away from the iron at a more convenient time.

"No, lads," said Jack, after we had laid it on the stone which contained our little all, "I propose that we should go to the tail of the island, where the ship struck, which is only a quarter of a mile off, and see if anything else has been thrown ashore. I don't expect anything, but it is well to see. When we get back here it will be time to have our supper and prepare our beds."

"Agreed!" cried Peterkin and I together, as, indeed, we would have agreed to any proposal that Jack made, for besides his being older and much stronger and taller than either of us, he was a very clever fellow, and I think would have induced people much older than himself to choose him for their leader, especially if they required to be led on a bold enterprise.

Now, as we hastened along the white beach, which shone so brightly in the rays of the setting sun that our eyes were quite dazzled by its glare, it suddenly came into Peterkin's head that we had nothing to eat except the wild berries which grew in profusion at our feet.

"What shall we do, Jack?" said he, with a rueful look; "perhaps they may be poisonous!"

"No fear," replied Jack confidently; "I have observed that a few of them are not unlike some of the berries that grow wild on our own native hills. Besides, I saw one or two strange birds eating them just a few minutes ago, and what won't kill the birds won't kill us. But look up there, Peterkin," continued Jack, pointing to the branched head of a coco-nut palm. "There are nuts for us in all stages."

"So there are!" cried Peterkin, who, being of a very unobservant nature, had been too much taken up with other things to notice anything so high above his head as the fruit of a palm tree. But whatever faults my young comrade had, he could not be blamed for want of activity or animal spirits. Indeed, the nuts had scarcely been pointed out to him when he bounded up the tall stem of the tree like a squirrel, and in a few minutes returned with three nuts, each as large as a man's fist.

"You had better keep them till we return," said Jack. "Let us finish our work before eating."

"So be it, captain; go ahead," cried Peterkin, thrusting the nuts into his trousers pocket. "In fact, I don't want to eat just now, but I would give a good deal for a drink. Oh that I could find a spring! but I don't see the smallest sign of one hereabouts. I say, Jack, how does it happen that you seem to be up to everything? You have told us the names of half a dozen trees already, and yet you say that you were never in the South Seas before."

"I'm not up to *everything*, Peterkin, as you'll find out ere long," replied Jack, with a smile; "but I have been a great reader of books of travel and adventure all my life, and that has put me up to a good many things that you are, perhaps, not acquainted with."

"Oh, Jack, that's all humbug. If you begin to lay everything to the credit of books, I'll quite lose my opinion of you," cried Peterkin, with a look of contempt. "I've seen a lot of fellows that were *always* poring over books, and when they came to try to *do* anything, they were no better than baboons!"

"You are quite right," retorted Jack; "and I have seen a lot of fellows who never looked into books at all, who knew nothing about anything except the things they had actually seen, and very little they knew even about these. Indeed, some were so ignorant that they did not know that coco-nuts grew on coco-nut trees!"

I could not refrain from laughing at this rebuke, for there was much truth in it, as to Peterkin's ignorance.

"Humph! maybe you're right," answered Peterkin; "but I would not give *tuppence* for a man of books, if he had nothing else in him."

"Neither would I," said Jack; "but that's no reason why you should run books down, or think less of me for having read them. Suppose, now, Peterkin, that you wanted to build a ship, and I were to give you a long and particular account of the way to do it, would not that be very useful?"

"No doubt of it," said Peterkin, laughing.

"And suppose I were to write the account in a letter instead of telling you in words, would that be less useful?"

"Well—no, perhaps not."

"Well, suppose I were to print it, and send it to you in the form of a book, would it not be as good and useful as ever?"

"'Oh, bother! Jack, you're a philosopher, and that's worse than anything!" cried Peterkin, with a look of pretended horror.

"Very well, Peterkin, we shall see," returned Jack, halting under the shade of a coco-nut tree. "You said you were thirsty just a minute ago; now jump up that tree and bring down a nut—not a ripe one, bring a green, unripe one."

Peterkin looked surprised, but seeing that Jack was in earnest, he obeyed.

"Now cut a hole in it with your penknife, and clap it to your mouth, old fellow," said Jack.

Peterkin did as he was directed, and we both burst into uncontrollable laughter at the changes that instantly passed over his expressive countenance. No sooner had he put the nut to his mouth, and thrown back his head in order to catch what came out of it, than his eyes opened to twice their ordinary size with astonishment, while his throat moved vigorously in the act of swallowing. Then a smile and look of intense delight overspread his face, except, indeed, the mouth, which being firmly fixed to the hole in the nut, could not take part in the expression; but he endeavoured to make up for this by winking at us excessively with his right eye. At length he stopped, and, drawing a long breath, exclaimed:

"Nectar! perfect nectar! I say, Jack, you're a Briton—the best fellow I ever met in my life. Only taste that!" said he, turning to me and holding the nut to my mouth. I immediately drank, and certainly I was much surprised at the delightful liquid that flowed copiously down my throat. It was extremely cool, and had a sweet taste, mingled with acid; in fact, it was the likest thing to lemonade I ever tasted, and was most grateful and refreshing. I handed the nut to Jack, who, after tasting it, said, "Now, Peterkin, you unbeliever, I never saw or tasted a coco-nut in my life before, except those sold in shops at home; but I once read that the green nuts contain that stuff, and you see it is true!"

"And pray," asked Peterkin, "what sort of 'stuff' does the ripe nut contain?"

"A hollow kernel," answered Jack, "with a liquid like milk in it; but it does not satisfy thirst so well as hunger. It is very wholesome food, I believe."

"Meat and drink on the same tree!" cried Peterkin; "washing in the sea, lodging on the ground—and all for nothing! My dear boys, we're set up for life; it must be the ancient Paradise—hurrah!" and Peterkin tossed his straw hat in the air, and ran along the beach hallooing like a madman with delight.

We afterwards found, however, that these lovely islands were very unlike Paradise in many things. But more of this in its proper place.

We had now come to the point of rocks on which the ship had struck, but did not find a single article, although we searched carefully among the coral rocks, which at this place jutted out so far as nearly to join the reef that encircled the island. Just as we were about to return, however, we saw something black floating in a little cove that had escaped our observation. Running forward, we drew it from the water, and found it to be a long, thick leather boot, such as fishermen at home wear; and a few paces farther on we picked up its fellow. We at once recognized these as having belonged to our captain, for he had worn them during the whole of the storm, in order to guard his legs from the waves and spray that constantly washed over our decks. My first thought on seeing them was that our dear captain had been drowned; but Jack soon put my mind more at rest on that point, by saying that if the captain had been drowned with the boots on, he would certainly have been washed ashore along with them, and that he had no doubt whatever he had kicked them off while in the sea, that he might swim more easily.

Peterkin immediately put them on, but they were so large that, as Jack said, they would have done for boots, trousers, and vest too. I also tried them, but although I was long enough in the legs for them, they were much too large in the feet for me; so we handed them to Jack who was anxious to make me keep them; but as they fitted his large limbs and feet as if they had been made for him, I would not hear of it, so he consented at last to use them. I may remark, however, that Jack did not use them often, as they were extremely heavy.

It was beginning to grow dark when we returned to our encampment; so we put off our visit to the top of a hill till next day, and employed the light that yet remained to us in cutting down a quantity of boughs and the broad leaves of a tree of which none of us knew the name. With these we erected a sort of rustic bower, in which we meant to pass the night. There was no absolute necessity for this, because the air of our island was so genial and balmy that we could have slept quite well without any shelter; but we were so little used to sleeping in the open air, that we did not quite relish the idea of lying down without any cover over us; besides, our bower would shelter us from the night dews or rain, if any should happen to fall. Having strewed the floor with leaves and dry grass, we bethought ourselves of supper.

But it now occurred to us, for the first time, that we had no means of making a fire.

"Now, there's a fix! What shall we do?" said Peterkin, while we both turned our eyes to Jack, to whom we always looked in our difficulties. Jack seemed not a little perplexed.

"There are flints enough, no doubt, on the beach," said he, "but they are of no use at all without a steel. However, we must try." So saying, he went to the beach, and soon returned with two flints. On one of these he placed the tinder, and endeavoured to ignite it; but it was with great difficulty that a very small spark was struck out of the flints, and the tinder, being a bad, hard piece, would not catch. He then tried the bit of hoop iron, which would not strike fire at all; and after that the back of the axe with no better success. During all these trials Peterkin sat with his hands in his pockets, gazing with a most melancholy visage at our comrade, his face growing longer and more miserable at each successive failure.

"Oh dear!" he sighed; "I would not care a button for the cooking of our victuals—perhaps they don't need it—but it's so dismal to eat one's supper in the dark, and we have had such a capital day, that it's a pity to finish off in this glum style. Oh, I have it!" he cried, starting up: "the spyglass—the big glass at the end is a burning-glass!"

"You forget that we have no sun," said I.

Peterkin was silent. In his sudden recollection of the telescope he had quite overlooked the absence of the sun.

"Ah, boys, I've got it now!" exclaimed Jack, rising, and cutting a branch from a neighbouring bush, which he stripped of its leaves. "I recollect seeing this done once at home. Hand me the bit of whip-cord." With the cord and branch Jack soon formed a bow. Then he cut a piece, about three inches long, off the end of a dead branch, which he pointed at the two ends. Round this he passed the cord of the bow, and placed one end against his chest, which was protected from its point by a chip of wood; the other point he placed against the bit of tinder, and then began to saw vigorously with the bow, just as a blacksmith does with his drill while boring a hole in a piece of iron. In a few seconds the tinder began to smoke; in less than a minute it caught fire, and in less than a quarter of an hour we were drinking our lemonade and eating coco-nuts round a fire that would have roasted an entire sheep, while the smoke, flames, and sparks flew up among the broad leaves of the overhanging palm trees, and cast a warm glow upon our leafy bower.

That night the starry sky looked down through the gently rustling trees upon our slumbers, and the distant roaring of the surf upon the coral reef was our lullaby.

Chapter 5

What a joyful thing it is to awaken, on a fresh glorious morning, and find the rising sun staring into your face with dazzling brilliancy! to see the birds twittering in the bushes, and to hear the murmuring of a rill, or the soft hissing ripples as they fall upon the sea shore! At any time and in any place such sights and sounds are most charming, but more especially are they so when one awakens to them, for the first time, in a novel and romantic situation, with the soft sweet air of a tropical climate mingling with the fresh smell of the sea, and stirring the strange leaves that flutter overhead and around one, or ruffling the plumage of the stranger birds that fly inquiringly around, as if to demand what business we have to intrude on their domains. When I awoke on the morning after the shipwreck, I found myself in this most delightful condition; and as I lay on my back upon my bed of leaves, gazing up through the branches of the coco-nut trees into the clear blue sky, and watched the few fleecy clouds that passed slowly across it, my heart expanded more and more with an exulting gladness, the like of which I had never felt before. While I meditated, my thoughts again turned to the great and kind Creator of this beautiful world, as they had done on the previous day, when I first beheld the sea and the coral reef, with the mighty waves dashing over it into the calm waters of the lagoon.

While thus meditating, I naturally bethought me of my Bible, for I had faithfully kept the promise, which I gave at parting to my beloved mother, that I would read it every morning; and it was with a feeling of dismay that I remembered I had left it in the ship. I was much troubled about this. However, I consoled myself with reflecting that I could keep the second part of my promise to her—namely, that I should never omit to say my prayers. So I rose quietly, lest I should disturb my companions, who were still asleep, and stepped aside into the bushes for this purpose.

On my return I found them still slumbering, so I again lay down to think over our situation. Just at that moment I was attracted by the sight of a very small parrot, which Jack afterwards told me was called a paroquet. It was seated on a twig that overhung Peterkin's head, and I was speedily lost in admiration of its bright green plumage, which was mingled with other gay colours. While I looked I observed that the bird turned its head slowly from side to side and looked downwards, first with the one eye and then with the other. On glancing downwards I observed that Peterkin's mouth was wide open, and that this remarkable bird was looking into it. Peterkin used to say that I had not an atom of fun in my composition, and that I never could understand a joke. In regard to the latter, perhaps he was right; yet I think that, when they were explained to me, I understood jokes as well as most people: but in regard to the former he must certainly have been wrong, for this bird seemed to me to be extremely funny; and I could not help thinking that, if it should happen to faint, or slip its foot, and fall off the twig into Peterkin's mouth, he would perhaps think it funny too! Suddenly the paroquet bent down its head and uttered a loud scream in his face. This awoke him, and, with a cry of surprise, he started up, while the foolish bird flew precipitately away.

"Oh, you monster!" cried Peterkin, shaking his fist at the bird. Then he yawned, and rubbed his eyes, and asked what o'clock it was.

I smiled at this question, and answered that, as our watches were at the bottom of the sea, I could not tell, but it was a little past sunrise.

Peterkin now began to remember where we were. As he looked up into the bright sky, and snuffed the scented air, his eyes glistened with delight, and he uttered a faint "Hurrah!" and yawned again. Then he gazed slowly round till, observing the calm sea through an opening in the bushes he started suddenly up as if he had received an electric shock, uttered a vehement shout, flung off his garments, and, rushing over the white sands, plunged into the water. The cry awoke Jack, who rose on his elbow with a look of grave surprise; but this was followed by a quiet smile of intelligence on seeing Peterkin in the water. With an energy that he only gave way to in moments of excitement, Jack bounded to his feet, threw off his clothes, shook back his hair, and, with a lion-like spring, dashed over the sands and plunged into the sea with such force as quite to envelop Peterkin in a shower of spray. Jack was a remarkably good swimmer and diver, so that after his plunge we saw no sign of him for nearly a minute; after which he suddenly emerged, with a cry of joy, a good many yards out from the shore. My spirits were so much raised by seeing all this that I, too, hastily threw off my garments and endeavoured to imitate Jack's vigorous bound; but I was so awkward that my foot caught on a stump, and I fell to the ground; then I slipped on a stone while running over the sand, and nearly fell again, much to the amusement of Peterkin, who laughed heartily, and called me a "slow-coach", while Jack cried out, "Come along, Ralph, and I'll help you." However, when I got into the water I managed very well, for I was really a good swimmer, and diver too. I could not, indeed, equal Jack, who was superior to any Englishman I ever saw, but I infinitely surpassed Peterkin, who could only swim a little, and could not dive at all.

While Peterkin enjoyed himself in the shallow water and in running along the beach, Jack and I swam out into the deep water, and occasionally dived for stones. I shall never forget my surprise and delight on first beholding the bottom of the sea. As I have before stated, the water within the reef was as calm as a pond; and, as there was no wind, it was quite clear, from the surface to the bottom, so that we could see down easily even at a depth of twenty or thirty yards. When Jack and I dived in shallower water, we expected to have found sand and stones, instead of which we found ourselves in what appeared really to be an enchanted garden. The whole of the bottom of the lagoon, as we called the calm water within the reef, was covered with coral of every shape, size and hue. Some portions were formed like large mushrooms; others appeared like the brain of a man, having stalks or necks attached to them; but the most common kind was a species of branching coral, and some portions were of a lovely pale pink colour, others pure white. Among this there grew large quantities of seaweed of the richest hues imaginable, and of the most graceful forms; while innumerable fishes—blue, red, yellow, green, and striped—sported in and out amongst the flower-beds of this submarine garden, and did not appear to be at all afraid of our approaching them.

On darting to the surface for breath, after our first dive, Jack and I rose close to each other.

"Did you ever in your life, Ralph, see anything so lovely?" said Jack, as he flung the spray from his hair.

"Never," I replied. "It appears to me like fairy realms. I can scarcely believe that we are not dreaming."

"Dreaming!" cried Jack; "do you know, Ralph, I'm half tempted to think that we really are dreaming. But if so, I am resolved to make the most of it, and dream another dive; so here goes—down again, my boy!"

We took the second dive together, and kept beside each other while under water; and I was greatly surprised to find that we could keep down much longer than I ever recollect having done in our own seas at home. I believe that this was owing to the heat of the water, which was so warm that we afterwards found we could remain in it for two and three hours at a time without feeling any unpleasant effects such as we used to experience in the sea at home. When Jack reached the bottom, he grasped the coral stems, and crept along on his hands and knees, peeping under the seaweed and among the rocks. I observed him also pick up one or two large oysters, and retain them in his grasp, as if he meant to take them up with him, so

I also gathered a few. Suddenly he made a grasp at a fish with blue and yellow stripes on its back, and actually touched its tail, but did not catch it. At this he turned towards me and attempted to smile; but no sooner had he done so than he sprang like an arrow to the surface, where, on following him, I found him gasping and coughing, and spitting water from his mouth. In a few minutes he recovered, and we both turned to swim ashore.

"I declare, Ralph," said he, "that I actually tried to laugh under water."

"So I saw," I replied; "and I observed that you very nearly caught that fish by the tail. It would have done capitally for breakfast if you had."

"Breakfast enough here," said he, holding up the oysters, as we landed and ran up the beach. "Hallo, Peterkin! here you are, boy. Split open these fellows while Ralph and I put on our clothes. They'll agree with the coco-nuts excellently, I have no doubt."

Peterkin, who was already dressed, took the oysters, and opened them with the edge of our axe, exclaiming, "Now, that *is* capital! There's nothing I'm so fond of."

"Ah! that's lucky," remarked Jack. "I'll be able to keep you in good order now, Master Peterkin. You know you can't dive any better than a cat. So, sir, whenever you behave ill, you shall have no oysters for breakfast."

"I'm very glad that our prospect of breakfast is so good," said I, "for I'm very hungry."

"Here, then, stop your mouth with that, Ralph," said Peterkin, holding a large oyster to my lips. I opened my mouth and swallowed it in silence, and really it was remarkably good.

We now set ourselves earnestly about our preparations for spending the day. We had no difficulty with the fire this morning, as our burning-glass was an admirable one; and while we roasted a few oysters and ate our coco-nuts, we held a long, animated conversation about our plans for the future. What those plans were, and how we carried them into effect, the reader shall see hereafter.

Chapter 6

Our first care, after breakfast, was to place the few articles we possessed in the crevice of a rock at the farther end of a small cave which we discovered near our encampment. This cave, we hoped, might be useful to us afterwards as a store-house. Then we cut two large clubs off a species of very hard tree which grew near at hand. One of these was given to Peterkin, the other to me, and Jack armed himself with the axe. We took these precautions because we proposed to make an excursion to the top of the mountains of the interior, in order to obtain a better view of our island. Of course we knew not what dangers might befall us by the way, so thought it best to be prepared.

Having completed our arrangements and carefully extinguished our fire, we sallied forth and walked a short distance along the sea-beach, till we came to the entrance of a valley, through which flowed the rivulet before mentioned. Here we turned our backs on the sea and struck into the interior.

The prospect that burst upon our view on entering the valley was truly splendid. On either side of us there was a gentle rise in the land, which thus formed two ridges, about a mile apart on each side of the valley. These ridges—which, as well as the low grounds between them, were covered with trees and shrubs of the most luxuriant kind—continued to recede inland for about two miles, when they joined the foot of a small mountain. This hill rose rather abruptly from the head of the valley, and was likewise entirely covered even to the top with trees, except on one particular spot near the left shoulder, where was a bare and rocky place of a broken and savage character. Beyond this hill we could not see, and we therefore directed our course up the banks of the rivulets toward the foot of it, intending to climb to the top, should that be possible, as, indeed, we had no doubt it was.

Jack being the wisest and boldest among us, took the lead, carrying the axe on his shoulder. Peterkin, with his enormous club, came second, as he said he should like to be in a position to defend me if any danger should threaten. I brought up the rear, but, having been more taken up with the wonderful and curious things I saw at starting than with thoughts of possible danger, I had very foolishly left my club behind me. Although, as I have said, the trees and bushes were very luxuriant, they were not so thickly crowded together as to hinder our progress among them. We were able to

26

wind in and out, and to follow the banks of the stream quite easily, although, it is true, the height and thickness of the foliage prevented us from seeing far ahead. But sometimes a jutting-out rock on the hillsides afforded us a position whence we could enjoy the romantic view and mark our progress towards the foot of the hill. I was particularly struck, during the walk, with the richness of the undergrowth in most places, and recognized many berries and plants that resembled those of my native land, especially a tall, elegantly formed fern, which emitted an agreeable perfume. There were several kinds of flowers, too, but I did not see so many of these as I should have expected in such a climate. We also saw a great variety of small birds of bright plumage, and many paroquets similar to the one that awoke Peterkin so rudely in the morning.'

Thus we advanced to the foot of the hill, without encountering anything to alarm us, except, indeed, once, when we were passing close under a part of the hill which was hidden from our view by the broad leaves of the banana trees, which grew in great luxuriance in that part. Jack was just preparing to force his way through this thicket, when we were startled and arrested by a strange pattering or rumbling sound which appeared to us quite different from any of the sounds we had heard during the previous part of our walk.

"Hallo!" cried Peterkin, stopping short and grasping his club with both hands, "what's that?"

Neither of us replied; but Jack seized his axe in his right hand, while with the other he pushed aside the broad leaves and endeavoured to peer amongst them.

"I can see nothing," he said, after a short pause. "I think it——"

Again the rumbling sound came, louder than before, and we all sprang back and stood on the defensive. For myself, having forgotten my club, and not having taken the precaution to cut another, I buttoned my jacket, doubled my fists, and threw myself into a boxing attitude. I must say, however, that I felt somewhat uneasy; and my companions afterwards confessed that their thoughts at this moment had been instantly filled with all they had ever heard or read of wild beasts and savages, torturings at the stake, roastings alive, and such-like horrible things. Suddenly the pattering noise increased with tenfold violence. It was followed by a fearful crash among the bushes, which was rapidly repeated, as if some gigantic animal were bounding towards us. In another moment an enormous rock came crashing through the shrubbery, followed by a cloud of dust and small stones, and flew close past the spot where we stood, carrying bushes and young trees along with it.

"Pooh! is that all?" exclaimed Peterkin, wiping the perspiration off his forehead. "Why, I thought it was all the wild men and beasts in the South Sea Islands galloping on in one grand charge to sweep us off the face of the earth, instead of a mere stone tumbling down the mountainside."

"Nevertheless," remarked Jack, "if that same stone had hit any of us, it would have rendered the charge you speak of quite unnecessary, Peterkin."

This was true, and I felt very thankful for our escape. On examining the spot more narrowly, we found that it lay close to the foot of a very rugged precipice, from which stones of various sizes were always tumbling at intervals. Indeed, the numerous fragments lying scattered all around might have suggested the cause of the sound, had we not been too suddenly alarmed to think of anything.

We now resumed our journey, resolving that, in our future excursions into the interior, we would be careful to avoid this dangerous precipice.

Soon afterwards we arrived at the foot of the hill, and prepared to ascend it. Here Jack made a discovery which caused us all very great joy. This was a tree of a remarkably beautiful appearance, which Jack confidently declared to be the celebrated bread-fruit tree.

"Is it celebrated?" inquired Peterkin, with a look of great simplicity.

"It is," replied Jack.

"That's odd, now," rejoined Peterkin; "I never heard of it before."

"Then it's not so celebrated as I thought it was," returned Jack, quietly squeezing Peterkin's hat over his eyes; "but listen you ignorant boobie! and hear of it now."

Peterkin readjusted his hat, and was soon listening with as much interest as myself, while Jack told us that this tree is one of the most valuable in the islands of the south; that it bears two, sometimes three, crops of fruit in the year; that the fruit is very like wheaten bread in appearance, and that it constitutes the principal food of many of the islanders.

"So," said Peterkin, "we seem to have everything ready prepared to our hands in this wonderful island—lemonade ready bottled in nuts, and loaf-bread growing on the trees!"

Peterkin, as usual, was jesting; nevertheless it is a curious fact that he spoke almost the literal truth.

"Moreover," continued Jack, "the bread-fruit tree affords a capital gum, which serves the natives for pitching their canoes; the bark of the young branches is made by them into cloth; and of the wood, which is durable and of a good colour, they build their houses. So you see, lads, that we have no lack of material here to make us comfortable, if we are only clever enough to use it."

"But are you sure that that's it?" asked Peterkin.

"Quite sure," replied Jack; "for I was particularly interested in the account I once read of it, and I remember the description well. I am sorry, however, that I have forgotten the descriptions of many other trees which I am sure we have seen today, if we could but recognize them. So you see, Peterkin, I'm not up to everything yet."

"Never mind, Jack," said Peterkin, with a grave, patronizing expression of countenance, patting his tall companion on the shoulder—"never mind, Jack; you know a good deal for your age. You're a clever boy, sir—a promising young man; and if you only go on as you have begun, sir, you will——"

The end of this speech was suddenly cut short by Jack tripping up Peterkin's heels and tumbling him into a mass of thick shrubs, where, finding himself comfortable, he lay still, basking in the sunshine, while Jack and I examined the bread-fruit tree.

Our hearts were now very much cheered by our good fortune, and it was with light and active steps that we clambered up the steep sides of the hill. On reaching the summit, a new and if possible a grander prospect met our gaze. We found that this was not the highest part of the island, but that another hill lay beyond, with a wide valley between it and the one on which we stood. This valley, like the first, was also full of rich trees, some dark and some light green, some heavy and thick in foliage, and others light, feathery, and graceful, while the beautiful blossoms on many of them threw a sort of rainbow tint over all, and gave to the valley the appearance of a garden of flowers. Among these we recognized many of the bread-fruit trees, laden with yellow fruit; and also a great many coco-nut palms. After gazing our fill we pushed down the hillside, crossed the valley, and soon began to ascend the second mountain. It was clothed with trees nearly to the top, but the summit was bare, and in some places broken.

While on our way up we came to an object which filled us with much interest. This was the stump of a tree that had evidently been cut down with an axe! So, then, we were not the first who had viewed this beautiful isle. The hand of man had been at work there before us. It now began to recur to us again that perhaps the island was inhabited, although we had not seen any traces of man until now; but a second glance at the stump convinced us that we had not more reason to think so now than formerly; for the surface of the wood was quite decayed, and partly covered with fungus and green matter, so that it must have been cut many years ago.

"Perhaps," said Peterkin, "some ship or other has touched here long ago for wood, and only taken one tree."

We did not think this likely, however, because, in such circumstances, the crew of a ship would cut wood of small size, and near the

shore, whereas this was a large tree and stood near the top of the
mountain. In fact, it was the highest large tree on the mountain, all
above it being wood of very recent growth.

"I can't understand it," said Jack, scratching the surface of the
stump with his axe. "I can only suppose that the savages have been
here and cut it for some purpose known only to themselves. But,
hallo! what have we here?"

As he spoke, Jack began carefully to scrape away the moss and
fungus from the stump, and soon laid bare three distinct traces of
marks, as if some inscription or initials had been cut thereon. But
although the traces were distinct, beyond all doubt, the exact form of
the letters could not be made out. Jack thought they looked like J. S.,
but we could not be certain. They had apparently been carelessly cut,
and long exposure to the weather had so broken them up that we
could not make out what they were. We were exceedingly perplexed
at this discovery, and stayed a long time at the place conjecturing
what these marks could have been, but without avail; so, as the day
was advancing, we left it and quickly reached the top of the
mountain.

We found this to be the highest point of the island, and from it we
saw our kingdom lying, as it were, like a map around us. As I have
always thought it impossible to get a thing properly into one's
understanding without comprehending it, I shall beg the reader's
patience for a little while I describe our island, thus, shortly:

It consisted of two mountains: the one we guessed at 500 feet; the
other, on which we stood, at 1000; between these lay a rich beautiful
valley, as already said. This valley crossed the island from one end to
the other, being high in the middle and sloping on each side towards
the sea. The large mountain sloped, on the side farthest from where
we had been wrecked, gradually towards the sea; but although, when
viewed at a glance, it had thus a regular sloping appearance, a more
careful observation showed that it was broken up into a multitude of
very small vales, or rather dells and glens, intermingled with little
rugged spots and small but abrupt precipices here and there, with
rivulets tumbling over their edges and wandering down the slopes in
little white streams, sometimes glistening among the broad leaves of
the bread-fruit and coco-nut trees, or hiding altogether beneath the
rich underwood. At the base of this mountain lay a narrow bright
green plain or meadow, which terminated abruptly at the shore. On
the other side of the island, whence we had come, stood the smaller
hill, at the foot of which diverged three valleys; one being that which
we had ascended, with a smaller vale on each side of it, and
separated from it by the two ridges before mentioned. In these
smaller valleys there were no streams, but they were clothed with

the same luxuriant vegetation.

The diameter of the island seemed to be about ten miles, and as it was almost circular in form, its circumference must have been thirty miles—perhaps a little more, if allowance be made for the numerous bays and indentations of the shore. The entire island was belted by a beach of pure white sand, on which laved the gentle ripples of the lagoon. We now also observed that the coral reef completely encircled the island; but it varied its distance from it here and there, in some places being a mile from the beach, in others a few hundred yards, but the average distance was half a mile. The reef lay very low, and the spray of the surf broke quite over it in many places. This surf never ceased its roar, for however calm the weather might be, there is always a gentle swaying motion in the great Pacific, which, although scarce noticeable out at sea, reaches the shore at last in a huge billow.

All this we noted, and a great deal more, while we sat on the top of the mountain. After we had satisfied ourselves we prepared to return; but here again we discovered traces of the presence of man. These were a pole or staff and one or two pieces of wood which had been squared with an axe. All of these were, however, very much decayed, and they had evidently not been touched for many years.

Full of these discoveries we returned to our encampment. On the way we fell in with the traces of some four-footed animal, but whether old or of recent date none of us were able to guess. This also tended to raise our hopes of obtaining some animal food on the island, so we reached home in good spirits, quite prepared for supper, and highly satisfied with our excursion.

After much discussion, in which Peterkin took the lead, we came to the conclusion that the island was uninhabited, and went to bed.

Chapter 7

For several days after the excursion related in the last chapter we did not wander far from our encampment, but gave ourselves up to forming plans for the future and making our present abode more comfortable.

There were various causes that induced this state of comparative inaction. In the first place, although everything around us was so delightful, and we could without difficulty obtain all that we required for our bodily comfort, we did not quite like the idea of settling down here for the rest of our lives, far away from our friends and our native land. To. set energetically about preparations for a permanent residence seemed so like making up our minds to saying adieu to home and friends for ever, that we tacitly shrank from it, and put off our preparations, for one reason and another, as long as we could. Then there was a little uncertainty still as to there being natives on the island, and we entertained a kind of faint hope that a ship might come and take us off. But as day after day passed, and neither savages nor ships appeared, we gave up all hope of an early deliverance, and set diligently to work at our homestead.

During this time, however, we had not been altogether idle. We made several experiments in cooking the coco-nut, most of which did not improve it. Then we removed our goods, and took up our abode in the cave, but found the change so bad that we returned gladly to the bower. Besides this, we bathed very frequently, and talked a great deal; at least Jack and Peterkin did—I listened. Among other useful things, Jack, who was ever the most active and diligent, converted about three inches of the hoop-iron into an excellent knife. First he beat it quite flat with the axe. Then he made a rude handle, and tied the hoop-iron to it with our piece of whip-cord, and ground it to an edge on a piece of sandstone. When it was finished he used it to shape a better handle, to which he fixed it with a strip of his cotton handkerchief—in which operation he had, as Peterkin pointed out, torn off one of Lord Nelson's noses. However, the whip-cord, thus set free, was used by Peterkin as a fishing-line. He merely tied a piece of oyster to the end of it. This the fish were allowed to swallow, and then they were pulled quickly ashore. But as the line was very short and we had no boat, the fish we caught were exceedingly small.

One day Peterkin came up from the beach, where he had been angling, and said in a very cross tone, "I'll tell you what, Jack, I'm not going to be humbugged with catching such contemptible things any longer. I want you to swim out with me on your back, and let me fish in deep water!"

"Dear me, Peterkin!" replied Jack, "I had no idea you were taking the thing so much to heart, else I would have got you out of that difficulty long ago. Let me see," and Jack looked down at a piece of timber on which he had been labouring, with a peculiar gaze of abstraction, which he always assumed when trying to invent or discover anything.

"What say you to building a boat?" he inquired, looking up hastily.

"Take far too long," was the reply; "can't be bothered waiting. I want to begin at once!"

Again Jack considered. "I have it!" he cried. "We'll fell a large tree and launch the trunk of it in the water, so that when you want to fish you've nothing to do but to swim out to it."

"Would not a small raft do better?" said I.

"Much better; but we have no ropes to bind it together with. Perhaps we may find something hereafter that will do as well, but in the meantime let us try the tree."

This was agreed on, so we started off to a spot not far distant, where we knew of a tree that would suit us, which grew near the water's edge. As soon as we reached it Jack threw off his coat, and, wielding the axe with his sturdy arms, hacked and hewed at it for a quarter of an hour without stopping. Then he paused, and while he sat down to rest I continued the work. Then Peterkin made a vigorous attack on it, so that when Jack renewed his powerful blows, a few minutes' cutting brought it down with a terrible crash.

"Hurrah! now for it," cried Jack; "let us off with its head."

So saying he began to cut through the stem again, at about six yards from the thick end. This done, he cut three strong, short poles or levers from the stout branches, with which to roll the log down the beach into the sea; for, as it was nearly two feet thick at the large end, we could not move it without such helps. With the levers, however, we rolled it slowly into the sea.

Having been thus successful in launching our vessel, we next shaped the levers into rude oars or paddles, and then attempted to embark. This was easy enough to do; but after seating ourselves astride the log, it was with the utmost difficulty we kept it from rolling round and plunging us into the water. Not that we minded that much; but we preferred, if possible, to fish in dry clothes. To be sure, our trousers were necessarily wet, as our legs were dangling in the water on each side of the log; but as they could be easily dried, we did not care. After half an hour's practice, we became expert enough to keep our balance pretty steadily. Then Peterkin laid down his paddle, and having baited his line with a whole oyster, dropped it into deep water.

"Now then, Jack," said he, "be cautious; steer clear o' that seaweed. There! that's it; gently now, gently. I see a fellow at least a foot long down there, coming to—ha! that's it. Oh bother! he's off."

"Did he bite?" said Jack, urging the log onwards a little with his paddle.

"Bite? ay! He took it into his mouth, but the moment I began to haul he opened his jaws and let it out again."

"Let him swallow it next time," said Jack, laughing at the melancholy expression of Peterkin's visage.

"There he's again," cried Peterkin, his eyes flashing with excitement. "Look out! Now then! No! Yes! No! Why, the brute *won't* swallow it!"

"Try to haul him up by the mouth, then," cried Jack. "Do it gently."

A heavy sigh and a look of blank despair showed that poor Peterkin had tried and failed again.

"Never mind, lad," said Jack, in a voice of sympathy; "we'll move on, and offer it to some other fish." So saying, Jack plied his paddle; but scarcely had he moved from the spot, when a fish with an enormous head and a little body darted from under a rock and swallowed the bait at once.

"Got him this time—that's a fact!" cried Peterkin, hauling in the line. "He's swallowed the bait right down to his tail, I declare. Oh, what a thumper!"

As the fish came struggling to the surface, we leaned forward to see it, and overbalanced the log. Peterkin threw his arms round the fish's neck, and in another instant we were all floundering in the water!

A shout of laughter burst from us as we rose to the surface like three drowned rats, and seized hold of the log. We soon recovered our position, and sat more warily, while Peterkin secured the fish, which had well-nigh escaped in the midst of our struggles. It was little worth having, however; but, as Peterkin remarked, it was better than the smouts he had been catching for the last two or three days; so we laid it on the log before us, and having rebaited the line, dropped it in again for another.

Now, while we were thus intent upon our sport, our attention was suddenly attracted by a ripple on the sea, just a few yards away from us. Peterkin shouted to us to paddle in that direction, as he thought it was a big fish, and we might have a chance of catching it. But Jack, instead of complying, said, in a deep, earnest tone of voice, which I never before heard him use——

"Haul up your line, Peterkin; seize your paddle; quick—it's a shark!"

The horror with which we heard this may well be imagined, for it must be remembered that our legs were hanging down in the water, and we could not venture to pull them up without upsetting the log. Peterkin instantly hauled up the line, and grasping his paddle, exerted himself to the utmost, while we also did our best to make for shore. But we were a good way off, and the log being, as I have before said, very heavy, moved but slowly through the water. We now saw the shark quite distinctly swimming round and round us, its sharp fin every now and then protruding above the water. From its active and unsteady motions, Jack knew it was making up its mind to attack us, so he urged us vehemently to paddle for our lives, while he himself set us the example. Suddenly he shouted, "Look out! there he comes!" and in a second we saw the monstrous fish dive close under us, and turn half over on his side. But we all made a great commotion with our paddles, which no doubt frightened it away for that time, as we saw it immediately after circling round us as before.

"Throw the fish to him," cried Jack, in a quick, suppressed voice; "we'll make the shore in time yet if we can keep him off for a few minutes."

Peterkin stopped one instant to obey the command, and then plied his paddle again with all his might. No sooner had the fish fallen on the water than we observed the shark to sink. In another second we saw its white breast rising; for sharks always turn over on their sides when about to seize their prey, their mouths being not at the point of their heads like those of other fish, but, as it were, under their chins. In another moment his snout rose above the water; his wide jaws, armed with a terrific double row of teeth, appeared. The dead fish was engulfed, and the shark sank out of sight. But Jack was mistaken in supposing that it would be satisfied. In a very few minutes it returned to us, and its quick motions led us to fear that it would attack us at once.

"Stop paddling," cried Jack suddenly. "I see it coming up behind us. Now, obey my orders *quickly*. Our lives may depend on it. Ralph, Peterkin, do your best to *balance* the log. Don't look out for the shark. Don't glance behind you. Do nothing but balance the log."

Peterkin and I instantly did as we were ordered, being only too glad to do anything that afforded us a chance or a hope of escape, for we had implicit confidence in Jack's courage and wisdom. For a few seconds, that seemed long minutes to my mind, we sat thus silently; but I could not resist glancing backward, despite the orders to the contrary. On doing so, I saw Jack sitting rigid like a statue, with his paddle raised, his lips compressed, and his eyebrows bent over his eyes, which glared savagely from beneath them down into the water. I also saw the shark, to my horror, quite close under the log, in the act of darting towards Jack's foot. I could scarcely suppress a cry on beholding this. In another moment the shark rose. Jack drew his leg suddenly from the water, and threw it over the log. The monster's snout rubbed against the log as it passed, and revealed its hideous jaws, into which Jack instantly plunged the paddle, and thrust it down its throat. So violent was this act that Jack rose to his feet in performing it; the log was thereby rolled completely over, and we were once more plunged into the water. We all rose, spluttering and gasping, in a moment.

"Now, then, strike out for shore," cried Jack. "Here, Peterkin, catch hold of my collar, and kick out with a will."

Peterkin did as he was desired, and Jack struck out with such force that he cut through the water like a boat; while I, being free from all encumbrance, succeeded in keeping up with him. As we had by this time drawn pretty near to the shore, a few minutes more sufficed to carry us into shallow water; and, finally, we landed in safety, though very much exhausted, and not a little frightened by our terrible adventure.

Chapter 8

Our encounter with the shark was the first great danger that had befallen us since landing on this island, and we felt very seriously affected by it, especially when we considered that we had so often unwittingly incurred the same danger before while bathing. We were now forced to take to fishing again in the shallow water, until we should succeed in constructing a raft. What troubled us most, however, was, that we were compelled to forgo our morning swimming excursions. We did, indeed, continue to enjoy our bathe in the shallow water, but Jack and I found that one great source of our enjoyment was gone, when we could no longer dive down among the beautiful coral groves at the bottom of the lagoon. We had come to be so fond of this exercise, and to take such an interest in watching the formations of coral and the gambols of the many beautiful fish amongst the forests of red and green seaweeds, that we had become quite familiar with the appearance of the fish and the localities that they chiefly haunted. We had also become expert divers. But we made it a rule never to stay long under water at a time. Jack told me that to do so often was bad for the lungs, and, instead of affording us enjoyment, would ere long do us a serious injury.

Now all this pleasure we were to forgo, and when we thought thereon, Jack and I felt very much depressed in our spirits. I could see, also, that Peterkin grieved and sympathized with us, for when talking about this matter he refrained from jesting and bantering us upon it.

As, however, a man's difficulties usually set him upon devising methods to overcome them, whereby he often discovers better things than those he may have lost, so this our difficulty induced us to think of searching for a large pool among the rocks, where the water should be deep enough for diving, yet so surrounded by rocks as to prevent sharks from getting at us. And such a pool we afterwards found, which proved to be very much better than our most sanguine hopes anticipated. It was situated not more than ten minutes' walk from our camp, and was in the form of a small deep bay or basin, the entrance to which, besides being narrow, was so shallow that no fish so large as a shark could get in, at least not unless he should be a remarkably thin one.

Inside of this basin, which we called our Water Garden, the coral formations were much more wonderful, and the seaweed plants far more lovely and vividly coloured, than in the lagoon itself. And the water was so clear and still, that, although very deep, you could see

37

the minutest object at the bottom. Besides this, there was a ledge of rock which overhung the basin at its deepest part, from which we could dive pleasantly, and whereon Peterkin could sit and see not only all the wonders I had described to him, but also see Jack and me creeping amongst the marine shrubbery at the bottom, like—as he expressed it—"two great white sea-monsters". During these excursions of ours to the bottom of the sea, we began to get an insight into the manners and customs of its inhabitants, and to make discoveries of wonderful things, the like of which we never before conceived. Among other things, we were deeply interested with the operations of the little coral insect which, I was informed by Jack, is supposed to have entirely constructed many of the numerous islands in the Pacific Ocean. And certainly, when we considered the great reef which these insects had formed round the island on which we were cast, and observed their ceaseless activity in building their myriad cells, it did at first seem as if this might be true; but then, again, when I looked at the mountains of the island, and reflected that there were thousands of such, many of them much higher, in the South Seas, I doubted that there must be some mistake here. But more of this hereafter.

I also became much taken up with the manners and appearance of the anemones, and star-fish, and crabs, and sea-urchins, and suchlike creatures; and was not content with watching those I saw during my dives in the Water Garden, but I must needs scoop out a hole in the coral rock close to it, which I filled with salt water, and stocked with sundry specimens of anemones and shell-fish, in order to watch more closely how they were in the habit of passing their time. Our burning-glass also now became a great treasure to me, as it enabled me to magnify, and so to perceive more clearly the forms and actions of these curious creatures of the deep.

Having now got ourselves into a very comfortable condition, we began to talk of a project which we had long had in contemplation —namely, to travel entirely round the island; in order, first, to ascertain whether it contained any other productions which might be useful to us; and, second, to see whether there might be any place more convenient and suitable for our permanent residence than that on which we were now encamped. Not that we were in any degree dissatisfied with it; on the contrary, we entertained quite a home-feeling to our bower and its neighbourhood; but if a better place did exist, there was no reason why we should not make use of it. At any rate, it would be well to know of its existence.

We had much earnest talk over this matter. But Jack proposed that, before undertaking such an excursion, we should supply ourselves with good defensive arms; for as we intended not only to go round all the shore, but to ascend most of the valleys, before returning home, we should be likely to meet in with, he would not say *dangers*, but at least with everything that existed on the island, whatever that might be.

"Besides," said Jack, "it won't do for us to live on coco-nuts and oysters always. No doubt they are very excellent in their way, but I think a little animal food now and then would be agreeable as well as good for us; and as there are many small birds among the trees, some of which are probably very good to eat, I think it would be a capital plan to make bows and arrows, with which we could easily knock them over."

"First rate!" cried Peterkin. "You will make the bows, Jack, and I'll try my hand at the arrows. The fact is, I'm quite tired of throwing stones at the birds. I began the very day we landed, I think, and have persevered up to the present time, but I've never hit anything yet."

"You forget," said I, "you hit me one day on the shin."

"Ah, true," replied Peterkin, "and a precious shindy you kicked up in consequence. But you were at least four yards away from the impudent paroquet I aimed at; so you see what a horribly bad shot I am."

"But," said I, "Jack, you cannot make three bows and arrows before tomorrow, and would it not be a pity to waste time, now that we have made up our minds to go on this expedition? Suppose that you make one bow and arrow for youself, and we can take our clubs?"

"That's true, Ralph. The day is pretty far advanced, and I doubt if I can make even one bow before dark. To be sure, I might work by firelight, after the sun goes down."

We had, up to this time, been in the habit of going to bed with the sun, as we had no pressing call to work of nights; and indeed, our work during the day was usually hard enough—what between fishing, and improving our bower, and diving in the Water Garden, and rambling in the woods; so that, when night came, we were usually very glad to retire to our beds. But now that we had a desire to work at night, we felt a wish for candles.

"Won't a good blazing fire give you light enough?" inquired Peterkin.

"Yes," replied Jack, "quite enough; but then it will give us a great deal more than enough of heat in this warm climate of ours."

"True," said Peterkin, "I forgot that. It will roast us."

"Well, as you're always doing that at any rate," remarked Jack, "we could scarcely call it a change. But the fact is, I've been thinking over this subject before. There is a certain nut growing in these islands which is called the candle-nut, because the natives use it instead of candles, and I know all about it, and how to prepare it for burning——"

"Then why don't you do it?" interrupted Peterkin. "Why have you kept us in the dark so long, you vile philosopher?"

"Because," said Jack, "I have not seen the tree yet, and I'm not sure that I should know either the tree or the nuts if I did see them. I believe the nut is about the size of a walnut; and I think that the leaves are white, but I am not sure."

"Eh! ha! hum!" exclaimed Peterkin, "I saw a tree answering to that description this very day."

"Did you?" cried Jack. "Is it far from this?"

"No, not half a mile."

"Then lead me to it," said Jack, seizing his axe.

In a few minutes we were all three pushing through the under-wood of the forest, headed by Peterkin.

We soon came to the tree in question, which, after Jack had closely examined it, we concluded must be the candle-nut tree. Its leaves were of a beautiful silvery white, and formed a fine contrast to the dark-green foliage of the surrounding trees. We immediately filled our pockets with the nuts, after which Jack said——

"Now, Peterkin, climb that coco-nut tree and cut me one of the long branches."

This was soon done, but it cost some trouble, for the stem was very high, and as Peterkin usually pulled nuts from the younger trees, he was not much accustomed to climbing the high ones. The leaf or branch was a very large one, and we were surprised at its size and strength. Viewed from a little distance, the coco-nut tree seems to be a tall, straight stem, without a single branch except at the top, where there is a tuft of feathery-looking leaves, that seem to wave like soft plumes in the wind. But when we saw one of these leaves or branches at our feet, we found it to be a strong stalk, about fifteen feet long, with a number of narrow, pointed leaflets ranged alternately on each side. But what seemed to us the most wonderful thing about it was a curious substance resembling cloth, which was wrapped round the thick end of the stalk, where it had been cut from the tree. It had a seam or fibre down the centre of it, from which diverged other fibres, about the size of a bristle. There were two layers of these fibres, very long and tough, the one layer crossing the other obliquely, and the whole was cemented together with a still finer fibrous and adhesive substance. When we regarded it attentively, we could with difficulty believe that it had not been woven by human hands. This remarkable piece of cloth we stripped carefully off, and found it to be above two feet long by a foot broad, and we carried it home with us as a great prize.

Jack now took one of the leaflets, and, cutting out the central spine or stalk, hurried back with it to our camp. Having made a small fire, he baked the nuts slightly, and then peeled off the husks. After this he wished to bore a hole in them, which, not having anything better at hand at the time, he did with the point of our useless pencil-case. Then he strung them on the coco-nut spine, and on putting a light to the topmost nut, we found to our joy that it burned with a clear, beautiful flame; upon seeing which, Peterkin sprang up and danced round the fire for at least five minutes in the excess of his satisfaction.

"Now, lads," said Jack, extinguishing our candle, "the sun will set in an hour, so we have no time to lose. I shall go and cut a young tree to make my bow out of, and you had better each of you go and select good strong sticks for clubs, and we'll set to work at them after dark."

So saying he shouldered his axe and went off, followed by Peterkin, while I took up the piece of newly discovered cloth, and fell to examining its structure. So engrossed was I in this that I was still sitting in the same attitude and occupation when my companions returned.

"I told you so!" cried Peterkin, with a loud laugh. "Oh, Ralph, you're incorrigible. See, there's a club for you. I was sure, when we left you looking at that bit of stuff, that we would find you poring over it when we came back, so I just cut a club for you as well as for myself."

"Thank you, Peterkin," said I. "It was kind of you to do that, instead of scolding me for a lazy fellow, as I confess I deserve."

"Oh, as to that," returned Peterkin, "I'll blow you up yet, if you wish it; only it would be of no use if I did, for you're a perfect mule!"

As it was now getting dark we lighted our candle, and placing it in a holder made of two crossing branches, inside of our bower, we seated ourselves on our leafy beds and began to work.

"I intend to appropriate the bow for my own use," said Jack, chipping the piece of wood he had brought with his axe. "I used to be a pretty fair shot once. But what's that you're doing?" he added, looking at Peterkin, who had drawn the end of a long pole into the tent, and was endeavouring to fit a small piece of hoop-iron to the end of it.

"I'm going to enlist into the Lancers," answered Peterkin. "You see, Jack, I find the club rather an unwieldy instrument for my delicately formed muscles, and I flatter myself I shall do more execution with a spear."

"Well, if length constitutes power," said Jack, "you'll certainly be invincible."

The pole which Peterkin had cut was full twelve feet long, being a very strong but light and tough young tree, which merely required thinning at the butt to be a serviceable weapon.

"That's a very good idea," said I.

"Which—this?" inquired Peterkin, pointing to the spear.

"Yes," I replied.

"Humph!" said he; "you'd find it a pretty tough and matter-of-fact idea if you had it stuck through your gizzard, old boy!"

"I mean the idea of making it is a good one," said I, laughing. "And, now I think of it, I'll change my plan too. I don't think much of a club, so I'll make me a sling out of this piece of cloth. I used to be very fond of slinging, ever since I read of David slaying Goliath the Philistine and I was once thought to be expert at it."

While we were thus engaged, we were startled by a distant but most strange and horrible cry. It seemed to come from the sea, but was so far away that we could not clearly distinguish its precise direction. Rushing out of our bower, we hastened down to the beach and stayed to listen. Again it came quite loud and distinct on the night air, a prolonged, hideous cry, something like the braying of an ass. The moon had risen, and we could see the islands in and beyond the lagoon quite plainly, but there was no object visible to account for such a cry. A strong gust of wind was blowing from the point whence the sound came, but this died away while we were gazing out to sea.

"What can it be?" said Peterkin, in a low whisper, while we all involuntarily crept closer to each other.

"Do you know," said Jack, "I have heard that mysterious sound twice before, but never so loud as tonight. Indeed, it was so faint that I thought I must have merely fancied it, so, I did not wish to alarm you, I said nothing about it."

We listened for a long time for the sound again, but as it did not come, we returned to the bower and resumed our work.

"Very strange," said Peterkin, quite gravely. "Do you believe in ghosts, Ralph?"

"No," I answered, "I do not. Nevertheless I must confess that strange, unaccountable sounds, such as we have just heard, make me feel a little uneasy."

"What say you to it, Jack?"

"I neither believe in ghosts nor feel uneasy," he replied. "I never saw a ghost myself, and I never met with anyone who had; and I have generally found that strange and unaccountable things have almost always been accounted for, and found to be quite simple, on close examination. I certainly can't imagine what *that* sound is; but I'm quite sure I shall find out before long, and if it's a ghost

I'll—I'll——"

"Eat it," cried Peterkin.

"Yes, I'll eat it! Now, then, my bow and two arrows are finished; so if you're ready we'd better turn in."

By this time Peterkin had thinned down his spear and tied an iron point very cleverly to the end of it; I had formed a sling, the lines of which were composed of thin strips of the coco-nut cloth, plaited; and Jack had made a stout bow, nearly five feet long, with two arrows, feathered with two or three large plumes which some birds had dropped. They had no barbs, but Jack said that if arrows were well feathered they did not require iron points, but would fly quite well if merely sharpened at the point; which I did not know before.

"A feathered arrow without a barb," said he, "is a good weapon, but a barbed arrow without feathers is utterly useless."

The string of the bow was formed of our piece of whipcord, part of which, as he did not like to cut it, was rolled round the bow.

Although thus prepared for a start on the morrow, we thought it wise to exercise ourselves a little in the use of our weapons before starting, so we spent the whole of the next day in practising. And it was well we did so, for we found that our arms were very imperfect, and that we were far from perfect in the use of them. First, Jack found that the bow was much too strong, and he had to thin it. Also the spear was much too heavy, and so had to be reduced in thickness, although nothing would induce Peterkin to have it shortened. My sling answered very well, but I had fallen so much out of practice that my first stone knocked off Peterkin's hat, and narrowly missed making a second Goliath of him. However, after having spent the whole day in diligent practice, we began to find some of our former expertness returning—at least Jack and I did. As for Peterkin, being naturally a neat-handed boy, he soon handled his spear well, and could run full tilt at a coco-nut, and hit it with great precision once out of every five times.

But I feel satisfied that we owed much of our rapid success to the unflagging energy of Jack, who insisted that, since we had made him captain, we should obey him, and he kept us at work from morning till night, perseveringly, at the same thing. Peterkin wished very much to run about and stick his spear into everything he passed; but Jack put up a coco-nut, and would not let him leave off running at that for a moment, except when he wanted to rest. We laughed at Jack for this, but we were both convinced that it did us much good.

That night we examined and repaired our arms ere we lay down to rest, although we were much fatigued, in order that we might be in readiness to set out our expedition at daylight on the following morning.

Chapter 9

Scarcely had the sun shot its first ray across the bosom of the broad Pacific, when Jack sprang to his feet, and, hallooing in Peterkin's ear to awaken him, ran down the beach to take his customary dip in the sea. We did not, as was our wont, bathe that morning in our Water Garden, but, in order to save time, refreshed ourselves in the shallow water, just opposite the bower. Our breakfast was also dispatched without loss of time, and in less than an hour afterwards all our preparations for the journey were completed.

We did not consider it necessary to carry any food with us, as we knew that wherever we went we should be certain to fall in with coco-nut trees; having which, we were amply supplied, as Peterkin said, with meat and drink and pocket handkerchiefs! I took the precaution, however, to put the burning-glass into my pocket, lest we should want fire.

The morning was exceedingly lovely. It was one of that very still and peaceful sort which made the few noises that we heard seem to be *quiet* noises. I know no other way of expressing this idea. Noises which, so far from interrupting the universal tranquillity of earth, sea, and sky, rather tended to reveal to us how quiet the world around us really was. Such sounds as I refer to were the peculiarly melancholy—yet, it seemed to me, cheerful-plaint of sea-birds floating on the glassy water or sailing in the sky, also the subdued twittering of little birds among the bushes, the faint ripples in the beach, and the solemn boom of the surf upon the distant coral reef. We felt very glad as we walked along the sands side by side.

We had two ways of walking about our island. When we travelled through the woods, we always did so in single file, as by this method we advanced with greater facility, the one treading in the other's footsteps. In such cases Jack always took the lead, Peterkin followed, and I brought up the rear. But when we travelled along the sands, which extended in an unbroken line of glistening white round the island, we marched abreast, as we found this method more sociable, and every way more pleasant. Jack, being the tallest, walked next to the sea, and Peterkin marched between us, as by this arrangement either of us could talk to him or he to us, while if Jack and I happened to wish to converse together, we could conveniently do so over Peterkin's head. Peterkin used to say, in reference to this arrrangement, that had he been as tall as either of us, our order of march might have been the same; for as Jack often used to scold him for letting everything we said to him pass in at one ear and out at the other, his head could of course form no interruption to our discourse.

We were now fairly started. Half a mile's walk conveyed us round a bend in the land which shut out our bower from view, and for some time we advanced at a brisk pace without speaking, though our eyes were not idle, but noted everything, in the woods, on the shore, or in the sea, that was interesting. After passing the ridge of land that formed one side of our valley—the Valley of the Wreck—we beheld another small vale lying before us in all the luxuriant loveliness of tropical vegetation. We had, indeed, seen it before from the mountain-top, but we had no idea that it would turn out to be so much more lovely when we were close to it. We were about to commence the exploration of this valley, when Peterkin stopped us, and directed our attention to a very remarkable appearance in advance along the shore.

"What's yon, think you?" said he, levelling his spear, as if he expected an immediate attack from the object in question, though it was full half a mile distant.

As he spoke, there appeared a white column above the rocks, as if of steam of spray. It rose upwards to a height of several feet, and then disappeared. Had this been near the sea, we would not have been so greatly surprised, as it might in that case have been the surf, for at this part of the coast the coral reef approached so near to the island that in some parts it almost joined it. There were therefore no lagoon between, and the heavy surf of the ocean beat almost up to the rocks. But this white column appeared about fifty yards inland. The rocks at the place were rugged, and they stretched across the sandy beach into the sea. Scarce had we ceased expressing our surprise at this sight, when another column flew upwards for a few seconds, not far from the spot where the first had been seen, and disappeared and so, at long, irregular intervals, these strange sights recurred. We were now quite sure that the columns were watery or composed of spray, but what caused them we could not guess, so we determined to go and see.

In a few minutes we gained the spot, which was very rugged and precipitous, and, moreover, quite damp with the falling of the spray. We had much ado to pass over dry-shod. The ground also was full of holes here and there. Now, while we stood anxiously waiting for the reappearance of these waterspouts, we heard a low, rumbling sound near us, which quickly increased to a gurgling and hissing noise, and a moment afterwards a thick spout of water burst upwards from a hole in the rock, and spouted into the air with much violence, and so close to where Jack and I were standing that it nearly touched us. We sprang to one side, but not before a cloud of spray descended, and drenched us both to the skin.

Peterkin, who was standing farther off, escaped with a few drops, and burst into an uncontrollable fit of laughter on beholding our miserable plight.

'Mind your eye!" he shouted eagerly, "there goes another!" The words were scarcely out of his mouth when there came up a spout from another hole, which served us exactly in the same manner as before.

Peterkin now shrieked with laughter; but his merriment was abruptly put a stop to by the gurgling noise occurring close to where he stood.

"Where'll it spout this time, I wonder?" he said, looking about with some anxiety, and preparing to run. Suddenly there came a loud hiss or snort; a fierce spout of water burst up between Peterkin's legs, blew him off his feet, enveloped him in its spray, and hurled him to the ground. He fell with so much violence that we feared he must have broken some of his bones, and ran anxiously to his assistance but fortunately he had fallen on a clump of tangled herbage, in which he lay sprawling in a most deplorable condition.

It was now our turn to laugh; but as we were not yet quite sure that he was unhurt, and as we knew not when or where the next spout might arise, we assisted him hastily to jump up and hurry from the spot.

I may here add, that although I am quite certain that the spout of water was very strong, and that it blew Peterkin completely off his legs, I am not quite certain of the exact height to which it lifted him, being somewhat startled by the event, and blinded partially by the spray, so that my power of observation was somewhat impaired for the moment.

"What's to be done now?" inquired Peterkin ruefully.

"Make a fire, lad, and dry ourselves," replied Jack.

"And here is material ready to our hand," said I, picking up a dried branch of a tree, as we hurried up to the woods.

In about an hour after this mishap our clothes were again dried. While they were hanging up before the fire, we walked down to the beach, and soon observed that these curious spouts took place immediately after the fall of a huge wave, never before it; and, moreover, that the spouts did not take place excepting when the billow was an extremely large one. From this we concluded that there must be a subterraneous channel in the rock into which the water was driven by the larger waves, and finding no way of escape except through these small holes, was thus forced up violently through them. At any rate, we could not conceive any other reason for these strange waterspouts, and as this seemed a very simple and probable one, we forthwith adopted it.

"I say, Ralph, what's that in the water? is it a shark?" said Jack, just as we were about to quit the place.

I immediately ran to the overhanging ledge of rock, from which he was looking down into the sea, and bent over it. There I saw a very faint pale object of a greenish colour, which seemed to move slightly while I looked at it.

"It's like a fish of some sort," said I.

"Hallo, Peterkin!" cried Jack, "fetch your spear; here's work for it."

But when we tried to reach the object, the spear proved to be too short.

"There now," said Peterkin, with a sneer, "you were always telling me it was too long."

Jack now drove the spear forcibly towards the object, and let go his hold; but although it seemed to be well aimed, he must have missed, for the handle soon rose again; and when the spear was drawn up, there was the pale green object in exactly the same spot, slowly moving its tail.

"Very odd," said Jack.

But although it was undoubtedly very odd, and although Jack and all of us plunged the spear at it repeatedly, we could neither hit it nor drive it away, so we were compelled to continue our journey without discovering what it was. I was very much perplexed at this strange appearance in the water, and could not get it out of my mind for a long time afterwards. However, I quieted myself by resolving that I would pay a visit to it again at some more convenient season.

Chapter 10

Our examination of the little valley proved to be altogether most satisfactory. We found in it not only similar trees to those we had already seen in our own valley, but also one or two others of a different species. We had also the satisfaction of discovering a peculiar vegetable, which Jack concluded must certainly be that of which he had read as being very common among the South Sea islanders, and which was named *taro*. Also we found a large supply of yams, and another root like a potato in appearance. As these were all quite new to us, we regarded our lot as a most fortunate one, in being thus cast on an island which was so prolific and so well stored with all the necessaries of life. Long afterwards we found out that this island of ours was no better in these respects than thousands of other islands in those seas. Indeed, many of them were much richer and more productive; but that did not render us the less grateful for our present good fortune. We each put one of these roots in our pocket, intending to use them for our supper; of which more hereafter. We also saw many beautiful birds here, and traces of some four-footed animal again. Meanwhile the sun began to descend, so we returned to the shore, and pushed on round the spouting rocks into the next valley. This was that valley of which I have spoken as running across the entire island. It was by far the largest and most beautiful that we had yet looked upon. Here were trees of every shape and size and hue which it is possible to conceive of, many of which we had not seen in the other valleys; for, the stream in this valley being larger, and the mould richer than in the Valley of the Wreck, it was clothed with a more luxuriant growth of trees and plants. Some trees were dark glossy green, others of a rich and warm hue, contrasting well with those of a pale light green, which were everywhere abundant. Among these we recognized the broad dark heads of the bread-fruit, with its golden fruit; the pure, silvery foliage of the candle-nut, and several species which bore a strong resemblance to the pine; while here and there, in groups and in single trees, rose the tall forms of the coco-nut palms, spreading abroad, and waving their graceful plumes high above all the rest, as if they were a superior race of stately giants keeping guard over these luxuriant forests. Oh, it was a most enchanting scene, and I thanked God for having created such delightful spots for the use of man.

Now, while we were gazing around us in silent admiration, Jack uttered an exclamation of surprise, and pointing to an object a little to one side of us, said—

"That's a banyan tree."

"And what's a banyan tree?" inquired Peterkin, as we walked towards it.

"A very curious one, as you shall see presently," replied Jack. "It is called the *aoa* here, if I recollect rightly, and has a wonderful peculiarity about it. What an enormous one it is, to be sure!"

"*It!*" repeated Peterkin; "why, there are dozens of banyans here! What do you mean by talking bad grammar? Is your philosophy deserting you, Jack?"

"There is but one tree here of this kind," returned Jack, "as you will perceive if you will examine it." And, sure enough, we did find that what we had supposed was a forest of trees was in reality only one. Its bark was of a light colour, and had a shining appearance, the leaves being lance-shaped, small, and of a beautiful pea-green. But the wonderful thing about it was, that the branches, which grew out from the stem horizontally, sent down long shoots or fibres to the ground, which, taking root, had themselves become trees, and were covered with bark like the tree itself. Many of these fibres had descended from the branches at various distances, and thus supported them on natural pillars, some of which were so large and strong that it was not easy at first to distinguish the offspring from the parent stem.

Shortly after this we came upon another remarkable tree, which, as its peculiar formation afterwards proved extremely useful to us, merits description. It was a splendid chestnut, but its proper name Jack did not know. However, there were quantities of fine nuts upon it, some of which we put in our pockets. But its stem was the wonderful part of it. It rose to about twelve feet without a branch, and was not of great thickness: on the contrary, it was remarkably slender for the size of the tree; but, to make up for this, there were four or five wonderful projections in this stem, which I cannot better describe than by asking the reader to suppose that five planks of two inches thick and three feet broad had been placed round the trunk of the tree, with their *edges* closely fixed to it, from the ground up to the branches, and that these planks had been covered over with the bark of the tree and incorporated with it. In short, they were just natural buttresses without which the stem could not have supported its heavy and umbrageous top. We found these chestnuts to be very numerous. They grew chiefly on the banks of the stream, and were of all sizes.

While we were examining a small tree of this kind, Jack chipped a piece off a buttress with his axe, and found the wood to be firm and easily cut. He then struck the axe into it with all his force, and very soon split it off, close to the tree, first, however, having cut it across

transversely above and below. By this means he satisfied himself that
we could now obtain short planks, as it were all ready sawn, of any
size and thickness that we desired; which was a very great discovery
indeed, perhaps the most important we had yet made.

We now wended our way back to the coast, intending to encamp
near the beach, as we found that the mosquitoes were troublesome in
the forest. On our way we could not help admiring the birds which
flew and chirped around us. Among them we observed a pretty kind
of paroquet, with a green body, a blue head, and a red breast; also a
few beautiful turtle-doves, and several flocks of wood-pigeons. The
hues of many of these birds were extremely vivid-bright green, blue,
and scarlet being the prevailing tints. We made several attempts
throughout the day to bring down one of these, both with the bow
and the sling—not for mere sport, but to ascertain whether they
were good for food. But we invariably missed, although once or
twice we were very near hitting. As evening drew on, however, a
flock of pigeons flew past. I slung a stone into the midst of them at a
venture, and had the good fortune to kill one. We were startled,
soon after, by a loud whistling noise above our heads; and on looking
up, saw a flock of wild ducks making for the coast. We watched
these, and observing where they alighted, followed them up until we
came upon a most lovely blue lake, not more than two hundred
yards long.

Now, as we neared the shore, Jack and I said we would go a little
out of our way to see if we could procure one of those ducks; so,
directing Peterkin to go straight to the shore and kindle a fire, we
separated, promising to rejoin him speedily. But we did not find the
ducks, although we made a diligent search for half an hour. We were
about to retrace our steps, when we were arrested by one of the
strangest sights that we had yet beheld.

Just in front of us, at the distance of about ten yards, grew a
superb tree, which certainly was the largest we had yet seen on the
island. Its trunk was at least five feet in diameter, with a smooth grey
bark; above this the spreading branches were clothed with light
green leaves, amid which were clusters of bright yellow fruit, so
numerous as to weigh down the boughs with their great weight. This
fruit seemed to be of the plum species, of an oblong form, and a
good deal larger than the magnum bonum plum. The ground at the
foot of this tree was thickly strewn with the fallen fruit, in the midst
of which lay sleeping, in every possible attitude, at least twenty hogs
of all ages and sizes, apparently quite surfeited with a recent
banquet.

Jack and I could scarce restrain our laughter as we gazed at these
coarse, fat ill-looking animals while they lay groaning and snoring

heavily amid the remains of their supper.

"Now, Ralph," said Jack, in a low whisper, "put a stone in your sling—a good big one—and let fly at that fat fellow with his back toward you. I'll try to put an arrow into yon little pig."

"Don't you think we had better put them up first?" I whispered; "it seems cruels to kill them while asleep."

"If I wanted *sport*, Ralph, I would certainly set them up; but as we only want *pork*, we'll let them lie. Besides, we're not sure of killing them; so, fire away."

Thus admonished, I slung my stone with so good aim that it went bang against the hog's flank as if against the head of a drum; but it had no other effect than that of causing the animal to start to its feet, with a frightful yell of surprise, and scamper away. At the same instant Jack's bow twanged, and the arrow pinned the little pig to the ground by the ear.

"I've missed, after all," cried Jack, darting forward with uplifted axe, while the little pig uttered a loud squeal, tore the arrow from the ground, and ran away with it, along with the whole drove, into the bushes and disappeared, though we heard them screaming long afterwards in the distance.

"That's very provoking, now," said Jack, rubbing the point of his nose.

"Very," I replied, stroking my chin.

"Well, we must make haste and rejoin Peterkin," said Jack. "It's getting late." And without further remark we threaded our way quickly through the woods towards the shore.

When we reached it, we found wood laid out, the fire lighted and beginning to kindle up, with other signs of preparation for our encampment, but Peterkin was nowhere to be found. We wondered very much at this; but Jack suggested that he might have gone to fetch water; so he gave a shout to let him know that we had arrived, and sat down upon a rock, while I threw off my jacket, and seized the axe, intending to split up one or two billets of wood. But I had scarce moved from the spot when, in the distance, we heard a most appalling shriek, which was followed up by a chorus of yells from the hogs, and a loud hurrah.

"I do believe," said I, "that Peterkin has met with the hogs."

"When Greek meets Greek," said Jack, soliloquizing, "then comes the tug of——"

"Hurrah!" shouted Peterkin in the distance.

We turned hastily towards the direction whence the sound came, and soon descried Peterkin walking along the beach towards us with a little pig transfixed on the end of his long spear!

"Well done, my boy!" exclaimed Jack, slapping him on the

shoulder when he came up; "you're the best shot amongst us."

"Look here, Jack!" cried Peterkin, as he disengaged the animal from his spear. "Do you recognise that hole?" said he, pointing to the pig's ear; "and are you familiar with this arrow, eh?"

"Well, I declare!" said Jack.

"Of course you do," interrupted Peterkin; "but, pray, restrain your declarations at this time, and let's have supper, for I'm uncommonly hungry, I can tell you; and it's no joke to charge a whole herd of swine with their great-grandmother bristling like a giant porcupine at the head of them!"

We now set about preparing supper; and, truly, a good display of viands we made, when all was laid out on a flat rock in the light of the blazing fire. There was, first of all, the little pig; then there was the taro-root, and the yam, and the potato, and six plums; and, lastly, the wood-pigeon. To these Peterkin added a bit of sugar-cane, which he had cut from a little patch of that plant which he had found not long after separating from us; "and," said he, "the patch was somewhat in a square form, which convinces me it must have been planted by man."

"Very likely," replied Jack. "From all we have seen, I'm inclined to think that some of the savages must have dwelt here long ago."

We found no small difficulty in making up our minds how we were to cook the pig. None of us had ever cut up one before, and we did not know exactly how to begin; besides, we had nothing but the axe to do it with, our knife having been forgotten. At last Jack started up and said——

"Don't let us waste more time talking about it, boys. Hold it up, Peterkin. There, lay the hind leg on this block of wood—so;" and he cut it off, with a large portion of the haunch, at a single blow of the axe. "Now the other—that's it." And having thus cut off the two hind legs, he made several deep gashes in them, thrust a sharp-pointed stick through each, and stuck them up before the blaze to roast. The wood-pigeon was then split open, quite flat, washed clean in salt water, and treated in a similar manner. While these were cooking, we scraped a hole in the sand and ashes under the fire, into which we put our vegetables, and covered them up. This was decidedly the most luxurious supper we had enjoyed for many a day; and Jack said it was out-of-sight better than we ever got on board ship; and Peterkin said he feared that if we should remain long on the island he would infallibly become a glutton or an epicure; whereat Jack remarked that he need not fear that, for he was *both* already! And so, having eaten our fill, not forgetting to finish off with a plum, we laid ourselves comfortably down to sleep upon a couch of branches, under the overhang of a coral rock.

Chapter 11

When we awoke on the following morning, we found that the sun was already a good way above the horizon, so I came to the conclusion that a heavy supper is not conducive to early rising. Nevertheless, we felt remarkably strong and well, and much disposed to have our breakfast. First, however, we had our customary morning bathe, which refreshed us greatly.

We had not advanced on our journey much above a mile or so, and were just beginning to feel the pleasant glow that usually accompanies vigorous exercise, when, on turning a point that revealed to us a new and beautiful cluster of islands, we were suddenly arrested by the appalling cry which had so alarmed us a few nights before. But this time we were by no means so much alarmed as on the previous occasion, because whereas at that time it was night, now it was day; and I have always found, though I am unable to account for it, that daylight banishes many of the fears that are apt to assail us in the dark.

On hearing the sound, Peterkin hastily threw forward his spear.

"Now, what can it be?" said he, looking round at Jack. "I tell you what it is: if we are to go on being pulled up in a constant state of horror and astonishment, as we have been for the last week, the sooner we're out o' this island the better, notwithstanding the yams and lemonade, and pork and plums!"

Peterkin's remark was followed by a repetition of the cry, louder than before.

"It comes from one of these islands," said Jack.

"It must be the ghost of a jackass, then," said Peterkin, "for I never heard anything so like."

We all turned our eyes towards the cluster of islands, where, on the largest, we observed curious objects moving on the shore.

"Soldiers they are—that's flat!" cried Peterkin, gazing at them in the utmost amazement.

And, in truth, Peterkin's remark seemed to me to be correct; for, at the distance from which we saw them, they appeared to be an army of soldiers. There they stood, rank and file, in lines and in squares, marching and countermarching, with blue coats and white trousers. While we were looking at them, the dreadful cry came again over the water, and Peterkin suggested that it must be a regiment sent out to massacre the natives in cold blood. At this remark Jack laughed and said,

53

"Why, Peterkin, they are penguins!"

"Penguins?" repeated Peterkin.

"Ay, penguins, Peterkin, penguins—nothing more or less than big seabirds, as you shall see one of these days, when we pay them a visit in our boat, which I mean to set about building the moment we return to our bower."

"So, then, our dreadful yelling ghosts and our murdering army of soldiers," remarked Peterkin, "have dwindled down to penguins —big seabirds! Very good. Then I propose that we continue our journey as fast as possible, lest our island should be converted into a dream before we get completely round it."

Now, as we continued on our way, I pondered much over this new discovery, and the singular appearance of these birds, of which Jack could only give us a very slight and vague account; and I began to long to commence at our boat, in order that we might go and inspect them more narrowly. But by degrees these thoughts left me, and I began to be much taken up again with the interesting peculiarities of the country which we were passing through.

The second night we passed in a manner somewhat similar to the first, at about two-thirds of the way round the island, as we calculated, and we hoped to sleep on the night following at our bower. I will not here note so particularly all that we said and saw during the course of this second day, as we did not make any further discoveries of great importance. The shore along which we travelled, and the various parts of the woods through which we passed, were similar to those which have been already treated of.

We found several more droves of hogs in the woods, but abstained from killing any of them, having more than sufficient for our present necessities. We saw also many of their footprints in this neighbourhood. Among these we also observed the footprints of a smaller animal, which we examined with much care, but could form no certain opinion as to them. Peterkin thought they were those of a little dog, but Jack and I thought differently. We became very curious on this matter, the more so that we observed these footprints to lie scattered about in one locality, as if the animal which had made them was wandering round about in a very irregular manner, and without any object in view. Early in the forenoon of our third day we observed these footprints to be much more numerous than ever, and in one particular spot they diverged off into the woods in a regular beaten track, which was, however, so closely beset with bushes that we pushed through it with difficulty. We had now become so anxious to find out what animal this was and where it went to, that we determined to follow the track, and, if possible, clear up the mystery. Peterkin said, in a bantering tone, that he was sure it would be cleared up as usual, in some frightfully simple way, and prove to be no mystery at all!

The beaten track seemed much too large to have been formed by the animal itself, and we concluded that some larger animal had made it, and that the smaller one made use of it. But everywhere the creeping plants and tangled bushes crossed our path, so that we forced our way along with some difficulty. Suddenly, as we came upon an open space, we heard a faint cry, and observed a black animal standing in the track before us.

"A wild-cat!" cried Jack, fitting an arrow to his bow, and discharging it so hastily that he missed the animal, and hit the earth about half a foot to one side of it. To our surprise the wild-cat did not fly, but walked slowly towards the arrow, and snuffed at it.

"That's the most comical wild-cat I ever saw!" cried Jack.

"It's a tame wild-cat, I think," said Peterkin, levelling his spear to make a charge.

"Stop!" cried I, laying my hand on his shoulder; "I do believe the poor beast is blind. See, it strikes against the branches as it walks along. It must be a very old one;" and I hastened towards it.

"Only think," said Peterkin, with a suppressed laugh, "of a superannuated wild-cat!"

We now found that the poor cat was not only blind, or nearly so, but extremely deaf, as it did not hear our footsteps until we were quite close behind it. Then it sprang round, and putting up its back and tail, while the black hair stood all on end, uttered a hoarse mew and a fuff.

"Poor thing!" said Peterkin, gently extending his hand, and endeavouring to pat the cat's head. "Poor pussy; chee, chee, chee; puss, puss, puss; cheetie pussy!"

No sooner did the cat hear these sounds than all signs of anger fled, and advancing eagerly to Peterkin, it allowed itself to be stroked, and rubbed itself against his legs, purring loudly all the time, and showing every symptom of the most extreme delight.

"It's no more a wild-cat than I am!" cried Peterkin, taking it in his arms; "it's quite tame. Poor pussy, cheetie pussy!"

We now crowded around Peterkin, and were not a little surprised, and, to say truth, a good deal affected, by the sight of the poor animal's excessive joy. It rubbed its head against Peterkin's cheek, licked his chin, and thrust its head almost violently into his neck, while it purred more loudly than I ever heard a cat purr before, and appeared to be so much overpowered by its feelings, that it occasionally mewed and purred almost in the same breath. Such demonstrations of joy and affection led us at once to conclude that this poor cat must have known man before, and we conjectured that it had either been left accidentally or by design on the island many years ago, and was now evincing its extreme joy at meeting once more with human beings. While we were fondling the cat and talking about it, Jack glanced round the open space in which we stood.

"Hallo!" exclaimed he; "this looks something like a clearing. The axe has been at work here. Just look at these tree-stumps."

We now turned to examine these, and without doubt we found trees that had been cut down here and there, also stumps and broken branches; all of which, however, were completely covered over with moss, and bore evidence of having been in this condition for some years. No human footprints were to be seen either on the track or among the bushes, but those of the cat were found everywhere. We now determined to follow up the track as far as it went, and Peterkin put the cat down; but it seemed to be so weak, and mewed so very pitifully, that he took it up again and carried it in his arms, where in a few minutes it fell sound asleep.

About ten yards farther on, the felled trees became more numerous, and the track, diverging to the right, followed for a short space the banks of a stream. Suddenly we came to a spot where once must have been a rude bridge, the stones of which were scattered in the stream, and those on each bank entirely covered over with moss. In silent surprise and expectancy we continued to advance, and, a few yards farther on, beheld, under the shelter of some bread-fruit trees, a small hut or cottage. I cannot hope to convey to my readers a very correct idea of the feelings that affected us on witnessing this unexpected sight. We stood for a long time in silent wonder, for there was a deep and most melancholy stillness about the place that quite overpowered us; and when we did at length speak, it was in subdued whispers, as if we were surrounded by some awful or supernatural influence. Even Peterkin's voice, usually so quick and lively on all occasions, was hushed now; for there was a dreariness about this silent, lonely, uninhabited cottage—so strange in its appearance, so far away from the usual dwellings of man, so old, decayed, and deserted in its aspect—that fell upon our spirits like a thick cloud, and blotted out as with a pall the cheerful sunshine that had filled us since the commencement of our tour round the island.

The hut or cottage was rude and simple in its construction. It was not more than twelve feet long by ten feet broad, and about seven or eight feet high. It had one window, or rather a small frame in which a window might perhaps once have been, but which was now empty. The door was exceedingly low, and formed of rough boards and the roof was covered with broad coco-nut and plantain leaves. But every part of it was in a state of the utmost decay. Moss and green matter grew in spots all over it. The woodwork was quite perforated with holes; the roof had nearly fallen in, and appeared to be prevented from doing so altogether by the thick matting of creeping plants and the interlaced branches which years of neglect had allowed to cover it almost entirely; while the thick, luxuriant branches of the bread-fruit and other trees spread above it, and flung a deep, sombre shadow over the spot, as if to guard it from the heat and the light of day. We conversed long and in whispers about this strange habitation ere we ventured to approach it; and when at length we did so, it was, at least on my part, with feelings of awe.

At first Jack endeavoured to peep in at the window, but from the deep shadow of the trees already mentioned, and the gloom within, he could not clearly discern objects; so we lifted the latch and pushed open the door. We observed that the latch was made of iron, and almost eaten away with rust. In the like condition were also the hinges, which creaked as the door swung back. On entering, we stood still and gazed around us, while we were much impressed with the dreary stillness of the room. But what we saw there surprised and shocked us not a little. There was no furniture in the apartment save a little wooden stool and an iron pot, the latter almost eaten through with rust. In the corner farthest from the door was a low bedstead, on which lay two skeletons, embedded in a little heap of dry dust. With beating hearts we went forward to examine them. One was the skeleton of a man, the other that of a dog, which was extended close beside that of the man, with its head resting on his bosom.

Now we were very much concerned about this discovery, and could scarce refrain from tears on beholding these sad remains. After some time, we began to talk about what we had seen, and to examine in and around the hut, in order to discover some clue to the name or history of this poor man, who had thus died in solitude, with none to mourn his loss save his cat and his faithful dog. But we found nothing—neither a book nor a scrap of paper. We found, however, the decayed remnants of what appeared to have been clothing, and an old axe. But none of these things bore marks of any kind; and, indeed, they were so much decayed as to convince us that they had lain in the condition in which we found them for many years.

This discovery now accounted to us for the tree-stump at the top of the mountain with the initials cut on it; also for the patch of sugar-cane and other traces of man which we had met with in the course of our rambles over the island. And we were much saddened by the reflection that the lot of this poor wanderer might possibly be our own, after many years' residence on the island, unless we should be rescued by the visit of some vessel or the arrival of natives. Having no clue whatever to account for the presence of this poor human being in such a lonely spot, we fell to conjecturing what could have brought him there. I was inclined to think that he must have been a shipwrecked sailor, whose vessel had been lost here, and all the crew been drowned except himself and his dog and cat. But Jack thought it more likely that he had run away from his vessel and had taken the dog and cat to keep him company.

While we were thinking on these things, and examining into everything about the room, we were attracted by an exclamation from Peterkin.

"I say, Jack," said he, "here is something that will be of use to us."

"What is it?" said Jack, hastening across the room.

"An old pistol," replied Peterkin, holding up the weapon, which he had just pulled from under a heap of broken wood and rubbish that lay in a corner.

"That, indeed, might have been useful," said Jack, examining it, "if we had any powder; but I suspect the bow and the sling will prove more serviceable."

"True, I forgot that," said Peterkin; "but we may as well take it with us, for the flint will serve to strike fire with when the sun does not shine."

After having spent more than an hour at this place without discovering anything of further interest, Peterkin took up the old cat, which had lain very contentedly asleep on the stool whereon he had placed it, and we prepared to take our departure. In leaving the hut, Jack stumbled heavily against the door-post, which was so much decayed as to break across, and the whole fabric of the hut seemed ready to tumble about our ears. This put into our heads that we might as well pull it down, and so form a mound over the skeleton. Jack, therefore, with his axe, cut down the other door-post, which, when it was done, brought the whole hut in ruins to the ground, and thus formed a grave to the bones of the poor recluse and his dog. Then we left the spot, having brought away the iron pot, the pistol and the old axe, as they might be of much use to us hereafter.

During the rest of this day we pursued our journey, and examined the other end of the large valley, which we found to be so much alike to the parts already described, that I shall not recount the particulars of what we saw in this place. I may, however, remark that we did not quite recover our former cheerful spirits until we arrived at our bower, which we did late in the evening, and found everything just in the same condition as we had left it three days before.

Chapter 12

We stood much in need of rest on our return home, and we found it exceedingly sweet when we indulged in it after completing the journey just related. It had not, indeed, been a very long journey, nevertheless we had pursued it so diligently that our frames were not a little prostrated. Our minds were also very much exhausted in consequence of the many surprises, frequent alarms, and much profound thought to which they had been subjected; so that when we lay down on the night of our return under the shelter of the bower, we fell immediately into very deep repose. I can state this with much certainty, for Jack afterwards admitted the fact, and Peterkin, although he stoutly denied it, I heard snoring loudly at least two minutes after lying down. In this condition we remained all night and the whole of the following day without awakening once, or so much as moving our positions. When we did awake it was near sunset, and we were all in such a state of lassitude that we merely rose to swallow a mouthful of food. As Peterkin remarked, in the midst of a yawn, we took breakfast at tea-time, and then went to bed again, where we lay till the following forenoon.

After this we arose very greatly refreshed, but much alarmed lest we had lost count of a day. I say we were much alarmed on this head, for we had carefully kept count of the days since we were cast upon our island, in order that we might remember the Sabbath-day, which day we had hitherto with one accord kept as a day of rest, and refrained from all work whatsoever. However, on considering the subject, we all three entertained the same opinion as to how long we had slept, and so our minds were put at ease.

We now hastened to our Water Garden to enjoy a bathe, and to see how did the animals which I had placed in the tank. We found the garden more charming, pellucid, and inviting than ever, and Jack and I plunged into its depth and gambolled among its radiant coral groves, while Peterkin wallowed at the surface, and tried occasionally to kick us as we passed below. Having dressed, I then hastened to the tank, but what was my surprise and grief to find nearly all the animals dead, and the water in a putrid condition! I was greatly distressed at this, and wondered what could be the cause of it.

"Why, you precious humbug," said Peterkin, coming up to me, "how could you expect it to be otherwise? When fishes are accustomed to live in the Pacific Ocean, how can you expect them to exist in a hole like that?"

"Indeed, Peterkin," I replied, "there seems to be truth in what you say. Nevertheless, now I think of it, there must be some error in your reasoning; for if I put in but a few very small animals, they will bear the same proportion to this pond that the millions of fish bear to the ocean."

"I say, Jack," cried Peterkin, waving his hand, "come here, like a good fellow. Ralph is actually talking philosophy. Do come to our assistance, for he's out o' sight beyond me already!"

"What's the matter?" inquired Jack, coming up, while he endeavoured to scrub his long hair dry with a towel of coco-nut cloth.

I repeated my thoughts to Jack, who, I was happy to find, quite agreed with me. "Your best plan," he said, "will be to put very few animals at first into your tank, and add more as you find it will bear them. And look here," he added, pointing to the sides of the tank, which for the space of two inches above the water-level, were incrusted with salt, "you must carry your philosophy a little farther, Ralph. That water has evaporated so much that it is too salt for anything to live in. You will require to add *fresh* water now and then, in order to keep it at the same degree of saltness as the sea."

"Very true, Jack; that never struck me before," said I.

"And, now I think of it," continued Jack, "it seems to me that the surest way of arranging your tank so as to get it to keep pure and in good condition, will be to *imitate* the ocean in it. In fact, make it a miniature Pacific. I don't see how you can hope to succeed unless you do that."

"Most true," said I, pondering what my companion said. "But I fear that that will be very difficult."

"Not at all," said Jack, rolling his towel up into a ball and throwing it into the face of Peterkin, who had been grinning and winking at him during the last five minutes—"not at all. Look here. There is water of a certain saltness in the sea; well, fill your tank with sea-water, and keep it at that saltness by marking the height at which the water stands on the sides. When it evaporates a little, pour in *fresh* water from the brook till it comes up to the mark, and then it will be right, for the salt does not evaporate with the water. Then there's lots of sea-weed in the sea; well, go and get one or two bits of sea-weed, and put them into your tank. Of course the weed must be alive, and growing to little stones; or you can chip a bit off the rocks with the weed sticking to it. Then, if you like, you can throw a little sand and gravel into your tank, and the thing's complete."

Now I considered well the advice which Jack had given me about preparing my tank, and the more I thought of it the more I came to regard it as very sound and worthy of being acted on. So I forthwith put his plan in execution, and found it to answer excellently well, indeed much beyond my expectation.

For many days after this, while Peterkin and Jack were busily employed in building a little boat out of the curious natural planks of the chestnut tree, I spent much of my time in examining with the burning-glass the marvellous operations that were constantly going on in my tank.

Chapter 13

"Come, Jack," cried Peterkin, one morning about three weeks after our return from our long excursion, "let's be jolly today, and do something vigorous. I'm quite tired of hammering and bammering, hewing and screwing, cutting and butting, at that little boat of ours, that seems as hard to build as Noah's ark. Let us go on an excursion to the mountain-top, or have a hunt after the wild ducks, or make a dash at the pigs. I'm quite flat—flat as bad ginger-beer—flat as a pancake; in fact, I want something to rouse me, to toss me up, as it were. Eh! what do you say to it?"

"Well," answered Jack, throwing down the axe with which he was just about to proceed towards the boat, "if that's what you want, I would recommend you to make an excursion to the waterspouts. The last one we had to do with tossed you up a considerable height; perhaps the next will send you higher, who knows, if you're at all reasonable or moderate in your expectations!"

"Jack, my dear boy," said Peterkin gravely, "you are really becoming too fond of jesting. It's a thing I don't at all approve of, and if you don't give it up, I fear that, for our mutual good, we shall have to part."

"Well, then, Peterkin," replied Jack, with a smile, "what would you have?"

"Have?" said Peterkin; "I would *have* nothing. I didn't say I wanted to *have*; I said that I wanted to *do*."

"By the by," said I, interrupting their conversation, "I am reminded by this that we have not yet discovered the nature of yon curious appearance that we saw near the waterspouts, on our journey round the island. Perhaps it would be well to go for that purpose."

"Humph!" ejaculated Peterkin, "I know the nature of it well enough."

"What was it?" said I.

"It was of a *mysterious* nature to be sure?" said he, with a wave of his hand, while he rose from the log on which he had been sitting and buckled on his belt, into which he thrust his enormous club.

"Well, then, let us away to the waterspouts," cried Jack, going up to the bower for his bow and arrows; "and bring your spear, Peterkin. It may be useful."

We now, having made up our minds to examine into this matter, sallied forth eagerly in the direction of the waterspout rocks, which, as I have before mentioned, were not far from our present place of abode. On arriving there we hastened down to the edge of the rocks and gazed over into the sea, where we observed the pale-green object still distinctly visible, moving its tail slowly to and fro in the water.

"Most remarkable!" said Jack.

"Exceedingly curious!" said I.

"Beats everything!" said Peterkin.

"Now, Jack," he added, "you made such a poor figure in your last attempt to stick that object, that I would advise you to let me try it. If it has got a heart at all, I'll engage to send my spear right through the core of it; if it hasn't got a heart, I'll send it through the spot where its heart ought to be."

"Fire away then, my boy," replied Jack with a laugh.

Peterkin immediately took the spear, poised it for a second or two above his head, then darted it like an arrow into the sea. Down it went straight into the centre of the green object, passed quite through it, and came up immediately afterwards, pure and unsullied, while the mysterious tail moved quietly as before!

"Now," said Peterkin gravely, "that brute is a heartless monster; I'll have nothing more to do with it."

"I'm pretty sure now," said Jack, "that it is merely a phosphoric light; but I must say I'm puzzled at its staying always in that exact spot."

I also was much puzzled, and inclined to think with Jack that it must be phosphoric light, of which luminous appearance we had seen much while on our voyage to these seas. "But," said I, "there is nothing to hinder us from diving down to it, now that we are sure it is not a shark."

"True," returned Jack, stripping off his clothes; "I'll go down, Ralph, as I'm better at diving than you are.—Now then, Peterkin, out o' the road!" Jack stepped forward, joined his hands above his head, bent over the rocks, and plunged into the sea. For a second or two the spray caused by his dive hid him from view; then the water became still, and we saw him swimming far down in the midst of the green object. Suddenly he sank below it, and vanished altogether from our sight! We gazed anxiously down at the spot where he had disappeared for nearly a minute, expecting every moment to see him rise again for breath; but fully a minute passed, and still he did not reappear. Two minutes passed! and then a flood of alarm rushed in upon my soul, when I considered that, during all my acquaintance with him, Jack had never stayed under water more than a minute at a time; indeed, seldom so long.

"Oh, Peterkin!" I said, in a voice that trembled with increasing anxiety, "something has happened. It is more than three minutes now." But Peterkin did not answer, and I observed that he was gazing down into the water with a look of intense fear mingled with anxiety, while his face was overspread with a deadly paleness. Suddenly he sprang to his feet and rushed about in a frantic state, wringing his hands, and exclaiming, "Oh, Jack, Jack! he is gone! It must have been a shark, and he is gone for ever!"

For the next five minutes I know not what I did; intensity of my feelings almost bereft me of my senses. But I was recalled to myself by Peterkin seizing me by the shoulder and staring wildly into my face, while he exclaimed, "Ralph! Ralph! perhaps he has only fainted. Dive for him, Ralph!"

It seemed strange that this did not occur to me sooner. In a moment I rushed to the edge of the rocks, and, without waiting to throw off my garments, was on the point to spring into the waves when I observed something black rising up through the green object. In another moment Jack's head rose to the surface, and he gave a wild shout, flinging back the spray from his locks, as was his wont after a dive. Now we were almost as much amazed at seeing him reappear, well and strong, as we had been at first at his non-appearance; for, to the best of our judgement, he had been nearly ten minutes under water, perhaps longer, and it required no exertion of our reason to convince us that this was utterly impossible for mortal man to do and retain his strength and faculties. It was therefore with a feeling akin to superstitious awe that I held down my hand and assisted him to clamber up the steep rocks. But no such feeling affected Peterkin. No sooner did Jack gain the rocks and seat himself on one, panting for breath, than he threw his arms round his neck and burst into a flood of tears. "Oh, Jack, Jack!" said he, "where were you? What kept you so long?"

"Now, lads," said Jack, when we were composed enough to listen to him, "yon green object is not a shark; it is a stream of light issuing from a cave in the rocks. Just after I made my dive, I observed that this light came from the side of the rock above which we are now sitting; so I struck out for it, and saw an opening into some place or other that appeared to be luminous within. For one instant I paused to think whether I ought to venture. Then I made up my mind, and dashed into it. For you see, Peterkin, although I take some time to tell this, it happened in the space of a few seconds, so that I knew I had wind enough in me to serve to bring me out o' the hole and up to the surface again. Well, I was just on the point of turning—for I began to feel a little uncomfortable in such a place—when it seemed to me as if there was a faint light right above me. I darted upwards, and found my head out of water. This relieved me greatly, for I now felt that I could take in air enough to enable me to return the way I came. Then it all at once occurred to me that I might not be able to find the way out again; but on glancing downwards, my mind was put quite at rest by seeing the green light below me streaming into the cave, just like the light that we had seen streaming out of it, only what I now saw was much brighter.

"At first I could scarcely see anything as I gazed around me, it was so dark; but gradually my eyes became accustomed to it, and I found that I was in a huge cave, part of the walls of which I observed on each side of me. The ceiling just above me was also visible, and I fancied that I could perceive beautiful glittering objects there; but the farther end of the cave was shrouded in darkness. While I was looking around me in great wonder, it came into my head that you two would think I was drowned; so I plunged down through the passage again in a great hurry, rose to the surface, and—here I am!"

When Jack concluded his recital of what he had seen in this remarkable cave, I could not rest satisfied till I had dived down to see it; which I did, but found it so dark, as Jack had said, that I could scarcely see anything. When I returned, we had a long conversation about it, during which I observed that Peterkin had a most lugubrious expression on his countenance.

"What's the matter, Peterkin?" said I.

"The matter?" he replied. "It's all very well for you two to be talking away like mermaids about the wonders of this cave but you know I must be content to hear about it, while you are enjoying yourselves down there like mad dolphins. It's really too bad."

"I'm very sorry for you, Peterkin, indeed I am," said Jack, "but we cannot help you. If you would only learn to dive——".

"Learn to fly, you might as well say!" retorted Peterkin in a very sulky tone.

"If you would only consent to keep still," said I, "we would take you down with us in ten seconds."

"Hum?" returned Peterkin; "suppose a salamander was to propose to you 'only to keep still', and he would carry you through a blazing fire in a few seconds, what would you say?"

We both laughed and shook our heads, for it was evident that nothing was to be made of Peterkin in the water. But we could not rest satisfied till we had seen more of this cave; so, after further consultation, Jack and I determined to try if we could take down a torch with us, and set fire to it in the cavern. This we found to be an undertaking of no small difficulty, but we accomplished it at last by the following means: First, we made a torch of a very inflammable nature out of the bark of a certain tree, which we cut into strips, and, after twisting, cemented together with a kind of resin or gum, which we also obtained from another tree; neither of which trees, however, was known by name to Jack. This, when prepared, we wrapped up in a great number of plies of coco-nut cloth, so that we were confident it could not get wet during the short time it should be under water. Then we took a small piece of the tinder, which we had carefully treasured up lest we should require it, as before said, when the sun should fail us; also, we rolled up some dry grass and a few chips, which, with a little bow and drill like those described before, we made into another bundle, and wrapped it up in coco-nut cloth. When all was ready we laid aside our garments, with the exception of our trousers, which, as we did not know what rough scraping against the rocks we might be subjected to, we kept on.

Then we advanced to the edge of the rocks, Jack carrying one bundle with the torch, I the other, with the things for producing fire.

"Now don't weary for us, Peterkin, should we be gone some time," said Jack; "we'll be sure to return in half an hour at the very latest, however interesting the cave should be, that we may relieve your mind."

"Farewell!" said Peterkin, coming up to us with a look of deep but pretended solemnity, while he shook hands and kissed each of us on the cheek. "Farewell! and while you are gone I shall repose my weary limbs under the shelter of this bush, and meditate on the changefulness of all things earthly, with special reference to the forsaken condition of a poor shipwrecked sailor boy!" So saying, Peterkin waved his hand, turned from us, and cast himself upon the ground with a look of melancholy resignation, which was so well feigned that I would have thought it genuine had he not accompanied it with a gentle wink. We both laughed, and, springing from the rocks together, plunged head first into the sea.

We gained the interior of the submarine cave without difficulty, and, on emerging from the waves, supported ourselves for some time by treading water, while we held the two bundles above our heads. This we did in order to let our eyes become accustomed to the obscurity. Then, when we could see sufficiently, we swam to a shelving rock, and landed in safety. Having wrung the water from our trousers, and dried ourselves as well as we could under the circumstances, we proceeded to ignite the torch. This we accomplished without difficulty in a few minutes; and no sooner did it flare up than we were struck dumb with the wonderful objects that were revealed to our gaze. The roof of the cavern just above us seemed to be about ten feet high, but grew higher as it receded into the distance, until it was lost in darkness. It seemed to be made of coral, and was supported by massive columns of the same material. Immense icicles (as they appeared to us) hung from it in various places. These, however, were formed, not of ice, but of a species of limestone, which seemed to flow in a liquid form towards the point of each, where it became solid. A good many drops fell, however, to the rock below, and these formed little cones, which rose to meet the points above. Some of them had already met, and thus we saw how the pillars were formed, which at first seemed to us as if they had been placed there by some human architect to support the roof. As we advanced farther in, we saw that the floor was composed of the same material as the pillars; and it presented the curious appearance of ripples, such as are formed on water when gently ruffled by the wind. There were several openings on either hand in the walls, that seemed to lead into other caverns; but these we did not explore at this time. We also observed that the ceiling was curiously marked in many places, as if it were fretwork of a noble cathedral; and the walls, as well as the roof, sparkled in the light of our torch, and threw back gleams and flashes, as if they were covered with precious stones. Although we proceeded far into this cavern, we did not come to the end of it; and we were obliged to return more speedily than we would otherwise have done, as our torch was nearly expended. We did not observe any openings in the roof, or any indications of places whereby light might enter; but near the entrance to the cavern stood an immense mass of pure white coral rock, which caught and threw back the little light that found an entrance through the cave's mouth, and thus produced, we conjectured, the pale-green object which had first attracted our attention. We concluded, also, that the reflecting power of this rock was that which gave forth the dim light that faintly illumined the first part of the cave.

Before diving through the passage again we extinguished the small piece of our torch that remained, and left it in a dry spot; conceiving that we might possible stand in need of it, if at any future time we should chance to wet our torch while diving into the cavern. As we stood for a few minutes after it was out, waiting till our eyes became accustomed to the gloom, we could not help remarking the deep, intense stillness and the unutterable gloom of all around us; and, as I thought of the stupendous dome above, and the countless gems that had sparkled in the torchlight a few minutes before, it came into my mind to consider how strange it is that God should make such wonderful and exquisitely beautiful works never to be seen at all, except, indeed, by chance visitors such as ourselves.

I afterwards found that there were many such caverns among the islands of the South Seas, some of them larger and more beautiful than the one I have just described.

"Now, Ralph, are you ready?" said Jack, in a low voice, that seemed to echo up into the dome above.

"Quite ready."

"Come along, then," said he; and plunging off the ledge of the rock into the water, we dived through the narrow entrance. In a few seconds we were panting on the rocks above, and receiving the congratulations of our friend Peterkin.

Chapter 14

For many days after this Jack applied himself with unremitting assiduity to the construction of our boat, which at length began to look somewhat like one. But those only who have had the thing to do can entertain a right idea of the difficulty involved in such an undertaking, with no other implements than an axe, a bit of hoop-iron, a sailneedle, and a broken penknife. But Jack did it. He was of that disposition which *will* not be conquered. When he believed himself to be acting rightly, he overcame all obstacles. I have seen Jack, when doubtful whether what he was about to do were right or wrong, as timid and vacillating as a little girl; and I honour him for it!

As this boat was a curiosity in its way, a few words here relative to the manner of its construction may not be amiss.

I have already mentioned the chestnut tree with its wonderful buttresses or planks. This tree, then, furnished us with the chief part of our material. First of all, Jack sought out a limb of a tree of such a form and size as, while it should form the keel, a bend at either end should form the stem and stern posts. Such a piece, however, was not easy to obtain; but at last he procured it, by rooting up a small tree which had a branch growing at the proper angle about ten feet up its stem, with two strong roots growing in such a form as enabled him to make a flat-sterned boat. This placed, he procured three branching roots of suitable size, which he fitted to the keel at equal distances, thus forming three strong ribs. Now the squaring and shaping of these, and the cutting of the grooves in the keel, was an easy enough matter, as it was all work for the axe, in the use of which Jack had become wonderfully expert; but it was quite a different affair when he came to nailing the ribs to the keel, for we had no instrument capable of boring a large hole, and no nails to fasten them with. We were, indeed, much perplexed here; but Jack at length devised an instrument that served very well. He took the remainder of our hoop-iron and beat it into the form of a pipe or cylinder, about as thick as a man's finger. This he did by means of our axe and the old rusty axe we had found at the house of the poor man at the other side of the island. This, when made red hot, bored slowly through the timbers; and, the better to retain the heat, Jack shut up one end of it and filled it with sand. True, the work was very slowly done, but it mattered not, we had little else to do. Two holes were bored in each timber, about an inch and a half apart, and also down into the keel, but not quite through. Into these were placed stout pegs made of a tree called iron-wood; and, when they were hammered well home, the timbers were as firmly fixed as if they had been nailed with iron. The gunwales, which were very stout, were fixed in a similar manner. But, besides the wooden nails, they were firmly lashed to the stem and stern posts and ribs by means of a species of cordage which we had contrived to make out of the fibrous husk of the coco-nut. This husk was very tough, and when a number of the threads were joined together they formed excellent cordage. At first we tied the different lengths together; but this was such a clumsy and awkward complication of knots that we contrived, by careful interlacing of the ends together before twisting, to make good cordage of any size or length we chose. Of course it cost us much time and infinite labour, but Jack kept up our spirits when we grew weary, and so all that we required was at last constructed.

Planks were now cut off the chestnut trees of about an inch thick. These were dressed with the axe—but clumsily, for an axe is ill adapted for such work. Five of these planks on each side were sufficient; and we formed the boat in a very rounded, barrel-like shape, in order to have as little twisting of the planks as possible, for although we could easily bend them, we could not easily twist them. Having no nails to rivet the planks with, we threw aside the ordinary fashion of boat-building and adopted one of our own. The planks were therefore placed on each other's edges, and sewed together with the tough cordage already mentioned. They were also thus sewed to the stem, the stern, and the keel. Each stitch or tie was six inches apart, and was formed thus: Three holes were bored in the upper plank and three in the lower—the holes being above each other, that is, in a vertical line. Through these holes the cord was passed, and, when tied, formed a powerful stitch of three-ply. Besides this, we placed between the edges of the planks layers of coco-nut fibre, which, as it swelled when wetted, would, we hoped, make our little vessel water-tight. But in order further to secure this end, we collected a large quantity of pitch from the bread-fruit tree, with which, when boiled in our old iron pot, we payed the whole of the inside of the boat, and, while it was yet hot, placed large pieces of coco-nut cloth on it, and then gave it another coat above that. Thus the interior was covered with a tough water-tight material; while the exterior, being uncovered and so exposed to the swelling action of the water, was, we hoped, likely to keep the boat quite dry.

While Jack was thus engaged, Peterkin and I sometimes assisted him; but as our assistance was not much required, we more frequently went a hunting on the extensive mudflats at the entrance of the long valley which lay nearest to our bower. Here we found large flocks of ducks of various kinds, some of them bearing so much resemblance to the wild ducks of our own country that I think they must have been the same. On these occasions we took the bow and the sling, with both of which we were often successful, though I must confess I was the least so. Our suppers were thus pleasantly varied, and sometimes we had such a profusion spread out before us that we frequently knew not with which of the dainties to begin.

I must also add that the poor old cat which we had brought home had always a liberal share of our good things, and so well was it looked after, especially by Peterkin, that it recovered much of its former strength, and seemed to improve in sight as well as hearing.

The large flat stone, or rock of coral, which stood just in front of the entrance to our bower, was our table. On this rock we had spread out the few articles we possessed the day we were shipwrecked; and on the same rock during many a day afterwards, we spread out the bountiful supply with which we had been blessed on our Coral Island. Sometimes we sat down at this table to a feast consisting of hot rolls—as Peterkin called the newly baked bread-fruit—a roast pig, roast duck, boiled and roasted yams, coco-nuts, taro, and sweet potatoes; which we followed up with a dessert of plums, apples, and plantains—the last being a large-sized and delightful fruit, which grew on a large shrub or tree not more than twelve feet high, with light-green leaves of enormous length and breadth. These luxurious feasts were usually washed down with coco-nut lemonade.

Occasionally Peterkin tried to devise some new dish—"a conglomerate", as he used to say; but these generally turned out such atrocious compounds that he was ultimately induced to give up his attempts in extreme disgust—not forgetting, however, to point out to Jack that his failure was a direct contradiction to the proverb which he, Jack, was constantly thrusting down his throat—namely, that "where there's a will there's a way". For he had a great will to become a cook, but could by no means find a way to accomplish that end.

One day, while Peterkin and I were seated beside our table on which dinner was spread, Jack came up from the beach, and, flinging down his axe, exclaimed—

"There, lads, the boat's finished at last! so we've nothing to do now but shape two pair of oars, and then we may put to sea as soon as we like."

This piece of news threw us into a state of great joy; for although we were aware that the boat had been gradually getting near its completion, it had taken so long that we did not expect it to be quite ready for at least two or three weeks. But Jack had wrought hard and said nothing, in order to surprise us.

"My dear fellow," cried Peterkin, "you're a perfect trump. But why did you not tell us it was so nearly ready? Won't we have a jolly sail tomorrow, eh?"

"Don't talk so much, Peterkin," said Jack; "and, pray, hand me a bit of that pig."

"Certainly, my dear," cried Peterkin, seizing the axe. "What part will you have? a leg, or a wing, or a piece of the breast—which?"

"A hind leg, if you please," answered Jack; "and, pray, be so good as to include the tail."

"With all my heart," said Peterkin, exchanging the axe for his hoop-iron knife, with which he cut off the desired portion. "I'm only too glad, my dear boy, to see that your appetite is so wholesale, and there's no chance whatever of its dwindling down into re-tail again, at least in so far as this pig is concerned. Ralph, lad, why don't you laugh, eh?" he added, turning suddenly to me with a severe look of inquiry.

"Laugh!" said I; "what at, Peterkin? Why should I laugh?"

Both Jack and Peterkin answered this inquiry by themselves laughing so immoderately that I was induced to believe I had missed noticing some good joke, so I begged that it might be explained to me; but as this only produced repeated roars of laughter, I smiled and helped myself to another slice of plantain.

"Well, but," continued Peterkin, "I was talking of a sail tomorrow. Can't we have one, Jack?"

"No," replied Jack, "we can't have a sail, but I hope we shall have a row, as I intend to work hard at the oars this afternoon, and, if we can't get them finished by sunset, we'll light our candle-nuts, and turn them out of hands before we turn into bed."

"Very good," said Peterkin, tossing a lump of pork to the cat, who received it with a mew of satisfaction. "I'll help you, if I can."

"Afterwards," continued Jack, "we will make a sail out of the coco-nut cloth, and rig up a mast, and then we shall be able to sail to some of the other islands, and visit our old friends the penguins."

The prospect of being so soon in a position to extend our observations to the other islands and enjoy a sail over the beautiful sea afforded us much delight, and after dinner we set about making the oars in good earnest. Jack went into the woods and blocked them roughly out with the axe, and I smoothed them down with the knife, while Peterkin remained in the bower spinning, or rather twisting, some strong thick cordage with which to fasten them to the boat.

We worked hard and rapidly, so that when the sun went down Jack and I returned to the bower with four stout oars, which required little to be done to them save a slight degree of polishing with the knife.

After supper we retired to rest and to dream of wonderful adventures in our little boat and distant voyages upon the sea.

Chapter 15

It was a bright, clear, beautiful morning, when we first launched our little boat and rowed out upon the placid waters of the lagoon. Not a breath of wind ruffled the surface of the deep. Not a cloud spotted the deep blue sky. Not a sound that was discordant broke the stillness of the morning, although there were many sounds, sweet, tiny, and melodious, that mingled in the universal harmony of nature. The sun was just rising from the Pacific's ample bosom and tipping the mountain-tops with a red glow. The sea was shining like a sheet of glass yet heaving with the long deep swell that, all the world round, indicates the life of ocean; and the bright sea-weeds and the brilliant corals shone in the depths of that pellucid water, as we rowed over it, like rare and precious gems. Oh! it was a sight fitted to stir the soul of man to its profoundest depths, and, if he owned a heart at all, to lift that heart in adoration and gratitude to the great Creator of this magnificent and glorious universe.

At first, in the strength of our delight, we rowed hither and thither without aim or object. But after the effervescence of our spirits was abated, we began to look about us and to consider what we should do.

"I vote that we row to the reef," cried Peterkin.

"And I vote that we visit the islands within the lagoon," said I.

"And I vote we do both," cried Jack; "so pull away, boys."

As I have already said, we had made four oars, but our boat was so small that only two were necessary. The extra pair were reserved in case any accident should happen to the others. It was therefore only needful that two of us should row, while the third steered, by means of an oar, and relieved the rowers occasionally.

First we landed on one of the small islands and ran all over it, but saw nothing worthy of particular notice. Then we landed on a larger island, on which were growing a few coco-nut trees. Not having eaten anything that morning, we gathered a few of the nuts and breakfasted. After this we pulled straight out to sea and landed on the coral reef.

This was indeed a novel and interesting sight to us. We had now been so long on shore that we had almost forgotten the appearance of breakers, for there were none within the lagoon; but now, as we stood beside the foam created billow of the open sea, all the enthusiasm of the sailor was awakened in our breasts, and as we gazed on the widerspread ruin of that single magnificent breaker that burst in thunder at our feet, we forgot the Coral Island behind us; we forgot our bower and the calm repose of the scented woods, we forgot all that had passed during the last few months, and remembered nothing but the storms, the calms, the fresh breezes, and the surging billows of the open sea.

This huge, ceaseless breaker, to which I have so often alluded, was a much larger and more sublime object than we had at all imagined it to be. It rose many yards above the level of the sea, and could be seen approaching at some distance from the reef. Slowly and majestically it came on, acquiring greater volume and velocity as it advanced, until it assumed the form of a clear watery arch, which sparkled in the bright sun. On it came with resistless and solemn majesty—the upper edge lipped gently over, and it fell with a roar that seemed as though the heart of Ocean were broken in the crash of tumultuous water, while the foam-clad coral reef appeared to tremble beneath the mighty shock!

Again at this time Jack and I pondered the formation of the large coral islands. We could now understand how the low ones were formed; but the larger islands cost us much consideration, yet we could arrive at no certain conclusion on the subject.

Having satisfied our curiosity and enjoyed ourselves during the whole day, in our little boat, we returned, somewhat wearied, and, withal, rather hungry, to our bower.

"Now," said Jack, "as our boat answers so well, we will get a mast and sail made immediately."

"So we will," cried Peterkin, as we all assisted to drag the boat above high-water mark; "we'll light our candle and set about it this very night. Hurrah, my boys, pull away!"

As we dragged our boat, we observed that she grated heavily on her keel, and as the sands were in this place mingled with broken coral rocks, we saw portions of the wood being scraped off.

"Hallo!" cried Jack, on seeing this; "that won't do. Our keel will be worn off in no time at this rate."

"So it will," said I, pondering deeply as to how this might be prevented. But I am not of a mechanical turn naturally, so I could conceive no remedy save that of putting a plate of iron on the keel; but as we had no iron, I knew not what was to be done. "It seems to me, Jack," I added, "that it is impossible to prevent the keel being worn off thus."

"Impossible!" cried Peterkin. "My dear Ralph, you are mistaken; there is nothing so easy."

"How?" I inquired, in some surprise.

"Why, by not using the boat at all!" replied Peterkin.

"Hold your impudent tongue, Peterkin," said Jack, as he

shouldered the oars; "come along with me and I'll give you work to do. In the first place, you will go and collect coco-nut fibre, and set to work to make sewing twine with it——"

"Please, captain," interrupted Peterkin, "I've got lots of it made already—more than enough, as a little friend of mine used to be in the habit of saying every day after dinner."

"Very well," continued Jack, "then you'll help Ralph to collect coco-nut cloth, and cut it into shape, after which we'll make a sail of it. I'll see to getting the mast and the gearing; so let's to work."

And to work we went right busily, so that in three days from that time we had set up a mast and sail, with the necessary rigging, in our little boat. The sail was not, indeed, very handsome to look at, as it was formed of a number of oblong patches of cloth; but we had sewed it well by means of our sail needle, so that it was strong, which was the chief point. Jack had also overcome the difficulty about the keel, by pinning to it a *false* keel. This was a piece of tough wood, of the same length and width as the real keel, and about five inches deep. He made it of this depth because the boat would be thereby rendered not only much more safe, but more able to beat against the wind, which, in a sea where the trade-winds blow so long and so steadily in one direction, was a matter of great importance. This piece of wood was pegged very firmly to the keel; and we now launched our boat with the satisfaction of knowing that when the false keel should be scraped off we could easily put on another; whereas, should the real keel have been scraped away, we could not have renewed it without taking our boat to pieces, which Peterkin said made his "marrow quake to think upon".

The mast and sail answered excellently, and we now sailed about in the lagoon with great delight, and examined with much interest the appearance of our island from a distance. Also, we gazed into the depths of the water, and watched for hours the gambols of the curious and brightcoloured fish among the corals and sea-weed. Peterkin also made a fishing-line, and Jack constructed a number of hooks, some of which were very good, others remarkably bad. Some of these hooks were made of iron-wood, which did pretty well, the wood being extremely hard, and Jack made them very thick and large. Fish there are not particular. Some of the crooked bones in fish-heads also answered for this purpose pretty well. But that which formed our best and most serviceable hook was the brass finger-ring belonging to Jack. It gave him not a little trouble to manufacture it. First he cut it with the axe, then twisted it into the form of a hook. The barb took him several hours to cut. He did it by means of constant sawing with the broken pen-knife. As for the point, an hour's rubbing on a piece of sandstone made an excellent one.

During these delightful fishing and boating excursions we caught a good many eels which we found to be very good to eat. We also found turtles among the coral rocks, and made excellent soup in our iron kettle. Moreover, we discovered many shrimps and prawns, so that we had no lack of variety in our food; and, indeed, we never passed a week without making some new and interesting discovery of some sort or other, either on the land or in the sea.

Chapter 16

One day, not long after our little boat was finished, we were sitting on the rocks at Spouting Cliff, and talking of an excursion which we intended to make to Penguin Island the next day.

"You see," said Peterkin, "it might be all very well for a stupid fellow like me to remain here and leave the penguins alone, but it would be quite inconsistent with your character as philosophers to remain any longer in ignorance of the habits and customs of these birds, so the sooner we go the better."

"Very true," said I; "there is nothing I desire so much as to have a closer inspection of them."

"And I think," said Jack, "that you had better remain at home, Peterkin, to take care of the cat; for I'm sure the hogs will be at it in your absence, out of revenge for your killing their great-grandmother so recklessly."

"Stay at home!" cried Peterkin. "My dear fellow, you would certainly lose your way, or get upset, if I were not there to take care of you."

"Ah, true," said Jack gravely; "that did not occur to me; no doubt you must go. Our boat does require a good deal of ballast; and all that you say, Peterkin, carries so much weight with it, that we won't need stones if you go."

Now, while my companions were talking, a notable event occurred, which, as it is not generally known, I shall be particular in recording here.

While we were talking, as I have said, we noticed a dark line, like a low cloud or fog-bank, on the seaward horizon. The day was a fine one, though cloudy, and a gentle breeze was blowing, but the sea was not rougher or the breaker on the reef higher than usual. At first we thought that this looked like a thunder-cloud, and as we had had a good deal of broken weather of late, accompanied by occasional peals of thunder, we supposed that a storm must be approaching. Gradually, however, this line seemed to draw nearer without spreading up over the sky, as would certainly have been the case if it had been a storm-cloud. Still nearer it came, and soon we saw that it was moving swiftly towards the island; but there was no sound till it reached the islands out at sea. As it passed these islands, we observed, with no little anxiety, that a cloud of white foam encircled them, and burst in spray into the air; it was accompanied by a loud roar. This led us to conjecture that the approaching object was an

78

enormous wave of the sea; but we had no idea how large it was till it came near to ourselves. When it approached the outer reef, however, we were awestruck with its unusual magnitude; and we sprang to our feet, and clambered hastily up to the highest point of the precipice, under an indefinable feeling of fear.

I have said before that the reef opposite Spouting Cliff was very near to the shore, while, just in front of the bower, it was at a considerable distance out to sea. Owing to this formation, the wave reached the reef at the latter point before it struck at the foot of Spouting Cliff. The instant it touched the reef we became aware, for the first time, of its awful magnitude. It burst completely over the reef at all points, with a roar that seemed louder to me than thunder; and this roar continued for some seconds, while the wave rolled gradually along towards the cliff on which we stood. As its crest reared before us, we felt that we were in great danger, and turned to flee; but we were too late. With a crash that seemed to shake the solid rocks the gigantic billow fell, and instantly the spouting holes sent up a gush of waterspouts with such force that they shrieked on issuing from their narrow vents. It seemed to us as if the earth had been blown up with water. We were stunned and confused by the shock, and so drenched and blinded with spray, that we knew not for a few moments whither to flee for shelter. At length we all three gained an eminence beyond the reach of the water; but what a scene of devastation met our gaze as we looked along the shore! This enormous wave not only burst over the reef, but continued its way across the lagoon, and fell on the sandy beach of the island with such force that it passed completely over it and dashed into the woods, levelling the smaller trees and bushes in its headlong course.

On seeing this, Jack said he feared our bower must have been swept away, and that the boat, which was on the beach, must have been utterly destroyed. Our hearts sank within us as we thought of this, and we hastened round through the woods towards our home. On reaching it we found, to our great relief of mind, that the force of the wave had been expended just before reaching the bower; but the entrance to it was almost blocked up by the torn-up bushes and tangled heaps of sea-weed. Having satisfied ourselves as to the bower, we hurried to the spot were the boat had been left; but no boat was there. The spot on which it had stood was vacant, and no sign of it could we see on looking around us.

"It may have been washed up into the woods," said Jack, hurrying up the beach as he spoke. Still no boat was to be seen, and we were about to give ourselves over to despair, when Peterkin called to Jack and said—

"Jack, my friend, you were once so exceedingly sagacious and wise as to make me acquainted with the fact that coco-nuts grow upon trees; will you now be so good as to inform me what sort of fruit that is growing on the top of yonder bush? for I confess to being ignorant, or, at least, doubtful on the point."

We looked towards the bush indicated, and there, to our surprise, beheld our little boat snugly nestled among the leaves. We were very much overjoyed at this, for we would have suffered any loss rather than the loss of our boat. We found that the wave had actually borne the boat on its crest from the beach into the woods, and there launched it into the heart of this bush; which was extremely fortunate, for had it been tossed against a rock or a tree, it would have been dashed to pieces, whereas it had not received the smallest injury. It was no easy matter, however, to get it out of the bush and down to the sea again. This cost us two days of hard labour to accomplish.

We had also much ado to clear away the rubbish from the bower, and spent nearly a week in constant labour ere we got the neighbourhood to look as clean and orderly as before; for the uprooted bushes and sea-weed that lay on the beach formed a more dreadfully confused-looking mass than one who had not seen the place after the inundation could conceive.

After we had got our home put to rights and cleared of the debris of the inundation, we again turned our thoughts to paying the penguins a visit. The boat was therefore overhauled and a few repairs done. Then we prepared a supply of provisions, for we intended to be absent at least a night or two, perhaps longer. This took us some time to do, for while Jack was busy with the boat, Peterkin was sent into the woods to spear a hog or two, and had to search long, sometimes, ere he found them. Peterkin was usually sent on this errand when he wanted a pork chop (which was not seldom), because he was so active and could run so wonderfully fast that he found no difficulty in overtaking the hogs; but being dreadfully reckless, he almost invariably tumbled over stumps and stones in the course of his wild chase, and seldom returned home without having knocked the skin off his shins.

But although Peterkin was often unfortunate in the way of getting tumbles, he was successful on the present occasion in hunting, and returned before evening with three very nice little hogs. I also was successful in my visit to the mudflats, where I killed several ducks. So that, when we launched and loaded our boat at sunrise the following morning, we found our store of provisions to be more than sufficient. Part had been cooked the night before, and on taking note of the different items, we found the account to stand thus:

10 Bread-fruits (two baked, eight unbaked).
20 Yams (six roasted, the rest raw).
 6 Taro roots.
50 Fine large plums.
 6 Coco-nuts, ripe.
 6 Ditto green (for drinking).
 4 Large ducks and two small ones, raw.
 3 Cold roast pigs, with stuffing.

I may here remark that the stuffing had been devised by Peterkin specially for the occasion. He kept the manner of its compounding a profound secret, so I cannot tell what it was; but I can say, with much confidence, that we found it to be atrociously bad, and, after the first tasting, scraped it carefully out and threw it overboard. We calculated that this supply would last us for several days; but we afterwards found that it was much more than we required, especially in regard to the coco-nuts, of which we found large supplies wherever we went. However, as Peterkin remarked, it was better to have too much than too little, as we knew not to what straits we might be put during our voyage.

It was a very calm sunny morning when we launched forth and rowed over the lagoon towards the outlet in the reef, and passed between the two green islets that guard the entrance. We experienced some difficulty and no little danger in passing the surf of the breaker, and shipped a good deal of water in the attempt; but, once past the billow, we found ourselves floating placidly on the long oily swell that rose and fell slowly as it rolled over the wide ocean.

Penguin Island lay on the other side of our own island, at about a mile beyond the outer reef, and we calculated that it must be at least twenty miles distant by the way we should have to go. We might, indeed, have shortened the way by coasting round our island inside of the lagoon, and going out at the passage in the reef nearly opposite to Penguin Island; but we preferred to go by the open sea—first, because it was more adventurous, and secondly, because we should have the pleasure of again feeling the motion of the deep, which we all loved very much, not being liable to sea-sickness.

"I wish we had a breeze," said Jack.

"So do I," cried Peterkin, resting on his oar and wiping his heated brow, "pulling is hard work. Oh dear, if we could only catch a hundred or two of these gulls, tie them to the boat with long strings and make them fly as we want them, how capital it would be!"

"Or bore a hole through a shark's tail, and reeve a rope through it, eh?" remarked Jack. "But, I say, it seems that my wish is going to be granted, for here comes a breeze. Ship your oar, Peterkin. Up with the mast, Ralph; I'll see to the sail. Mind your helm; look out for squalls!"

This last speech was caused by the sudden appearance of a dark-blue line on the horizon, which, in an incredibly short space of time, swept down on us, lashing up the sea in white foam as it went. We presented the stern of the boat to its first violence, and, after a few seconds, it moderated into a steady breeze, to which we spread our sail and flew merrily over the waves. Although the breeze died away soon afterwards, it had been so stiff while it lasted that we were carried over the greater part of our way before it fell calm again; so that, when the flapping of the sail against the mast told us that it was time to resume the oars, we were not much more than a mile from Penguin Island.

"There go the soldiers!" cried Peterkin, as we came in sight of it; "how spruce their white trousers look this morning! I wonder if they will receive us kindly. D'you think they are hospitable, Jack?"

"Don't talk, Peterkin, but pull away and you shall see shortly."

As we drew near to the island we were much amused by the manoeuvres and appearance of these strange birds. They seemed to be of different species, for some had crests on their heads while others had none, and while some were about the size of a goose others appeared nearly as large as a swan. We also saw a huge albatross soaring above the heads of the penguins. It was followed and surrounded by numerous flocks of sea-gulls. Having approached to within a few yards of the island, which was a low rock, with no other vegetation on it than a few bushes, we lay on our oars and gazed at the birds with surprise and pleasure, they returning our gaze with interest. We now saw that their soldier-like appearance was owing to the stiff, erect manner in which they sat on their short legs—"bolt-upright", as Peterkin expressed it. They had black heads, long sharp beaks, white breasts, and bluish backs. Their wings were so short that they looked more like the fins of a fish, and, indeed, we soon saw that they used them for the purpose of swimming under water. There were no quills on these wings, but a sort of scaly feathers, which also thickly covered their bodies.

"Pull in a bit," cried Peterkin, "I see some other animals. They must be fond of noisy company, to consort with such creatures."

To our surprise we found that these were no other than penguins which had gone down on all-fours, and were crawling among the bushes on their feet and wings, just like quadrupeds. Suddenly one big old bird, that had been sitting on a point very near to us, gazing in mute astonishment, became alarmed, and scuttling down the rocks, plumped or fell, rather than ran, into the sea. It dived in a moment, and, a few seconds afterwards, came out of the water far ahead, with such a spring, and such a dive back into the sea again, that we could scarcely believe it was not a fish that had leaped in sport.

"That beats everything," said Peterkin, rubbing his nose, and screwing up his face with an expression of exasperated amazement. "I've heard of a thing being neither fish, flesh, nor fowl, but I never did expect to live to see a brute that was all three together—at once—in one! But look there!" he continued, pointing with a look of resignation to the shore—"look there! there's no end to it. What *has* that brute got under its tail?"

We turned to look in the direction pointed out, and there saw a penguin walking slowly and very sedately along the shore with an egg under its tail. There were several others, we observed, burdened in the same way; and we found afterwards that these were a species of penguins that always carried their eggs so. Indeed, they had a most convenient cavity for the purpose, just between the tail and the legs. We were very much impressed with the regularity and order of this colony. The island seemed to be apportioned out into squares, of which each penguin possessed one, and sat in stiff solemnity in the middle of it, or took a slow march up and down the spaces between. Some were hatching their eggs, but others were feeding their young ones in a manner that caused us to laugh not a little. The mother stood on a mound or raised rock, while the young ones stood patiently below her on the ground. Suddenly the mother raised her head and uttered a series of the most discordant cackling sounds.

"She's going to choke," cried Peterkin.

But this was not the case, although, I confess, she looked like it. In a few seconds she put down her head and opened her mouth, into which the young one thrust its beak and seemed to suck something from her throat. Then the cackling was renewed, the sucking continued, and so the operation of feeding was carried on till the young one was satisfied; but what she fed her little one with we could not tell.

Scarcely had we finished making our remarks on this, when we were startled by about a dozen of the old birds hopping in the most clumsy and ludicrous manner towards the sea. The beach here was a sloping rock, and when they came to it some of them succeeded in hopping down in safety, but others lost their balance, and rolled and scrambled down the slope in the most helpless manner. The instant they reached the water, however, they seemed to be in their proper element. They dived and bounded out of it and into it again with the utmost agility; and so, diving and bounding and sputtering—for they could not fly—they went rapidly out to sea.

On seeing this Peterkin turned with a grave face to us and said,

"It's my opinion that these birds are all stark, staring mad, and that this is an enchanted island. I therefore propose that we should either put about ship and fly in terror from the spot, or land valorously on the island, and sell our lives as dearly as we can."

"I vote for landing: so pull in, lads," said Jack, giving a stroke with his oar that made the boat spin. In a few seconds we ran the boat into a little creek, where we made her fast to a projecting piece of coral, and running up the beach, entered the ranks of the penguins armed with our cudgels and our spear. We were greatly surprised to find that, instead of attacking us or showing signs of fear at our approach, these curious birds did not move from their places until we laid hands on them, and merely turned their eyes on us in solemn, stupid wonder as we passed. There was one old penguin, however, that began to walk slowly towards the sea, and Peterkin took it into his head that he would try to interrupt its progress, so he ran between it and the sea and brandished his cudgel in its face. But this proved to be a resolute old bird. It would not retreat; nay, more, it would not cease to advance, but battled with Peterkin bravely and drove him before it until it reached the sea. Had Peterkin used his club he could easily have felled it, no doubt; but as he had no wish to do so cruel an act merely out of sport, he let the bird escape.

We spent fully three hours on this island in watching the habits of these curious birds, and when we finally left them, we all three concluded after much consultation, that they were the most wonderful creatures we had ever seen; and further, we thought it probable that they were the most wonderful creatures in the world!

Chapter 17

For many months after this excursion we continued to live on Coral Island in uninterrupted harmony and happiness. Sometimes we went out a-fishing in the lagoon, and sometimes went a-hunting in the woods, or ascended to the mountain-top, by way of variety, although Peterkin always asserted that we went for the purpose of hailing any ship that might chance to heave in sight.

Now, while we were engaged with these occupations and amusements, an event occurred one day which was as unexpected as it was exceedingly alarming and very horrible.

Jack and I were sitting, as we were often wont to do, on the rocks at Spouting Cliff, and Peterkin was wringing the water from his garments, having recently fallen by accident into the sea—a thing he was constantly doing—when our attention was suddenly arrested by two objects which appeared on the horizon.

"What are yon, think you?" I said, addressing Jack.

"I can't imagine," answered he. "I've noticed them for some time, and fancied they were black sea-gulls, but the more I look at them the more I feel convinced they are much larger than gulls."

"They seem to be coming towards us," said I.

"Hallo! what's wrong?" inquired Peterkin, coming up.

"Look there," said Jack.

"Whales!" cried Peterkin, shading his eyes with his hand. "No—eh—*can* they be boats, Jack?"

Our hearts beat with excitement at the very thought of seeing human faces again.

"I think you are about right, Peterkin. But they seem to me to move strangely for boats," said Jack, in a low tone, as if he were talking to himself.

I noticed that a shade of anxiety crossed Jack's countenance as he gazed long and intently at the two objects, which were now nearing us fast. At last he sprang to his feet. "They are canoes, Ralph! whether war-canoes or not I cannot tell, but this I know, that all the natives of the South Sea Islands are fierce cannibals, and they have little respect for strangers. We must hide if they land here, which I earnestly hope they will not do."

I was greatly alarmed at Jack's speech, but I confess I thought less of what he said than of the earnest, anxious manner in which he said it, and it was with very uncomfortable feelings that Peterkin and I followed him quickly into the woods.

"How unfortunate," said I, as we gained the shelter of the bushes, "that we have forgotten our arms!"

"It matters not," said Jack, "here are clubs enough and to spare." As he spoke he laid his hand on a bundle of stout poles of various sizes, which Peterkin's ever-busy hands had formed during our frequent visits to the cliff, for no other purpose, apparently, than that of having something to do.

We each selected a stout club according to our several tastes, and lay down behind a rock, whence we could see the canoes approach, without ourselves being seen. At first we made an occasional remark on their appearance, but, after they entered the lagoon, and drew near the beach, we ceased to speak, and gazed with intense interest at the scene before us.

We now observed that the foremost canoe was being chased by the other, and that it contained a few women and children, as well as men—perhaps forty souls altogether, while the canoe which pursued it contained only men. They seemed to be about the same in number, but were better armed, and had the appearance of being a war-party. Both crews were paddling with all their might, and it seemed as if the pursuers exerted themselves to overtake the fugitives ere they could land. In this, however, they failed. The foremost canoe made for the beach close beneath the rocks behind which we were concealed. Their short paddles flashed like meteors in the water, and sent up a constant shower of spray. The foam curled from the prow, and the eyes of the rowers glistened in their black faces as they strained every muscle of their naked bodies; nor did they relax their efforts till the canoe struck the beach with a violent shock; then with a shout of defiance the whole party sprang, as if by magic, from the canoe to the shore. Three women, two of whom carried infants in their arms, rushed into the woods; and the men crowded to the water's edge, with stones in their hands, spears levelled and clubs brandished, to resist the landing of their enemies.

The distance between the two canoes had been about half a mile, and, at the great speed they were going, this was soon passed. As the pursuers neared the shore, no sign of fear or hesitation was noticeable. On they came like a wild charger—received but recked not of a shower of stones. The canoe struck and with a yell that seemed to issue from the throats of incarnate fiends, they leaped into the water, and drove their enemies up the beach.

The battle that immediately ensued was frightful to behold. Most of the men wielded clubs of enormous size and curious shapes, with which they dashed out each other's brains. As they were almost entirely naked, and had to bound, stoop, leap, and run in their terrible hand-to-hand encounters, they looked more like demons than human beings. I felt my heart grow sick at the sight of this bloody battle, and would fain have turned away, but a species of fascination seemed to hold me down and glue my eyes upon the combatants. I observed that the attacking party was led by a most extraordinary being, who, from his size and peculiarity, I concluded was a chief. His hair was frizzed out to an enormous extent, so that it resembled a large turban. It was of a light-yellow hue, which surprised me much for the man's body was as black as coal, and I felt convinced that the hair must have been dyed. He was tattooed from head to foot; and his face, besides being tattooed, was besmeared with red paint, and streaked with white. Altogether, with his yellow turban-like hair, his Herculean black frame, his glittering eyes and white teeth, he seemed the most terrible monster I ever beheld. He was very active in the fight, and had already killed four men.

Suddenly the yellow-haired chief was attacked by a man quite as strong and large as himself. He flourished a heavy club something like an eagle's beak at the point. For a second or two these giants eyed each other warily, moving round and round as if to catch each other at a disadvantage; but seeing that nothing was to be gained by this caution, and that the loss of time might effectually turn the tide of battle either way, they apparently made up their minds to attack at the same instant, for, with a wild shout and simultaneous spring, they swung their heavy clubs, which met with a loud report. Suddenly the yellow-haired savage tripped, his enemy sprang forward, the ponderous club was swung, but it did not descend, for at that moment the savage was felled to the ground by a stone from the hand of one who had witnessed his chief's danger. This was the turning-point in the battle. The savages who landed first turned and fled towards the bush, on seeing the fall of their chief. But not one escaped. They were all overtaken and felled to the earth. I saw, however, that they were not all killed. Indeed, their enemies, now that they were conquered, seemed anxious to take them alive; and they succeeded in securing fifteen, whom they bound hand and foot with cords, and carrying them up into the woods, laid them down among the bushes. Here they left them, for what purpose I knew not, and returned to the scene of the late battle, where the remnant of the party were bathing their wounds.

Out of the forty blacks that composed the attacking party, only twenty-eight remained alive, two of whom were sent into the bush to hunt for the women and children. Of the other party, as I have said, only fifteen survived, and these were lying bound and helpless on the grass.

Jack and Peterkin and I now looked at each other, and whispered our fears that the savages might clamber up the rocks to search for

fresh water, and so discover our place of concealment; but we were
so much interested in watching their movements that we agreed to
remain where we were—and, indeed, we could not easily have risen
without exposing ourselves to detection. One of the savages now
went up to the wood, and soon returned with a bundle of firewood,
and we were not a little surprised to see him set fire to it by the very
same means used by Jack the time we made our first fire—namely,
with the bow and drill. When the fire was kindled, two of the party
went again to the woods and returned with one of the bound men. A
dreadful feeling of horror crept over my heart as the thought
flashed upon me that they were going to burn their enemies. As they
bore him to the fire my feelings almost overpowered me. I gasped
for breath, and, seizing my club, endeavoured to spring to my feet;
but Jack's powerful arm pinned me to the earth. Next moment one
of the savages raised his club, and fractured the wretched creature's
skull. He must have died instantly; and strange though it may seem,
I confess to a feeling of relief when the deed was done, because I
now knew that the poor savage could not be burned alive. Scarcely
had his limbs ceased to quiver when the monsters cut slices of flesh
from his body, and, after roasting them slightly over the fire,
devoured them.

Suddenly there arose a cry from the woods, and in a few seconds
the two savages hastened towards the fire dragging the three women
and their two infants along with them. One of those women was
much younger than her companions, and we were struck with the
modesty of her demeanour and the gentle expression of her face,
which, although she had the flattish nose and thick lips of the others,
was of a light-brown colour, and we conjectured that she must be of
a different race. She and her companions wore short petticoats and a
kind of tippet on their shoulders. Their hair was jet black, but
instead of being long, was short and curly—though not woolly
—somewhat like the hair of a young boy. While we gazed with
interest and some anxiety at these poor creatures, the big chief
advanced to one of the elder females and laid his hand upon the
child. But the mother shrank from him, and, clasping the little one
to her bosom, uttered a wail of fear. With a savage laugh, the chief
tore the child from her arms and tossed it into the sea. A low groan
burst from Jack's lips as he witnessed this atrocious act and heard the
mother's shriek, as she fell insensible on the sand. The rippling
waves rolled the child on the beach, as if they refused to be a party in
such a foul murder, and we could observe that the little one still
lived.

The young girl was now brought forward, and the chief addressed
her; but although we heard his voice and even the words distinctly,

of course we could not understand what he said. The girl made no answer to his fierce questions and we saw by the way in which he pointed to the fire that he threatened her life.

"Peterkin," said Jack, in a hoarse whisper, "have you got your knife?"

"Yes," replied Peterkin, whose face was pale as death.

"That will do. Listen to me, and do my bidding quick. Here is the small knife, Ralph. Fly, both of you, through the bush, cut the cords that bind the prisoners, and set them free. There, quick, ere it be too late!" Jack sprang up, and seized a heavy but short bludgeon, while his strong frame trembled with emotion, and large drops rolled down his forehead.

At this moment the man who had butchered the savage a few minutes before advanced towards the girl with his heavy club. Jack uttered a yell that rang like a death-shriek among the rocks. With one bound he leaped over a precipice full fifteen feet high, and before the savages had recovered from their surprise, was in the midst of them; while Peterkin and I dashed through the bushes towards the prisoners. With one blow of his staff Jack felled the man with the club, then, turning round with a look of fury, he rushed upon the big chief with the yellow hair. Had the blow which Jack aimed at his head taken effect, the huge savage would have needed no second stroke; but he was agile as a cat, and avoided it by springing to one side, while, at the same time, he swung his ponderous club at the head of his foe. It was now Jack's turn to leap aside, and well was it for him that the first outburst of his blind fury was over, else he had become an easy prey to his gigantic antagonist; but Jack was cool now. He darted his blows rapidly and well, and the superiority of his light weapon was strikingly proved in this combat; for while he could easily evade the blows of the chief's heavy club, the chief could not so easily evade those of his light one. Nevertheless, so quick was he, and so frightfully did he fling about the mighty weapon, that although Jack struck him almost every blow, the strokes had to be delivered so quickly that they wanted force to be very effectual.

It was lucky for Jack that the other savages considered the success of their chief in this encounter to be so certain that they refrained from interfering. Had they doubted it, they would have probably ended the matter at once by felling him. But they contented themselves with awaiting the issue.

The force which the chief expended in wielding his club now began to be apparent. His movements became slower, his breath hissed through his clenched teeth, and the surprised savages drew nearer in order to render assistance. Jack observed this movement.

He felt that his fate was sealed, and resolved to cast his life upon the next blow. The chief's club was again about to descend on his head. He might have evaded it easily, but, instead of doing so, he suddenly shortened his grasp of his own club, rushed in under the blow, struck his adversary right between the eyes with all his force, and fell to the earth, crushed beneath the senseless body of the chief. A dozen clubs flew high in air, ready to descend on the head of Jack; but they hesitated a moment, for the massive body of the chief completely covered him. That moment saved his life. Ere the savages could tear the chief's body away, seven of their number fell prostrate beneath the clubs of the prisoners whom Peterkin and I had set free, and two others fell under our own hand. We could never have accomplished this had not our enemies been so engrossed with the fight between Jack and their chief that they had failed to observe us until we were upon them. They still outnumbered our party by three, but we were flushed with victory, while they were taken by surprise and dispirited by the fall of their chief. Moreover, they were awe-struck by the sweeping fury of Jack, who seemed to have lost his senses altogether, and had no sooner shaken himself free of the chief's body than he rushed into the midst of them, and in three blows equalized our numbers. Peterkin and I flew to the rescue, the savages followed us, and in less than ten minutes the whole of our opponents were knocked down or made prisoners, bound hand and foot, and extended side by side upon the seashore.

Chapter 18

After the battle was over, the savages crowded round us and gazed at us in surprise, while they continued to pour upon us a flood of questions, which, being wholly unintelligible, of course we could not answer. However, by way of putting an end to it, Jack took the chief (who had recovered from the effects of his wound) by the hand and shook it warmly. No sooner did the blacks see that this was meant to express good-will than they shook hands with us all round. After this ceremony was gone through Jack went up to the girl, who had never once moved from the rock where she had been left, but had continued an eager spectator of all that had passed. He made signs to her to follow him, and then, taking the chief by the hand, was about to conduct him to the bower, when his eyes fell on the poor infant which had been thrown into the sea and was still lying on the shore. Dropping the chief's hand he hastened towards it, and to his great joy found it to be still alive. We also found that the mother was beginning to recover slowly.

"Here, get out o' the way," said Jack, pushing us aside, as we stooped over the poor woman and endeavoured to restore her; "I'll soon bring her round." So saying, he placed the infant on her bosom and laid its warm cheek on hers. The effect was wonderful. The woman opened her eyes, felt the child, looked at it, and with a cry of joy clasped it in her arms, at the same time endeavouring to rise, for the purpose, apparently, of rushing into the woods.

"There, that's all right," said Jack, once more taking the chief by the hand. "Now, Ralph and Peterkin, make the women and these fellows follow me to the bower. We'll entertain them as hospitably as we can."

In a few minutes the savages were all seated on the ground in front of the bower making a hearty meal off a cold roast pig, several ducks, and a variety of cold fish, together with an unlimited supply of coco-nuts, bread-fruits, yams, taro, and plums; with all of which they seemed to be quite familiar and perfectly satisfied.

Meanwhile, we three, being thoroughly knocked up with our day's work, took a good draught of coco-nut lemonade, and throwing ourselves on our beds fell fast asleep. The savages, it seems, followed our example, and in half an hour the whole camp was buried in repose.

How long we slept I cannot tell, but this I know, that when we lay down the sun was setting, and when we awoke it was high in the heavens. I awoke Jack, who started up in surprise, being unable at first to comprehend our situation. "Now, then," said he, springing up, "let's see after breakfast. Hallo, Peterkin, lazy fellow! how long do you mean to lie there?"

Peterkin yawned heavily. "Well," said he, opening his eyes and looking up after some trouble, "if it isn't tomorrow morning, and me thinking it was today all this time! Hallo, Venus! where did you come from? you seem tolerably at home, anyhow. Bah! might as well speak to the cat as to you—better, in fact, for it understands me, and you don't."

This remark was called forth by the sight of one of the elderly females, who had seated herself on the rock in front of the bower, and, having placed her child at her feet, was busily engaged in devouring the remains of a roast pig.

By this time the natives outside were all astir, and breakfast in an advanced state of preparation. During the course of it we made sundry attempts to converse with the natives by signs, but without effect. At last we hit upon a plan of discovering their names. Jack pointed to his breast and said "Jack" very distinctly; then he pointed to Peterkin and to me, repeating our names at the same time. Then he pointed to himself again, and said "Jack", and laying his finger on the breast of the chief, looked inquiringly into his face. The chief instantly understood him, and said "Tararo" twice distinctly. Jack repeated it after him, and the chief, nodding his head approvingly, said "Chuck". On hearing which Peterkin exploded with laughter; but Jack turned, and with a frown rebuked him, saying, "I must look even more indignantly at you than I feel, Peterkin, you rascal, for the fellows don't like to be laughed at." Then turning towards the youngest of the women, who was seated at the door of the bower, he pointed towards her; whereupon the chief said "Avatea", and pointing towards the sun, raised his finger slowly towards the zenith, where it remained steadily for a minute or two.

"What can that mean, I wonder?" said Jack, looking puzzled.

Jack now made signs to the natives to follow him, and taking up his axe, he led them to the place where the battle had been fought. Here we found the prisoners, who had passed the night on the beach, having been totally forgotten by us, as our minds had been full of our guests, and were ultimately overcome by sleep. They did not seem the worse for their exposure, however, as we judged by the hearty appetite with which they devoured the breakfast that was soon after given to them. Jack then began to dig a hole in the sand, and after working a few seconds, he pointed to it and to the dead bodies that lay exposed on the beach. The natives immediately perceived what he wanted, and running for their paddles, dug a hole in the course of half an hour that was quite large enough to contain all the bodies of the slain. When it was finished they tossed their dead enemies into it with so much indifference that we felt assured they would not have put themselves to this trouble had we not asked them to do so. The body of the yellow-haired chief was the last thrown in. This wretched man would have recovered from the blow with which Jack felled him, and indeed he did endeavour to rise during the mêlée that followed his fall; but one of his enemies, happening to notice the action, dealt him a blow with his club that killed him on the spot.

While they were about to throw the sand over this chief, one of the savages stooped over him, and with a knife, made apparently of stone, cut a large slice of flesh from his thigh. We knew at once that he intended to make use of this for food, and could not repress a cry of horror and disgust.

"Come, come, you blackguard!' cried Jack, starting up and seizing the man by the arm, "pitch that into the hole. Do you hear?"

The savage, of course, did not understand the command, but he perfectly understood the look of disgust with which Jack regarded the flesh, and his fierce gaze as he pointed towards the hole. Nevertheless he did not obey. Jack instantly turned to Tararo and made signs to him to enforce obedience. The chief seemed to understand the appeal, for he stepped forward, raised his club, and was on the point of dashing out the brains of his offending subject, when Jack sprang forward and caught his uplifted arm.

"Stop," he shouted, "you blockhead! I don't want you to kill the man." He then pointed again to the flesh and to the hole. The chief uttered a few words, which had the desired effect; for the man threw the flesh into the hole, which was immediately filled up. This man was of a morose, sulky disposition, and during all the time he remained on the island, regarded us, especially Jack, with a scowling visage. His name, we found, was Mahine.

The next three or four days were spent by the savages in mending their canoe, which had been damaged by the violent shock it had sustained on striking the shore.

When the canoe was ready, we assisted the natives to carry the prisoners into it, and helped them to load it with provisions and fruit. Peterkin also went to the plum-tree for the purpose of making a special onslaught upon the hogs, and killed no less than six of them. These we baked and presented to our friends on the day of their departure. On that day Tararo made a great many energetic signs to us, which, after much consideration, we came to understand were proposals that we should go away with him to his island; but having no desire to do so, we shook our heads very decidedly.

However, we consoled him by presenting him with our rusty axe, which we thought we could spare, having the excellent one which had been so providentially washed ashore to us the day we were wrecked. We also gave him a piece of wood with our names carved on it, and a piece of string to hang it round his neck as an ornament.

In a few minutes we were all assembled on the beach. Being unable to speak to the savages, we went through the ceremony of shaking hands, and expected they would depart; but before doing so, Tararo went up to Jack and rubbed noses with him, after which he did the same with Peterkin and me! Seeing that this was their mode of salutation, we determined to conform to their custom, so we rubbed noses heartily with the whole party, women and all! The only disagreeable part of the process was when we came to rub noses with Mahine, and Peterkin afterwards said that when he saw his wolfish eyes glaring so close to his face, he felt much more inclined to *bang* than to *rub* his nose. Avatea was the last to take leave of us, and we experienced a feeling of real sorrow when she approached to bid us farewell. Besides her modest air and gentle manners, she was the only one of the party who exhibited the smallest sign of regret at parting from us. Going up to Jack, she put out her flat little nose to be rubbed, and thereafter paid the same compliment to Peterkin and me.

An hour later the canoe was out of sight, and we, with an indefinable feeling of sadness creeping round our hearts, were seated in silence beneath the shadow of our bower, meditating on the wonderful events of the last few days.

Chapter 19

One day we were all enjoying ourselves in the Water Garden, preparatory to going on a fishing excursion; for Peterkin had kept us in such constant supply of hogs that we had become quite tired of pork, and desired a change. Peterkin was sunning himself on the ledge of rock, while we were creeping among the rocks below. Happening to look up, I observed Peterkin cutting the most extraordinary capers and making violent gesticulations for us to come up, so I gave Jack a push and rose immediately.

"A sail! a sail!—Ralph, look; Jack, away on the horizon there, just over the entrance to the lagoon!" cried Peterkin, as we scrambled up the rocks.

"So it is, and a schooner too!" said Jack, as he proceeded hastily to dress.

Our hearts were thrown into a terrible flutter by this discovery, for if it should touch at our island we had no doubt the captain would be happy to give us a passage to some of the civilized islands, where we could find a ship sailing for England or some other part of Europe. Home, with all its associations, rushed in upon my heart like a flood, and much though I loved the Coral Island and the bower which had now been our home so long, I felt that I could have quitted all at that moment without a sigh. With joyful anticipations we hastened to the highest point of rock near our dwelling, and awaiting the arrival of the vessel for we now perceived that she was making straight for the island, under a steady breeze.

In less than an hour she was close to the reef, where she rounded to, and backed her topsails in order to survey the coast. Seeing this, and fearing that they might not perceive us, we all three waved pieces of coco-nut cloth in the air, and soon had the satisfaction of seeing them beginning to lower a boat and bustle about the decks as if they meant to land. Suddenly a flag was run up to the peak, a little cloud of white smoke rose from the schooner's side, and before we could guess their intentions, a cannon-shot came crashing through the bushes, carried away several coco-nut trees in its passage, and burst in atoms against the cliff a few yards below the spot on which we stood.

With feelings of terror we now observed that the flag at the schooner's peak was black, with a Death's-head and cross-bones upon it. As we gazed at each other in blank amazement, the word "pirate" escaped our lips simultaneously.

"What is to be done?" cried Peterkin, as we observed a boat shoot from the vessel's side and make for the entrance of the reef. "If they take us off the island, it will either be to throw us overboard for sport, or to make pirates of us."

I did not reply, but looked at Jack, as being our only resource in this emergency. He stood with folded arms, and his eyes fixed with a grave anxious expression on the ground. "There is but one hope," said he, turning with a sad expression of countenance to Peterkin; "perhaps, after all, we may not have to resort to it. If these villains are anxious to take us, they will soon overrun the whole island. But come, follow me."

Stopping abruptly in his speech, Jack bounded into the woods, and led us by a circuitous route to Spouting Cliff. Here he halted, and advancing cautiously to the rocks, glanced over their edge. We were soon by his side, and saw the boat, which was crowded with armed men, just touching the shore. In an instant the crew landed, formed line, and rushed up to our bower.

In a few seconds we saw them hurrying back to the boat, one of them swinging the poor cat round his head by the tail. On reaching the water's edge, he tossed it far into the sea, and joined his companions, who appeared to be holding a hasty council.

"You see what we may expect," said Jack bitterly. "The man who will wantonly kill a poor brute for sport will think little of murdering a fellow-creature. Now, boys, we have but one chance left—the Diamond Cave."

"The Diamond Cave!" cried Peterkin; "then my chance is a poor one, for I could not give into it if all the pirates on the Pacific were at my heels."

"Nay, but," said I, "we will take you down, Peterkin, if you will only trust us."

As I spoke, we observed the pirates scatter over the beach, and radiate, as if from a centre, towards the woods and along shore.

"Now, Peterkin," said Jack, in a solemn tone, "you must make up your mind to do it, or we must make up our minds to die in your company."

"Oh, Jack, my dear friend," cried Peterkin, turning pale, "leave me; I don't believe they'll think it worth while to kill me. Go, you and Ralph, and dive into the cave."

"That will not I," answered Jack quietly, while he picked up a stout cudgel from the ground. "So now, Ralph, we must prepare to meet these fellows. Their motto is, 'No quarter.' If we can manage to floor those coming in this direction, we may escape into the woods for a while."

"There are five of them," said I; "we have no chance."

"Come, then," cried Peterkin, starting up, and grasping Jack convulsively by the arm, "let us dive; I will go."

Those who are not naturally expert in the water know well the feelings of horror that overwhelm them, when in it, at the bare idea of being held down even for a few seconds—that spasmodic, involuntary recoil from compulsory immersion which has no connection whatever with cowardice; and they will understand the amount of resolution that it required in Peterkin to allow himself to be dragged down to a depth of ten feet, and then, through a narrow tunnel, into an almost pitch dark cavern. But there was no alternative. The pirates had already caught sight of us, and were now within a short distance of the rocks.

Jack and I seized Peterkin by the arms.

"Now, keep quite still, no struggling," said Jack, "or we are lost."

Peterkin made no reply, but the stern gravity of his marble features, and the tension of his muscles, satisfied us that he had fully made up his mind to go through with it. Just as the pirates gained the foot of the rocks, which hid us for a moment from their view, we bent over the sea, and plunged down together head foremost. Peterkin behaved like a hero. He floated passively between us like a log of wood, and we passed the tunnel and rose into the cave in a shorter space of time than I had ever done it before.

Peterkin drew a long deep breath on reaching the surface, and in a few seconds we were all standing on the ledge of rock in safety. Jack now searched for the tinder and torch which always lay in the cave. He soon found them, and lighting the torch, revealed to Peterkin's wondering gaze the marvels of the place. But we were too wet to waste much time in looking about us. Our first care was to take off our clothes and wring them as dry as we could. This done, we proceeded to examine into the state of our larder, for, as Jack truly remarked, there was no knowing how long the pirates might remain on the island.

"Perhaps," said Peterkin, "they may take it into their heads to stop here altogether, and so we shall be buried alive in this place."

"Don't you think, Peterkin, that it's the nearest thing to being drowned alive that you ever felt?" said Jack, with a smile. "But I've no fear of that. These villains never stay long on shore. The sea is their home, so you may depend upon it that they won't stay more than a day or two at the furthest."

We now began to make arrangements for spending the night in the cavern. At various periods Jack and I had conveyed coco-nuts and other fruits, besides rolls of coco-nut cloth, to this submarine cave, partly for amusement; and partly from a feeling that we might possibly be driven one day to take shelter here from the savages.

Little did we imagine that the first savages who would drive us into it would be white savages, perhaps our own countrymen. We found the coco-nuts in good condition, and the cooked yams, but the bread-fruits were spoiled. We also found the cloth where we had left it, and on opening it out there proved to be sufficient to make a bed; which was important, as the rock was damp. Having collected it all together, we spread out our bed, placed our torch in the midst of us, and ate our supper. It was indeed a strange chamber to feast in; and we could not help remarking on the cold, ghastly appearance of the walls, and the black water at our side, with the thick darkness beyond, and the sullen sound of the drops that fell at long intervals from the roof of the cavern into the still water, and the strong contrast between all this and our bed and supper, which, with our faces, were lit up with the deep red flame of the torch.

We sat long over our meal, talking together in subdued voices, for we did not like the dismal echoes that rang through the vault above when we happened to raise them. At last the faint light that came through the opening died away, warning us that it was night and time for rest. We therefore put out our torch and lay down to sleep.

On awaking, it was some time ere we could collect our faculties so as to remember where we were, and we were in much uncertainty as to whether it was early or late. We saw by the faint light that it was day, but could not guess at the hour; so Jack proposed that he should dive out and reconnoitre.

"No, Jack," said I; "do you rest here. You've had enough to do during the last few days. Rest yourself now, and take care of Peterkin, while I go out to see what the pirates are about. I'll be very careful not to expose myself, and I'll bring you word again in a short time."

"Very well, Ralph," answered Jack; "please yourself, but don't be long; and if you'll take my advice you'll go in your clothes, for I would like to have some fresh coco-nuts, and climbing trees without clothes is uncomfortable, to say the least of it."

"The pirates will be sure to keep a sharp look-out," said Peterkin, "so pray be careful."

"No fear," said I; "good-bye."

"Good-bye," answered my comrades.

And while the words were yet sounding in my ears, I plunged into the water, and in a few seconds found myself in the open air. On rising, I was careful to come up gently and to breathe softly, while I kept close in beside the rocks, but as I observed no one near me, I crept slowly out, and ascended the cliff a step at a time, till I obtained a full view of the shore. No pirates were to be seen—even their boat was gone but as it was possible they might have hidden themselves, I did not venture too boldly forward. Then it occurred to me to look out to sea, when, to my surprise, I saw the pirate schooner sailing away almost hull down on the horizon! On seeing this I uttered a shout of joy. Then my first impulse was to dive back to tell my companions the goods news; but I checked myself, and ran to the top of the cliff, in order to make sure that the vessel I saw was indeed the pirate schooner. I looked long and anxiously at her, and giving vent to a deep sigh of relief, said aloud, "Yes, there she goes; the villains have been balked of their prey this time at least."

"Not so sure of that!" said a deep voice at my side, while at the same moment a heavy hand grasped my shoulder, and held it as if in a vice.

Chapter 20

My heart seemed to leap into my throat at the words; and turning round, I beheld a man of immense stature and fierce aspect regarding me with a smile of contempt. He was a white man—that is to say, he was a man of European blood, though his face, from long exposure to the weather, was deeply bronzed. His dress was that of a common seaman except that he had on a Greek skull cap, and wore a broad shawl of the richest silk round his waist. In this shawl were placed two pairs of pistols and a heavy cutlass. He wore a beard and moustache, which, like the locks on his head, were short, curly and sprinkled with grey hairs.

"So, youngster," he said, with a sardonic smile, while I felt his grasp tighten on my shoulder, "the villains have been balked of their prey, have they? We shall see, we shall see. Now, you whelp, look yonder." As he spoke, the pirate uttered a shrill whistle. In a second or two it was answered, and the pirate boat rowed round the point at the Water Garden, and came rapidly towards us. "Now, go, make a fire on that point; and hark'ee, youngster, if you try to run away, I'll send a quick and sure messenger after you," and he pointed significantly at his pistols.

I obeyed in silence, and as I happened to have the burning-glass in my pocket, a fire was speedily kindled, and a thick smoke ascended into the air. It had scarcely appeared for two minutes when the boom of a gun rolled over the sea, and looking up, I saw that the schooner was making for the island again. It now flashed across me that this was a ruse on the part of the pirates, and that they had sent their vessel away, knowing that it would lead us to suppose that they had left altogether. But there was no use of regret now. I was completely in their power, so I stood helplessly beside the pirate watching the crew of the boat as they landed on the beach. For an instant I contemplated rushing over the cliff into the sea, but this I saw I could not now accomplish, as some of the men were already between me and the water.

There was a good deal of jesting at the success of their scheme, as the crew ascended the rocks and addressed the man who had captured me by the title of captain. They were a ferocious set of men, with shaggy beards and scowling brows. All of them were armed with cutlasses and pistols, and their costumes were, with trifling variations, similar to that of the captain. As I looked from one to the other, and observed the low, scowling brows, that never unbent, even when the men laughed, and the mean, rascally expression that sat on each face, I felt that my life hung by a hair.

"But where are the other cubs?" cried one of the men, with an oath that made me shudder. "I'll swear to it there were three, at least if not more."

"You hear what he says, whelp; where are the other dogs?" said the captain.

"If you mean my companions," said I, in a low voice, "I won't tell you."

A loud laugh burst from the crew at this answer.

The pirate captain looked at me in surprise. Then drawing a pistol from his belt, he cocked it and said, "Now, youngster, listen to me. I've no time to waste here. If you don't tell me all you know, I'll blow your brains out! Where are your comrades?"

For an instant I hesitated, not knowing what to do in this extremity. Suddenly a thought occurred to me.

"Villain," said I, shaking my clenched fist in his face, "to blow my brains out would make short work of me, and be soon over; death by drowning is as sure, and the agony prolonged: yet, I tell you to your face, if you were to toss me over yonder cliff into the sea, I would not tell you where my companions are, and I dare you to try me!"

The pirate captain grew white with rage as I spoke. "Say you so?" cried he, uttering a fierce oath. "Here, lads, take him by the legs and heave him in—quick!"

The men who were utterly silenced with surprise at my audacity, advanced and seized me and as they carried me towards the cliff, I congratulated myself not a little on the success of my scheme, for I knew that once in the water I should be safe, and could rejoin Jack and Peterkin in the cave. But my hopes were suddenly blasted by the captain crying out, "Hold on, lads, hold on! We'll give him a taste of the thumbscrews before throwing him in to the sharks. Away with him into the boat. Look alive, the breeze is freshening!"

The men instantly raised me shoulder high, and hurrying down the rocks, tossed me into the bottom of the boat, where I lay for some time stunned with the violence of my fall.

On recovering sufficiently to raise myself on my elbow, I perceived that we were already outside the coral reef and close alongside the schooner, which was of small size and clipper built. I had only time to observe this much, when I received a severe kick on the side from one of the men, who ordered me, in a rough voice, to jump aboard. Rising hastily, I clambered up the side. In a few minutes the boat was hoisted on deck, the vessel's head put close to the wind, and the Coral Island dropped slowly astern as we beat up against a head sea.

Immediately after coming aboard, the crew were too busily engaged in working the ship and getting in the boat to attend to me, so I remained leaning against the bulwarks close to the gangway, watching their operations. I was surprised to find that there were no guns or carronades of any kind in the vessel, which had more the appearance of a fast-sailing trader than a pirate. But I was struck with the neatness of everything. The brass-work of the binnacle and about the tiller, as well as the copper belaying-pins, were as brightly polished as if they had just come from the foundry. The decks were pure white, and smooth. The masts were clean-scraped and varnished, except at the cross-trees and truck, which were painted black. The standing and running rigging was in the most perfect order, and the sails as white as snow. In short, everything, from the single narrow red stripe on her low black hull to the trucks on her tapering masts, evinced an amount of care and strict discipline that would have done credit to a ship of the Royal Navy. There was nothing lumbering or unseemly about the vessel, excepting perhaps, a boat, which lay on the deck with its keel up between the fore and main masts. It seemed disproportionately large for the schooner; but when I saw that the crew amounted to between thirty and forty men, I concluded that this boat was held in reserve in case of any accident compelling the crew to desert the vessel.

But my thoughts soon reverted to the dear companions whom I had left on shore, and as I turned towards the Coral Island, which was now far away to leeward, I sighed deeply, and the tears rolled slowly down my cheeks as I thought that I might never see them more.

"So you're blubbering, are you, you obstinate whelp?" said the deep voice of the captain, as he came up and gave me a box on the ear that nearly felled me to the deck. "I don't allow any such weakness aboard o' this ship. So clap a stopper on your eyes, or I'll give you something to cry for."

I flushed with indignation at this rough and cruel treatment, but felt that giving way to anger would only make matters worse, so I made no reply, but took out my handkerchief and dried my eyes.

"I thought you were made of better stuff," continued the captain angrily. "I'd rather have a mad bull dog aboard than a watery-puppy. But I'll cure you, lad, or introduce you to the sharks before long. Now go below and stay there till I call you."

As I walked forward to obey, my eye fell on a small keg standing by the side of the main-mast, on which the word *gunpowder* was written in pencil. I immediately flashed across me that, as we were beating up against the wind, anything floating in the sea would be driven on the reef encircling the Coral Island. I also recollected—for thought is more rapid than the lightning—that my old companions had a pistol. Without a moment's hesitation, therefore, I lifted the keg from the deck and tossed it into the sea! An exclamation of surprise burst from the captain and some of the men who witnessed this act of mine.

Striding up to me, and uttering fearful imprecations, the captain raised his hand to strike me, while he shouted, "Boy! whelp! what mean you by that?"

"If you lower your hand," said I, in a loud voice, while I felt the blood rush to my temples, "I'll tell you. Until you do so, I'm dumb."

The captain stepped back and regarded me with a look of amazement.

"Now," continued I, "I threw that keg into the sea because the wind and waves willl carry it to my friends on the Coral Island, who happen to have a pistol but no powder. I hope that it will reach them soon; and my only regret is that the keg was not a bigger one. Moreover, pirate, you said just now that you thought I was made of better stuff. I don't know what stuff I am made of—I never thought much about that subject—but I'm quite certain of this, that I am made of such stuff as the like of you shall never tame, though you should do your worst."

To my surprise the captain, instead of flying into a rage, smiled, and thrusting his hand into the voluminous shawl that encircled his waist, turned on his heel and walked aft, while I went below.

Here, instead of being rudely handled, as I had expected, the men received me with a shout of laughter, and one of them, patting me on the back said, "Well done, lad! you're a brick, and I have no doubt will turn out a rare cove. Bloody Bill there was just such a fellow as you are, and he's now the biggest cut-throat of us all."

"Take a can of beer, lad," cried another, "and wet your whistle after that speech o' your'n to the captain. If any o' us had made it, youngster, he would have had no whistle to wet by this time."

"Stop your clapper, Jack," vociferated a third. "Give the boy a junk o' meat. Don't you see he's a'most goin' to kick the bucket?"

"And no wonder," said the first speaker, with an oath, "after the tumble you gave him into the boat. I guess it would have broke *your* neck if you had got it."

I did indeed feel somewhat faint, which was owing, doubtless to the combined effects of ill usage and hunger; for it will be recollected that I had dived out of the cave that morning before breakfast, and it was now near midday. I therefore gladly accepted a plate of boiled pork and a yam, which were handed to me by one of the men from the locker on which some of the crew were seated eating their dinner. But I must add that the zest with which I ate my meal was much abated in consequence of the frightful oaths and the terrible language that flowed from the lips of these godless men, even in the midst of their hilarity and good humour. The man who had been alluded to as Bloody Bill was seated near me, and I could not help wondering at the moody silence he maintained among his comrades. He did indeed reply to their questions in a careless, off-hand tone, but he never volunteered a remark. The only difference between him and the others was his taciturnity and his size, for he was nearly, if not quite, as large a man as the captain.

During the remainder of the afternoon I was left to my own reflections, which were anything but agreeable; for I could not banish from my mind the threat about the thumb-screws, of the nature and use of which I had a vague but terrible conception. I was still meditating on my unhappy fate, when, just after nightfall, one of the watch on deck called down the hatchway—

"Hallo there! one o' you tumble up and light the cabin lamp, and send that boy aft to the captain—sharp!"

"Now then, do you hear, youngster? The captain wants you. Look alive," said Bloody Bill, raising his huge frame from the locker on which he had been asleep for the last two hours. He sprang up the ladder, and I instantly followed him, and going aft was shown into the cabin by one of the men, who closed the door after me.

A small silver lamp which hung from a beam threw a dim soft light over the cabin, which was a small apartment, and comfortably but plainly furnished. Seated on a campstool at the table, and busily engaged in examining a chart of the Pacific, was the captain, who looked up as I entered, and in a quiet voice bade me be seated, while he threw down his pencil, and rising from the table, stretched himself on a sofa, at the upper end of the cabin.

"Boy," said he, looking me full in the face, "what is your name?"

"Ralph Rover," I replied.

"Where did you come from, and how came you to be on that island? How many companions had you on it? Answer me, now, and mind you tell no lies."

"I never tell lies," said I firmly.

The captain received this reply with a cold, sarcastic smile, and bade me answer his questions.

I then told him the history of myself and my companions from the time we sailed till the day of his visit to the island, taking care, however, to make no mention of the Diamond Cave. After I had concluded, he was silent for a few minutes then looking up, he said, "Boy, I believe you."

I was surprised at this remark, for I could not imagine why he should not believe me. However, I made no reply.

"And what," continued the captain, "makes you think that this schooner is a pirate?"

"The black flag," said I, "showed me what you are, and if any further proof were wanting, I have had it in the brutal treatment I have received at your hands."

The captain frowned as I spoke, but subduing his anger he continued, "Boy, you are too bold. I admit that we treated you roughly, but that was because you made us lose time and gave us a good deal of trouble. As to the black flag, that is merely a joke that my fellows play off upon people sometimes in order to frighten them. It is their humour, and does no harm. I am no pirate, boy, but a lawful trader—a rough one, I grant you, but one can't help that in these seas, where there are so many pirates on the water and such murderous blackguards on the land. I carry on a trade in sandal-wood with the Feejee Islands; and if you choose, Ralph, to behave yourself and be a good boy, I'll take you along with me and give you a good share of the profits. You see I'm in want of an honest boy like you to look after the cabin and keep the log and superintend the traffic on shore sometimes. What say you, Ralph: would you like to become a sandalwood trader?"

I was much surprised by this explanation, and a good deal relieved to find that the vessel, after all, was not a pirate; but instead of replying I said, "If it be as you state, then why did you take me from my island, and why do you not now take me back?"

The captain smiled as he replied, "I took you off in anger, boy, and I'm sorry for it. I would even now take you back, but we are too far away from it. See, there it is," he added, laying his finger on the chart, "and we are now here—fifty miles at least. It would not be fair to my men to put about now, for they have all an interest in the trade."

I could make no reply to this; so, after a little more conversation, I agreed to become one of the crew, at least until we could reach some civilized island where I might be put ashore. The captain assented to this proposition, and after thanking him for the promise, I left the cabin and went on deck with feelings that ought to have been lighter, but which were, I could not tell why, marvellously heavy and uncomfortable still.

Chapter 21

Three weeks after the conversation narrated in the last chapter, I was standing on the quarter deck of the schooner watching the gambols of a shoal of porpoises that swam round us. It was a dead calm—one of those still, hot, sweltering days so common in the Pacific, when nature seems to have gone to sleep, and the only thing in water or in air that proves her still alive is her long, deep breathing in the swell of the mighty sea. No cloud floated in the deep blue above, no ripple broke the reflected blue below. The sun shone fiercely in the sky, and a ball of fire blazed with almost equal power from out the bosom of the water. So intensely still was it, and so perfectly transparent was the surface of the deep, that had it not been for the long swell already alluded to, we might have believed the surrounding universe to be a huge blue liquid ball, and our little ship the one solitary material speck in all creation, floating in the midst of it.

No sound broke on our ears save the soft puff now and then of a porpoise, the slow creak of the masts as we swayed gently on the swell, the patter of the reef points, and the occasional flap of the hanging sails. An awning covered the fore and after parts of the schooner, under which the men composing the watch on deck lolled in sleepy indolence, overcome with excessive heat. Bloody Bill, as the men invariably called him, was standing at the tiller, but his post for the present was a sinecure, and he whiled away the time by alternately gazing in dreamy abstraction at the compass in the binnacle, and by walking to the taffrail in order to spit into the sea. In one of these turns he came near to where I was standing, and, leaning over the side, looked long and earnestly down into the blue wave.

This man, although he was always taciturn and often surly, was the only human being on board with whom I had the slightest desire to become better acquainted. The other men, seeing that I did not relish their company, and knowing that I was a protégé of the captain, treated me with total indifference. Bloody Bill, it is true, did the same, but as this was his conduct towards everyone else, it was not peculiar in reference to me. Once or twice I tried to draw him into conversation, but he always turned away after a few cold monosyllables. As he now leaned over the taffrail close beside me, I said to him—

"Bill, why is it that you are so gloomy? Why do you never speak to anyone?"

Bill smiled slightly as he replied, "Why, I s'pose it's because I hain't got nothin' to say!"

"That's strange," said I, musingly; "you look like a man that could think, and such men can usually speak."

"So they can, youngster," rejoined Bill, somewhat sternly; "and I could speak too if I had a mind to, but what's the use o' speakin' here? The men only open their mouths to curse and swear, an' they seem to find it entertainin', but I don't, so I hold my tongue."

"Well, Bill, that's true, and I would rather not hear you speak at all than hear you speak like the other men; but *I* don't swear, Bill, so you might talk to me sometimes, I think. Besides, I'm weary of spending day after day in this way, without a single soul to say a pleasant word to. I've been used to friendly conversation, Bill, and I really would take it kind if you would talk with me a little now and then."

Bill looked at me in surprise, and I thought I observed a sad expression pass across his sun-burned face.

"An' where have you been used to friendly conversation?" said Bill, looking down again into the sea; "not on that Coral Island, I take it?"

"Yes, indeed," said I energetically. "I have spent many of the happiest months in my life on that Coral Island;" and, without waiting to be further questioned, I launched out into a glowing account of the happy life that Jack and Peterkin and I had spent together, and related minutely every circumstance that befell us while on the island.

"Boy, boy," said Bill, in a voice so deep that it startled me, "this is no place for you."

"That's true," said I. "I am of little use on board, and I don't like my comrades; but I can't help it, and at any rate I hope to be free again soon."

"Free?" said Bill, looking at me in surprise.

"Yes, free," returned I, "the captain said he would put me ashore after this trip was over."

"*This trip!* Hark'ee, boy," said Bill, lowering his voice, "what said the captain to you the day you came aboard?"

"He said that he was a trader in sandal-wood, and no pirate, and told me that if I would join him for this trip he would give me a good share of the profits or put me on shore in some civilized island if I chose."

Bill's brows lowered savagely as he muttered, "Ay, he said truth when he told you he was a sandal-wood trader, but he lied when——"

"Sail ho!" shouted the look-out at the masthead.

"Where away?" cried Bill, springing to the tiller; while the men, startled by the sudden cry, jumped up and gazed round the horizon.

"On the starboard quarter, hull down, sir," answered the look-out.

At this moment the captain came on deck, and, mounting into the rigging, surveyed the sail through the glass. Then sweeping his eye round the horizon, he gazed steadily at a particular point.

"Take in top-sails," shouted the captain, swinging himself down on the deck by the main back-stay.

"Take in top-sails," roared the first mate.

"Ay, ay, sir-r-r," answered the men, as they sprang into the rigging and went aloft like cats.

Instantly all was bustle on board the hitherto quiet schooner. The top-sails were taken in and stowed, the men stood by the sheets and halyards, and the captain gazed anxiously at the breeze which was now rushing towards us like a sheet of dark blue. In a few seconds it struck us. The schooner trembled as if in surprise at the sudden onset, while she fell away, then bending gracefully to the wind, as though in acknowledgement of her subjection, she cut through the waves with her sharp prow like a dolphin, while Bill directed her course towards the strange sail.

In half an hour we neared her sufficiently to make out that she was a schooner, and from the clumsy appearance of her masts and sails we judged her to be a trader. She evidently did not like our appearance, for the instant the breeze reached her she crowded all sail and showed us her stern. As the breeze had moderated a little, our top-sails were again shaken out, and it soon became evident—despite the proverb, "A stern chase is a long one" — that we doubled her speed and would overhaul her speedily. When within a mile we hoisted British colours, but receiving no acknowledgement, the captain ordered a shot to be fired across her bows. In a moment, to my surprise, a large portion of the bottom of the boat amidships was removed, and in the hole thus exposed appeared an immense brass gun. It worked on a swivel, and was elevated by means of machinery. It was quickly loaded and fired. The heavy ball struck the water a few yards ahead of the chase, and ricocheting into the air, plunged into the sea a mile beyond it.

This produced the desired effect. The strange vessel backed her top-sails and hove-to, while we ranged up and lay to about a hundred yards off.

"Lower the boat," cried the captain.

In a second the boat was lowered and manned by a part of the crew, who were all armed with cutlasses and pistols. As the captain passed me to get into it, he said, "Jump into the stern-sheets, Ralph;

I may want you." I obeyed, and in ten minutes more we were standing on the stranger's deck. We were all much surprised at the sight that met our eyes. Instead of a crew of such sailors as we were accustomed to see, there were only fifteen blacks standing on the quarterdeck and regarding us with looks of undisguised alarm. They were totally unarmed, and most of them unclothed; one or two, however, wore portions of European attire. One had on a pair of duck trousers which were much too large for him, and stuck out in a most ungainly manner. Another wore nothing but the common scanty native garment round the loins and a black beaver hat. But the most ludicrous personage of all, and one who seemed to be chief, was a tall middle-aged man, of a mild, simple expression of countenance, who wore a white cotton shirt, a swallow-tailed coat, and a straw hat, while his black brawny legs were totally uncovered below the knees.

"Where's the commander of this ship?" inquired our captain, stepping up to this individual.

"I is capin," he answered, taking off his straw hat and making a low bow.

"You!" said our captain in surprise. "Where do you come from, and where are you bound? What cargo have you aboard?"

"We is come," answered the man with the swallow-tail, "from Aitutaki; we was go for Rarotonga. We is native miss'nary ship; our name is de *Olive Branch*; an' our cargo is two tons coco-nuts, seventy pigs, twenty cats, and de Gosp'l."

This announcement was received by the crew of our vessel with a shout of laughter, which, however, was peremptorily checked by the captain, whose expression instantly changed from one of severity to that of frank urbanity as he advanced towards the missionary and shook him warmly by the hand.

"I am very glad to have fallen in with you," said he, "and I wish you much success in your missionary labours. Pray take me to your cabin, as I wish to converse with you privately."

The missionary immediately took him by the hand, and as he led him away I heard him saying, "Me most glad to find you trader; we t'ought you be pirate. You very like one 'bout the masts."

What conversation the captain had with this man I never heard, but he came on deck again in a quarter of an hour, and shaking hands cordially with the missionary, ordered us into our boat and returned to the schooner, which was immediately put before the wind. In a few minutes the *Olive Branch* was left far behind us.

That afternoon, as I was down below at dinner, I heard the men talking about this curious ship.

"I wonder," said one, "why our captain looked so sweet on yon swallow-tailed supercargo o' pigs and Gospels. If it had been an ordinary trader, now, he would have taken as many o' the pigs as he required and sent the ship with all on board to the bottom."

"Why, Dick, you must be new to these seas if you don't know that," cried another. "The captain cares as much for the Gospel as you do (an' that's precious little), but he knows, and everybody knows, that the only place among the southern islands where a ship can put in and get what she wants in comfort is where the Gospel has been sent to. There are hundreds o' islands, at this blessed moment, where you might as well jump straight into a shark's maw as land without a band o' thirty comrades armed to the teeth to back you."

"Ay," said a man with a deep scar over his right eye, "Dick's new to the work. But if the captain takes us for a cargo o' sandal-wood to the Feejees, he'll get a taste o' these black gentry in their native condition. For my part, I don't know and I don't care what the Gospel does to them, but I know that when any o' the islands chance to get it, trade goes all smooth and easy; but where they ha'n't got it, Beelzebub himself would hardly desire better company."

"Well, you ought to be a good judge," cried another, laughing, "for you've never kept any company but the worst all your life!"

"Ralph Rover!" shouted a voice down the hatchway, "captain wants you aft."

Springing up the ladder, I hastened to the cabin, pondering as I went the strange testimony borne by these men to the effect of the Gospel on savage natures—testimony which, as was perfectly disinterested, I had no doubt whatever was strictly true.

On coming again on deck I found Bloody Bill at the helm, and as we were alone together I tried to draw him into conversation. After repeating to him the conversation in the forecastle about the missionaries, I said—

"Tell me, Bill, is this schooner really a trader in sandalwood?"

"Yes, Ralph, she is, but she's just as really a pirate. The black flag you saw flying at the peak was no deception."

"Then how can you say she's a trader?" asked I.

"Why, as to that, she trades when she can't take by force; but she takes by force when she can, in preference. Ralph," he added, lowering his voice, "if you had seen the bloody deeds that I have witnessed done on these decks, you would not need to ask if we were pirates. But you'll find it out soon enough. As for the missionaries, the captain favours them because they are useful to him. The South Sea islanders are such incarnate fiends that they are the better of being tamed, and the missionaries are the only men who can do it."

Our track after this lay through several clusters of small islets, among which we were becalmed more than once. During this part of our voyage the watch on deck and the lookout at the masthead were more than usually vigilant, as we were not only in danger of being attacked by the natives, who, I learned from the captain's remarks, were a bloody and deceitful tribe at this group, but we were also exposed to much risk from the multitudes of coral reefs that rose up in the channels between the islands, some of them just above the surface, others a few feet below it. Our precautions against the savages I found were indeed necessary.

One day we were becalmed among a group of small islands, most of which appeared to be uninhabited. As we were in want of fresh water, the captain sent the boat ashore to bring off a cask or two. But we were mistaken in thinking there were no natives; for scarcely had we drawn near to the shore when a band of naked blacks rushed out of the bush and assembled on the beach, brandishing their clubs and spears in a threatening manner. Our men were well armed, but refrained from showing any signs of hostility, and rowed nearer in order to converse with the natives; and I now found that more than one of the crew could imperfectly speak dialects of the language peculiar to the South Sea islanders. When within forty yards of the shore, we ceased rowing, and the first mate stood up to address the multitude; but instead of answering us, they replied with a shower of stones, some of which cut the men severely. Instantly our muskets were levelled, and a volley was about to be fired when the captain hailed us in a loud voice from the schooner, which lay not more than five or six hundred yards off the shore.

"Don't fire!" he shouted angrily. "Pull off to the point ahead of you."

The men looked surprised at this order, and uttered deep curses as they prepared to obey, for their wrath was roused and they burned for revenge. Three or four of them hesitated, and seemed disposed to mutiny.

"Don't distress yourselves, lads," said the mate, while a bitter smile curled his lip. "Obey orders. The captain's not the man to take an insult tamely. If Long Tom does not speak presently I'll give myself to the sharks."

The men smiled significantly as they pulled from the shore, which was now crowded with a dense mass of savages, amounting probably to five or six hundred. We had not rowed off above a couple of hundred yards when a loud roar thundered over the sea, and the big brass gun sent a withering shower of grape point blank into the midst of the living mass, through which a wide lane was cut, while a yell, the like of which I could not have imagined, burst from the miserable survivors as they fled to the woods. Amongst the heaps of dead that lay on the sand just where they had fallen, I could distinguish mutilated forms writhing in agony, while ever and anon one and another rose convulsively from out of the mass, endeavoured to stagger towards the wood, and ere they had taken a few steps, fell and wallowed on the bloody sand. My blood curdled within me as I witnessed this frightful and wanton slaughter, but I had little time to think, for the captain's deep voice came again over the water towards us: "Pull ashore, lads, and fill your water-casks." The men obeyed in silence, and it seemed to me as if even their hard hearts were shocked by the ruthless deed. On gaining the mouth of the rivulet at which we intended to take in water, we found it flowing with blood, for the greater part of those who were slain had been standing on the banks of the stream, a short way above its mouth. Many of the wretched creatures had fallen into it, and we found one body, which had been carried down, jammed between two rocks, with the staring eyeballs turned towards us, and his black hair waving in the ripples of the blood-red stream. No one dared to oppose our landing now, so we carried our casks to a pool above the murdered group, and, having filled them, returned on board. Fortunately a breeze sprang up soon afterwards and carried us away from the dreadful spot, but it could not waft me away from the memory of what I had seen.

"And this," thought I, gazing in horror at the captain, who, with a quiet look of indifference, leaned upon the taffrail smoking a cigar and contemplating the fertile green islets as they passed like a lovely picture before our eyes—"this is the man who favours the missionaries because they are useful to him and can tame the savages better than anyone else can do it!" Then I wondered in my mind whether it were possible for any missionary to tame *him*!

Chapter 22

It was many days after the events just narrated ere I recovered a little of my wonted spirits. I could not shake off the feeling for a long time that I was in a frightful dream, and the sight of our captain filled me with so much horror that I kept out of his way as much as my duties about the cabin would permit. Fortunately he took so little notice of me that he did not observe my changed feelings towards him, otherwise it might have been worse for me.

But I was now resolved that I would run away the very first island we should land at, and commit myself to the hospitality of the natives rather than remain an hour longer than I could help in the pirate schooner. I pondered this subject a good deal, and at last made up my mind to communicate my intention to Bloody Bill; for during several talks I had had with him of late, I felt assured that he too would willingly escape if possible. When I told him of my design he shook his head. "No, no, Ralph," said he, "you must not think of running away here. Among some of the groups of islands you might do so with safety, but if you tried it here you would find that you had jumped out of the fryin' pan into the fire."

"How so, Bill?" said I; "would the natives not receive me?"

"That they would, lad; but they would eat you too."

"Eat me!" said I, in surprise; "I thought the South Sea islanders never ate anybody except their enemies."

"Humph!" ejaculated Bill. "I s'pose 'twas yer tenderhearted friends in England that put that notion into your head. There's a set o' soft-hearted folk at home that I knows on who don't like to have their feelin's ruffled, and when you tell them anything they don't like—that shocks them, as they call it—no matter how true it be, they stop their ears and cry out, 'Oh, that is *too* horrible! We can't believe that!' An' they say truth. They can't believe it 'cause they won't believe it. Now, I believe there's thousands o' the people in England who are sich born drivellin' *won't-believers* that they think the black fellows hereaway at the worst eat an enemy only now an' then, out o' spite, whereas I know for certain, and many captains of the British and American navies know as well as me, that the Feejee islanders eat not only their enemies but one another, and they do it not for spite, but for pleasure. It's a *fact* that they prefer human flesh to any other. But they don't like white men's flesh so well as black; they say it makes them sick."

"Why, Bill," said I, "you told me just now that they would eat *me* if they caught me."

"So I did, and so I think they would. I've only heard some o' them say they don't like white men *so well* as black; but if they was hungry they wouldn't be particular. Anyhow, I'm sure they would kill you. You see, Ralph, I've been a good while in them parts, and I've visited the different groups of islands oftentimes as a trader. And thorough-goin' blackguards some o' them traders are; no better than pirates, I can tell you. One captain that I sailed with was not a chip better than the one we're with now. He was trading with a friendly chief one day, aboard his vessel. The chief had swum off to us with the things for trade tied atop of his head, for them chaps are like otters in the water. Well, the chief was hard on the captain, and would not part with some o' his things. When their bargainin' was over they shook hands, and the chief jumped overboard to swim ashore; but before he got forty yards from the ship the captain seized a musket and shot him dead. He then hove up anchor and put to sea, and as we sailed along shore, he dropped six black fellows with his rifle, remarkin' that 'that would spoil the trade for the next comers'. But as I was sayin', I'm up to the ways o' these fellows. One o' the laws o' the country is, that every shipwrecked person who happens to be cast ashore, be he dead or alive, is doomed to be roasted and eaten. There was a small tradin' schooner wrecked off one of these islands when we were lyin' there in harbour during a storm. The crew was lost, all but three men, who swam ashore. The moment they landed they were seized by the natives and carried up into the woods. We knew pretty well what their fate would be, but we could not help them for our crew was small, and if we had gone ashore they would likely have killed us all. We never saw the three men again; but we heard frightful yelling and dancing and merry-making that night; and one of the natives, who came aboard to trade with us next day, told us that the *long pigs,* as he called the men, had been roasted and eaten, and their bones were to be converted into sail needles. He also said that white men were bad to eat, and that most of the people on shore were sick."

I was very much shocked and cast down in my mind at this terrible account of the natives, and asked Bill what he would advise me to do. Looking round the deck to make sure that we were not overheard, he lowered his voice and said, "There are two or three ways that we might escape, Ralph, but none o' them's easy. If the captain would only sail for some o' the islands near Tahiti, we might run away there well enough, because the natives are all Christians; an' we find that wherever the savages take up with Christianity they always give over their bloody ways, and are safe to be trusted. I never cared for Christianity myself," he continued, in a soliloquizing voice, "and I don't well know what it means; but a man with half an eye can see what it does for these black critters. However, the captain always keeps a sharp look-out after us when we get to these islands, for he half suspects that one or two o' us are tired of his company. Then we might manage to cut the the boat adrift some fine night when it's our watch on deck, and clear off before they discovered that we were gone. But we would run the risk o' bein' caught by the blacks. I wouldn't like to try that plan. But you and I will think over it, Ralph, and see what's to be done. In the meantime it's our watch below, so I'll go and turn in."

Bill then bade me good night, and went below, while a comrade took his place at the helm; but feeling no desire to enter into conversation with him, I walked aft, and leaning over the stern, looked down into the phosphorescent waves that gurgled around the rudder, and streamed out like a flame of blue light in the vessel's wake. My thoughts were very sad, and I could scarce refrain from tears as I contrasted my present wretched position with the happy, peaceful time I had spent on the Coral Island with my dear companions. As I thought upon Jack and Peterkin anxious forebodings crossed my mind, and I pictured to myself the grief and dismay with which they would search every nook and corner of the island, in a vain attempt to discover my dead body; for I felt assured that if they did not see any sign of the pirate schooner or boat when they came out of the cave to look for me, they would never imagine that I had been carried away. I wondered, too, how Jack would succeed in getting Peterkin out of the cave without my assistance; and I trembled when I thought that he might lose presence of mind, and begin to kick when he was in the tunnel! These thoughts were suddenly interrupted and put to flight by a bright red blaze which lighted up the horizon to the southward and cast a crimson glow far over the sea. This appearance was accompanied by a low growling sound, as of distant thunder, and at the same time the sky above us became black, while a hot stifling wind blew around us in fitful gusts.

The crew assembled hastily on deck, and most of them were under the belief that a frightful hurricane was pending; but the captain coming on deck, soon explained the phenomena.

"It's only a volcano," said he. "I knew there was one hereabouts but thought it was extinct. Up there and furl top-gallant-sails, we'll likely have a breeze, and it's well to be ready."

As he spoke a shower began to fall, which we quickly observed was not rain but fine ashes. As we were many miles distant from the volcano, these must have been carried to us from it by the wind. As the captain had predicted, a stiff breeze soon afterwards sprang up, under the influence of which we speedily left the volcano far behind us; but during the greater part of the night we could see its lurid glare and hear its distant thunder. The shower did not cease to fall for several hours, and we must have sailed under it for nearly forty miles, perhaps further. When we emerged from the cloud, our decks and every part of the rigging were completely covered with a thick coat of ashes. I was much interested in this, and recollected that Jack had often spoken of many of the islands of the Pacific as being volcanoes, either active or extinct and had said that the whole region was more or less volcanic, and that some scientific men were of opinion that the islands of the Pacific were nothing more or less than the mountain-tops of a huge continent which had sunk under the influence of volcanic agency.

Three days after passing the volcano, we found ourselves a few miles to windward of an island of considerable size and luxuriant aspect. It consisted of two mountains, which seemed to be nearly four thousand feet high. They were separated from each other by a broad valley, whose thick, growing trees ascended a considerable distance up the mountain sides; and rich level plains, or meadow-land, spread round the base of the mountains, except at the point immediately opposite the large valley, where a river seemed to carry the trees, as it were, along, with it down to the white sandy shore. The mountain-tops, unlike those of our Coral Island, were sharp, needle-shaped, and bare, while their sides were more rugged and grand in outline than anything I had yet seen in those seas. Bloody Bill was beside me when the island first hove in sight.

"Ha!" he exclaimed, "I know that island well. They call it Emo."

"Have you been here before, then?" I inquired.

"Ay, that I have, often, and so has this schooner. 'Tis a famous island for sandal-wood. We have taken many cargoes off it already, and have paid for them, too; for the savages are so numerous that we dared not try to take it by force. But our captain has tried to cheat them so often that they're beginning not to like us overmuch now. Besides, the men behaved ill the last time we were here and I wonder the captain is not afraid to venture. But he's afraid o' nothing earthly, I believe."

We soon ran inside the barrier coral-reef, and let go our anchor in six fathoms water, just opposite the mouth of a small creek, whose shores were densely covered with mangroves and tall umbrageous trees. The principal village of the natives lay about half a mile from this point. Ordering the boat out, the captain jumped into it, and ordered me to follow him. The men, fifteen in number, were well armed; and the mate was directed to have Long Tom ready for emergencies.

"Give way, lads," cried the captain.

The oars fell into the water at the word, the boat shot from the schooner's side, and in a few minutes reached the shore. Here, contrary to our expectation, we were met with the utmost cordiality by Romata, the principal chief of the island, who conducted us to his house and gave us mats to sit upon. I observed in passing that the natives, of whom there were two or three thousand, were totally unarmed.

After a short preliminary palaver, a feast of baked pigs and various roots was spread before us; of which we partook sparingly, and then proceeded to business. The captain stated his object in visiting the island, regretted that there had been a slight misunderstanding during the last visit, and hoped that no ill will was borne by either party, and that a satisfactory trade would be accomplished.

Romata answered that he had forgotten there had been any differences between them, protested that he was delighted to see his friends again, and assured them they should have every assistance in cutting and embarking the wood. The terms were afterwards agreed on, and we rose to depart. All this conversation was afterwards explained to me by Bill, who understood the language pretty well.

Romata accompanied us on board, and explained that a great chief from another island was then on a visit to him, and that he was to be ceremoniously entertained on the following day. After begging to be allowed to introduce him to us, and receiving permission, he sent his canoe ashore to bring him off. At the same time he gave orders to bring on board his two favourites, a cock and a paroquet. While the canoe was gone on this errand, I had time to regard the savage chief attentively. He was a man of immense size, with massive but beautifully moulded limbs and figure, only parts of which, the broad chest and muscular arms, were uncovered; for although the lower orders generally wore no other clothing than a strip of cloth called *maro* round their loins, the chief, on particular occasions, wrapped his person in voluminous folds of a species of native cloth made from the bark of the Chinese paper-mulberry. Romata wore a magnificent black beard and moustache, and his hair was frizzed out to such an extent that it resembled a large turban, in which was stuck a long wooden pin! I afterwards found that this pin served for scratching the head, for which purpose the fingers were too short without disarranging the hair. But Romata put himself to much greater inconvenience on account of his hair, for we found that he slept with his head resting on a wooden pillow, in which was cut a hollow for the neck, so that the hair of the sleeper might not be disarranged.

In ten minutes the canoe returned, bringing the other chief, who certainly presented a most extraordinary appearance, having painted one half of his face red and the other half yellow, besides ornamenting it with various designs in black! Otherwise he was much the same in appearance as Romata, though not so powerfully built. As this chief had never seen a ship before, except, perchance, some of the petty traders that at long intervals visit these remote islands, he was much taken up with the neatness and beauty of all the fittings of the schooner. He was particularly struck with a musket which was shown to him, and asked where the white men got hatchets hard enough to cut the tree of which the barrel was made! While he was thus engaged, his brother chief stood aloof, talking with the captain, and fondling a superb cock and a little blueheaded paroquet, the favourites of which I have before spoken. I observed that all the other natives walked in a crouching posture while in the presence of Romata. Before our guests left us, the captain ordered the brass gun to be uncovered and fired for their gratification; and I have every reason to believe he did so for the purpose of showing our superior power, in case the natives should harbour any evil designs against us. Romata had never seen this gun before, as it had not been uncovered on previous visits, and the astonishment with which he viewed it was very amusing. Being desirous of knowing its power, he begged that the captain would fire it. So a shot was put into it. The chiefs were then directed to look at a rock about two miles out at sea, and the gun was fired. In a second the top of the rock was seen to burst asunder, and to fall in fragments into the sea.

Next day the crew went ashore to cut sandal-wood, while the captain, with one or two men, remained on board, in order to be ready, if need be, with the brass gun, which was unhoused and conspicuously elevated, with its capacious muzzle directed point-blank at the chief's house. The men were fully armed as usual; and the captain ordered me to go with them, to assist in the work. I was much pleased with this order, for it freed me from the captain's company, which I could not now endure, and it gave me an opportunity of seeing the natives.

As we wound along in single file through the rich fragrant groves of banana, coco-nut, bread-fruit, and other trees, I observed that there were many of the plum and banyan trees with which I had become familiar on the Coral Island. I noticed also large quantities of taro-roots, yams, and sweet potatoes growing in enclosures. On turning into an open glade of the woods, we came abruptly upon a cluster of native houses. They were built chiefly of bamboos and were thatched with the large thick leaves of the pandanus; but many of them had little more than a sloping roof and three sides with an open front, being the most simple shelter from the weather that could well be imagined. Within these and around them were groups of natives—men, women, and children—who all stood up to gaze at us as we marched along, followed by the party of men whom the chief had sent to escort us. About half a mile inland we arrived at the spot where the sandal-wood grew, and while the men set to work I clambered up an adjoining hill to observe the country.

About midday the chief arrived with several followers, one of whom carried a baked pig on a wooden platter, with yams and potatoes on several plantain leaves, which he presented to the men, who sat down under the shade of a tree to dine. The chief sat down to dine also; but to my surprise, instead of feeding himself, one of his wives performed that office for him! I was seated beside Bill, and asked him the reason of this.

"It is beneath his dignity, I believe, to feed himself," answered Bill; "but I dare say he's not particular, except on great occasions. They've a strange custom among them, Ralph, which is called *tabu*, and they carry it to great lengths. If a man chooses a particular tree for his god, the fruit o' that tree is tabued to him; and if he eats it, he is sure to be killed by his people, and eaten, of course, for killing means eating hereaway. Then, you see that great mop o' hair on the chief's head? Well, he has a lot o' barbers to keep it in order; and it's a law that whoever touches the head of a living chief or the body of a dead one, his hands are tabued; so in that way the barbers' hands are always tabued, and they daren't use them for their lives, but have to be fed like big babies, as they are, sure enough!"

"That's odd, Bill. But look there," said I, pointing to a man whose skin was of a much lighter colour than the generality of the natives. "I've seen a few of these light-skinned fellows among the Feejeeans. They seem to me to be of quite a different race."

"So they are," answered Bill. "These fellows come from the Tongan Islands, which lie a long way to the eastward. They come here to build their big war-canoes; and as these take two and sometimes four years to build, there's always some o' the brown-skins among the black sarpents o' these islands."

"By the way, Bill," said I, "your mentioning serpents reminds me that I have not seen a reptile of any kind since I came to this part of the world."

"No more there are any," said Bill, "there's none on the islands but a lizard or two and some sich harmless things. But I never seed any myself. If there's none on the land, however, there's more than enough in the water, and that minds me of a wonderful brute they have here. But come, I'll show it to you." So saying, Bill arose, and leaving the men still busy with the baked pig, led me into the forest. After proceeding a short distance we came upon a small pond of stagnant water. A native lad had followed us, to whom we called and beckoned him to come to us. On Bill saying a few words to him, which I did not understand, the boy advanced to the edge of the pond, and gave a low, peculiar whistle. Immediately the water became agitated, and an enormous eel thrust its head above the surface and allowed the youth to touch it. It was about twelve feet long, and as thick round the body as a man's thigh.

"There!" said Bill, his lip curling with contempt; "what do you think of that for a god, Ralph? This is one o' their gods, and it has been fed with dozens o' livin' babies already. How many more it'll get afore it dies is hard to say."

"Babies!" said I, with an incredulous look.

"Ay, babies," returned Bill. "Your soft-hearted folk at home would say, 'Oh, horrible! impossible!' to that, and then go away as comfortable and unconcerned as if their saying, 'horrible! impossible!' had made it a lie. But I tell you, Ralph, it's a *fact.* I've seed it with my own eyes the last time I was here, an' mayhap if you stop a while at this accursed place, and keep a sharp look out, you'll see it too. They don't feed it regularly with livin' babies, but they give it one now and then as a treat. Bah, you brute!" cried Bill in disgust, giving the reptile a kick on the snout with his heavy boot that sent it sweltering back in agony into its loathsome pool. I thought it lucky for Bill, indeed for all of us, that the native youth's back happened to be turned at the time; for I am certain that if the poor savages had come to know that we had so rudely handled their god, we should have had to fight our way back to the ship. As we retraced our steps I questioned my companion further on this subject.

"How comes it, Bill, that the mothers allow such a dreadful thing to be done?"

"Allow it? The mothers *do* it! It seems to me that there's nothing too fiendish or diabolical for these people to do. Why, in some of the islands they have an institution called the *Areoi,* and the persons connected with that body are ready for any wickedness that mortal man can devise. In fact they stick at nothing; and one o' their customs is to murder their infants the moment they are born. The mothers agree to it, and the fathers do it. And the mildest ways they have of murdering them is by sticking them through the body with sharp splinters of bamboo, strangling them with their thumbs, or burying them alive and stamping them to death while under the sod."

I felt sick at heart while my companion recited these horrors.

"But it's a curious fact," he continued, after a pause, during which we walked in silence towards the spot where we had left our comrades—"it's a curious fact, that wherever the missionaries get a footin' all these things come to an end at once, an' the savages take to doin' each other good and singin' psalms, just like Methodists."

"God bless the missionaries!" said I, while a feeling of enthusiasm filled my heart, so that I could speak with difficulty. "God bless and prosper the missionaries till they get a footing in every island of the sea!"

"I would say Amen to that prayer, Ralph, if I could," said Bill, in a deep, sad voice; "but it would be a mere mockery for a man to ask a blessing for others who dare not ask one for himself. But, Ralph," he continued, "I've not told you half o' the abominations I have seen durin' my life in these seas. If we pull long together, lad, I'll tell you more; and if times have not changed very much since I was here last, it's like that you'll have a chance o' seeing a little for yourself before long."

Chapter 23

Next day the wood-cutting party went ashore again, and I accompanied them as before. During the dinner hour I wandered into the woods alone, being disinclined for food that day. I had not rambled far when I found myself unexpectedly on the seashore, having crossed a narrow neck of land which separated the native village from a large bay. Here I found a party of the islanders busy with one of their war-canoes, which was almost ready for launching. I stood for a long time watching this party with great interest, and observed that they fastened the timbers and planks to each other very much in the same way in which I had seen Jack fasten those of our little boat. But what surprised me most was its immense length, which I measured very carefully, and found to be a hundred feet long; and it was so capacious that it could have held three hundred men. It had the unwieldy outrigger and enormously high stern posts which I had remarked on the canoe that came to us while I was on the Coral Island. Observing some boys playing at games a short way along the beach, I resolved to go and watch them but, as I turned from the natives who were engaged so busily and cheerfully at their work. I little thought of the terrible event that hung on the completion of that war-canoe.

Advancing towards the children, who were so numerous that I began to think this must be the general playground of the village, I sat down on a grassy bank under the shade of a plantain tree to watch them. And a happier or noisier crew I have never seen. There were at least two hundred of them, both boys and girls, all of whom were clad in no other garments than their own glossy little black skins, except the maro, or strip of cloth round the loins of the boys, and a very short petticoat or kilt on the girls. They did not all play at the same game, but amused themselves in different groups.

One band was busily engaged in a game exactly similar to our blind man's buff. Another set were walking on stilts, which raised the children three feet from the ground. They were very expert at this amusement, and seldom tumbled. In another place I observed a group of girls standing together, and apparently enjoying themselves very much; so I went up to see what they were doing, and found that they were opening their eyelids with their fingers till their eyes appeared of an enormous size, and then thrusting pieces of straw between the upper and lower lids, across the eyeball, to keep them in that position! This seemed to me, I must confess, a very foolish as well as dangerous amusement. Nevertheless, the children seemed to be greatly delighted with the hideous faces they made. I pondered this subject a good deal, and thought that if little children knew how silly they seem to grown-up people when they make faces, they would not be so fond of doing it. In another place were a number of boys engaged in flying kites, and I could not help wondering that some of the games of those little savages should be so like to our own, although they had never seen us at play. But the kites were different from ours in many respects, being of every variety of shape. They were made of very thin cloth, and the boys raised them to a wonderful height in the air by means of twine made from the coco-nut husk. Other games there were, some of which showed the natural depravity of the hearts of these poor savages, and made me wish fervently that missionaries might be sent out to them. But the amusement which the greatest number of the children of both sexes seemed to take chief delight in was swimming and diving in the sea, and the expertness which they exhibited was truly amazing. They seemed to have two principal games in the water, one of which was to dive off a sort of stage which had been erected near a deep part of the sea, and chase each other in the water. Some of them went down to an extraordinary depth; others skimmed along the surface, or rolled over and over like porpoises, or diving under each other, came up unexpectedly and pulled each other down by a leg or an arm. They never seemed to tire of this sport, and from the great heat of the water in the South Seas they could remain in it nearly all day without feeling chilled. Many of these children were almost infants scarce able to walk; yet they staggered down the beach, flung their round fat little black bodies fearlessly into deep water, and struck out to sea with as much confidence as ducklings.

The other game to which I have referred was swimming in the surf. But as this is an amusement in which all engage, from children of ten to grey-headed men of sixty, and as I had an opportunity of witnessing it the day following, I shall describe it more minutely.

I suppose it was in honour of their guest that this grand swimming-match was got up, for Romata came and told the captain that they were going to engage in it, and begged him to "come and see".

"What sort of amusement is this surf-swimming?" I inquired of Bill, as we walked together to a part of the shore on which several thousands of the natives were assembled.

"It's a very favourite lark with these 'xtr'or'nary critters," replied Bill, giving a turn to the quid of tobacco that invariably bulged out of his left cheek. "Ye see, Ralph, them fellows take to the water as soon a'most as they can walk, an' long before they can do that anything respectably, so that they are as much at home in the sea as on the land. Well, ye see, I s'pose they found swimmin' for miles out to sea, and divin' fathoms deep, wasn't exciting enough, so they invented this game o' swimmin' on the surf. Each man and boy, as you see, has got a short board or plank, with which he swims out for a mile or more to sea, and then, gettin' on the top o' yon thunderin' breaker, they come to shore on the top of it, yellin' and screechin' like fiends. It's a marvel to me that they're not dashed to shivers on the coral reef, for sure an' sartin am I that if any o' us tried it, we wouldn't be worth the fluke of a broken anchor after the wave fell. But there they go!"

As he spoke, several hundreds of the natives, amongst whom we were now standing, uttered a loud yell, rushed down the beach, plunged into the surf, and were carried off by the seething foam of the retreating wave.

At the point where we stood, the encircling coral reef joined the shore, so that the magnificent breakers, which a recent stiff breeze had rendered larger than usual, fell in thunder at the feet of the multitudes who lined the beach. For some time the swimmers continued to strike out to sea, breasting over the swell like hundreds of black seals. Then they all turned, and, watching an approaching billow, mounted its white crest, and each laying his breast on the short flat board, came rolling towards the shore, careering on the summit of the mighty wave, while they and the onlookers shouted and yelled with excitement. Just as the monster wave curled in solemn majesty to fling its bulky length upon the beach, most of the swimmers slid back into the trough behind; others slipping off their boards, seized them in their hands, and plunging through the watery waste, swam out to repeat the amusement; but a few, who seemed to me the most reckless, continued their career until they were launched upon the beach, and enveloped in the churning foam and spray. One of these last came in on the crest of the wave most manfully, and landed with a violent bound almost on the spot where Bill and I stood. I saw by his peculiar head-dress that he was the chief whom the tribe entertained as their guest. The seawater had removed nearly all the paint with which his face had been covered, and as he rose panting to his feet, I recognized, to my surprise, the features of Tararo, my old friend of the Coral Island!

Tararo at the same moment recognized me, and, advancing quickly, took me round the neck and rubbed noses; which had the effect of transferring a good deal of the moist paint from his nose to mine. Then, recollecting that this was not the white man's mode of salutation, he grasped me by the hand and shook it violently.

"Hallo, Ralph!" cried Bill, in surprise, "that chap seems to have taken a sudden fancy to you, or he must be an old acquaintance."

"Right, Bill," I replied; "he is indeed an old acquaintance;" and I explained in a few words that he was the chief whose party Jack and Peterkin and I had helped to save.

Tararo, having thrown away his surf-board, entered into an animated conversation with Bill, pointing frequently during the course of it to me; whereby I concluded he must be telling him about the memorable battle and the part we had taken in it. When he paused, I begged of Bill to ask him about the woman Avatea, for I had some hope that she might have come with Tararo on this visit. "And ask him," said I, "who she is, for I am persuaded she is of a different race from the Feejeeans." On the mention of her name the chief frowned, and seemed to speak with much anger.

"You're right, Ralph," said Bill, when the chief had ceased to talk: "she's not a Feejee girl, but a Samoan. How she ever came to this place the chief does not very clearly explain, but he says she was taken in war, and that he got her three years ago an' kept her as his daughter ever since. Lucky for her, poor girl, else she'd have been roasted and eaten like the rest."

"But why does Tararo frown and look so angry?" said I.

"Because the girl's somewhat obstinate, like most o' the sex, an' won't marry the man he wants her to. It seems that a chief of some other island came on a visit to Tararo and took a fancy to her, but she wouldn't have him on no account, bein' already in love and engaged to a young chief whom Tararo hates, and she kicked up a desperate shindy; so, as he was going on a war expedition in his canoe, he left her to think about it, sayin' he'd be back in six months or so, when he hoped she wouldn't be so obstropolous. This happened just a week ago, an' Tararo says that if she's not ready to go, when the chief returns, as his bride, she'll be sent to him as a *long pig*."

"As a long pig!" I exclaimed, in surprise, "why, what does he mean by that?"

"He means somethin' very unpleasant," answered Bill, with a frown. "You see these blackguards eat men an' women just as readily as they eat pigs; and as baked pigs and baked men are very like each other in appearance, they call men *long* pigs. If Avatea goes to this fellow as a long pig, it's all up with her, poor thing."

"Is she on the island now?" I asked eagerly.

"No, she's at Tararo's island."

"And where does it lie?"

"About fifty miles to the south'ard," returned Bill, "but I——"

At this moment we were startled by the cry of "Mao! mao!—a shark! a shark!" which was immediately followed by a shriek that rang clear and fearfully loud above the tumult of cries that arose from the savages in the water and on the land. We turned hastily towards the direction whence the cry came, and had just time to observe the glaring eyeballs of one of the swimmers as he tossed his arms in the air. Next instant he was pulled under the waves. A canoe was instantly launched, and the hand of the drowning man was caught, but only half of his body was dragged from the maw of the monster, which followed the canoe until the water became so shallow that it could scarcely swim. The crest of the next billow was tinged with red as it rolled towards the shore.

In most countries of the world this would have made a deep impression on the spectators, but the only effect it had upon these islanders was to make them hurry with all speed out of the sea, lest a similar fate should befall some of the others; but so utterly reckless were they of human life, that it did not for a moment suspend the progress of their amusements. It is true the surf swimming ended somewhat abruptly, but they immediately proceeded with other games. Bill told me that sharks do not often attack the surf-swimmers, being frightened away by the immense numbers of men and boys in the water, and by the shouting and splashing that they make. "But," said he, "such a thing as you have seen just now don't frighten them much. They'll be at it again tomorrow or next day just as if there wasn't a single shark between Feejee and Nova Zembla."

After this the natives had a series of wrestling and boxing matches and, being men of immense size and muscle, they did a good deal of injury to each other, especially in boxing, in which not only the lower orders but several of the chiefs and priests engaged.

During these exhibitions, which were very painful to me, though I confess I could not refrain from beholding them, I was struck with the beauty of many of the figures and designs that were tattooed on the persons of the chiefs and principal men. One figure, that seemed to me very elegant, was that of a palm tree tattooed on the back of a man's leg, the roots rising, as it were, from under his heel, the stem ascending the tendon of the ankle, and the graceful head branching out upon the calf. I afterwards learned that this process of tattooing is very painful, and takes long to do, commencing at the age of ten, and being continued at intervals up to the age of thirty. It is done by means of an instrument made of bone, with a number of sharp teeth with which the skin is punctured. Into these punctures a preparation made from the kernel of the candle-nut, mixed with coco-nut oil, is rubbed, and the mark thus made is indelible. The operation is performed by a class of men whose profession it is, and they tattoo as much at a time as the person on whom they are operating can bear, which is not much, the pain and inflammation caused by tattooing being very great, sometimes causing death.

Next day, while we were returning from the woods to our schooner, we observed Romata rushing about in the neighbourhood of his house, apparently mad with passion.

"Ah," said Bill to me, "there he's at his old tricks again. That's his way when he gets drink. The natives make a sort of drink o' their own, and it makes him bad enough; but when he gets brandy he's like a wild tiger. The captain, I suppose, has given him a bottle, as usual, to keep him in good humour. After drinkin' he usually goes to sleep, and the people know it well, and keep out of his way, for fear they should waken him. Even the babies are taken out of earshot; for when he's waked up he rushes out just as you see him now, and spears or clubs the first person he meets."

It seemed at the present time, however, that no deadly weapon had been in his way, for the infuriated chief was raging about without one. Suddenly he caught sight of an unfortunate man who was trying to conceal himself behind a tree. Rushing towards him, Romata struck him a terrible blow on the head which knocked out the poor man's eye and also dislocated the chief's finger. The wretched creature offered no resistance; he did not even attempt to parry the blow. Indeed, from what Bill said, I found that he might consider himself lucky in having escaped with his life, which would certainly have been forfeited had the chief been possessed of a club at the time.

"Have these wretched creatures no law among themselves," said I, "which can restrain such wickedness?"

"None," replied Bill. "The chief's word is law. He might kill and eat a dozen of his own subjects any day for nothing more than his own pleasure, and nobody would take the least notice of it."

This ferocious deed took place within sight of our party as we wended our way to the beach, but I could not observe any other expression on the faces of the men than that of total indifference or contempt. It seemed to me a very awful thing that it should be possible for men to come to such hardness of heart and callousness to the sight of bloodshed and violence; but, indeed, I began to find that such constant exposure to scenes of blood was having a slight effect upon myself, and I shuddered when I came to think that I too was becoming callous.

Chapter 24

Next morning I awoke with a feverish brow and a feeling of deep depression at my heart, and the more I thought on my unhappy fate, the more wretched and miserable did I feel.

When the captain came on deck, before the hour at which the men usually started for the woods, I begged of him to permit me to remain aboard that day, as I did not feel well; but he looked at me angrily, and ordered me, in a surly tone, to get ready to go on shore as usual. The fact was that the captain had been out of humour for some time past. Romata and he had had some differences, and high words had passed between them, during which the chief had threatened to send a fleet of war-canoes, with a thousand men, to break up and burn the schooner; whereupon the captain smiled sarcastically, and going up to the chief gazed sternly in his face, while he said, "I have only to raise my little finger just now, and my big guns will blow your whole village to atoms in five minutes!" Although the chief was a bold man, he quailed before the pirate's glance and threat, and made no reply; but a bad feeling had been raised, and old sores had been opened.

I had, therefore, to go with the wood-cutters that day. Before starting, however, the captain called me into his cabin, and said—

"Here, Ralph; I've got a mission for you, lad. That blackguard Romata is in the dumps, and nothing will mollify him but a gift; so do you go up to his house and give him these whale's teeth, with my compliments. Take with you one of the men who can speak the language."

I looked at the gift in some surprise for it consisted of six whale's teeth, and two of the same dyed bright red, which seemed to me very paltry things. However, I did not dare to hesitate or ask any questions so, gathering them up, I left the cabin, and was soon on my way to the chief's house, accompanied by Bill. On expressing my surprise at the gift, he said—

"They're paltry enough to you or me, Ralph, but they're considered of great value by them chaps. They're a sort o' cash among them. The red ones are the most prized, one of them bein' equal to twenty o' the white ones. I suppose the only reason for their bein' valuable is that there ain't many of them, and they're hard to be got."

On arriving at the house we found Romata sitting on a mat, in the midst of a number of large bales of native cloth and other articles, which had been brought to him as presents from time to time by inferior chiefs. He received us rather haughtily, but, on Bill explaining the nature of our errand, he became very condescending, and his eyes glistened with satisfaction when he received the whale's teeth, although he laid them aside with an assumption of kingly indifference.

"Go," said he, with a wave of the hand—"go tell your captain that he may cut wood today but not tomorrow. He must come ashore; I want to have a palaver with him."

As we left the house to return to the woods, Bill shook his head.

"There's mischief brewin' in that black rascal's head. I know him of old. But what comes here?"

As he spoke, we heard the sound of laughter and shouting in the wood, and presently there issued from it a band of savages, in the midst of whom were a number of men bearing burdens on their shoulders. At first I thought that these burdens were poles with something rolled round them, the end of each pole resting on a man's shoulder; but on a nearer approach I saw that they were human beings, tied hand and foot, and so lashed to the poles that they could not move. I counted twenty of them as they passed.

"More murder!" said Bill, in a voice that sounded between a hoarse laugh and a groan.

"Surely they are not going to murder them?" said I, looking anxiously into Bill's face.

"I don't know, Ralph," replied Bill, "what they're goin' to do with them; but I fear they mean no good when they tie fellows up in that way."

As we continued our way towards the wood-cutters, I observed that Bill looked anxiously over his shoulder in the direction where the procession had disappeared. At last he stopped, and, turning abruptly on his heel, said—

"I tell ye what it is, Ralph: I must be at the bottom o' that affair. Let us follow these black scoundrels and see what they're goin' to do."

I must say I had no wish to pry further into their bloody practices; but Bill seemed bent on it, so I turned and went. We passed rapidly through the brush, being guided in the right direction by the shouts of the savages. Suddenly there was a dead silence, which continued for some time, while Bill and I involuntarily quickened our pace until we were running at top of our speed across the narrow neck of land previously mentioned. As we reached the verge of the wood, we discovered the savages surrounding the large war-canoe, which they were apparently on the point of launching. Suddenly the multitude put their united strength to the canoe; but scarcely had the huge machine begun to move, when a yell, the most appalling that ever fell upon my ear, rose high above the shouting of the savages. It had not died away when another and another smote upon my throbbing ear; and then I saw that these inhuman monsters were actually launching their canoe over the living bodies of their victims. But there was no pity in the breasts of these men. Forward they went in ruthless indifference, shouting as they went, while high above their voices rang the dying shrieks of those wretched creatures, as, one after .another, the ponderous canoe passed ' over them, burst the eyeballs from their sockets, and sent the life's blood gushing from their mouths. Oh reader, this is no fiction. I would not, for the sake of thrilling you with horror, invent so terrible a scene. It was witnessed. It is true—true as that accursed sin which has rendered the human heart capable of such diabolical enormities!

When it was over I turned round and fell upon the grass with a deep groan; but Bill seized me by the arm, and, lifting me up as if I had been a child, cried—

"Come along, lad; let's away!"—and so, staggering and stumbling over the tangled underwood, we fled from the fatal spot.

During the remainder of that day I felt as if I were in a horrible dream. I scarce knew what was said to me, and was more than once blamed by the men for idling my time. At last the hour to return aboard came. We marched down to the beach and I felt relief for the first time when my feet rested on the schooner's deck.

In the course of the evening I overheard part of a conversation between the captain and the first mate, which startled me not a little. They were down in the cabin, and conversed in an undertone; but the skylight being off, I overheard every word that was said.

"I don't half like it," said the mate. "It seems to me that we'll only have hard fightin' and no pay."

"No pay!" repeated the captain, in a voice of suppressed anger. "Do you call a good cargo all for nothing no pay?"

"Very true," returned the mate; "but we've got the cargo aboard. Why not cut your cable and take French leave o' them? What's the use o' trying to lick the blackguards when it'll do us no manner o' good?"

"Mate," said the captain, in a low voice, "you talk like a fresh-water sailor. I can only attribute this shyness to some strange delusion; for surely" (his voice assumed a slightly sneering tone as he said this), "surely I am not to suppose that *you* have become soft-hearted! Besides, you are wrong in regard to the cargo being aboard; there's a good quarter of it lying in the woods, and that blackguard chief knows it and won't let me take it off. He defied us to do our worst yesterday."

"Defied us! did he?" cried the mate, with a bitter laugh. "Poor contemptible thing!"

"And yet he seems not so contemptible but that you are afraid to attack him."

"Who said I was afraid?" growled the mate sulkily. "I'm as ready as any man in the ship. But, captain, what is it that you intend to do?"

"I intend to muffle the sweeps and row the schooner up to the head of the creek there, from which point we can command the pile of sandal-wood with our gun. Then I shall land with all the men except two, who shall take care of the schooner and be ready with the boat to take us off. We can creep through the woods to the head of the village, where these cannibals are always dancing round their suppers of human flesh, and if the carbines of the men are loaded with a heavy charge of buck-shot, we can drop forty or fifty at the first volley. After that the thing will be easy enough. The savages will take to the mountains in a body, and we shall take what we require, up anchor, and away."

To this plan the mate at length agreed. As he left the cabin I heard the captain say—

"Give the men an extra glass of grog and don't forget the buck-shot."

The reader may conceive the horror with which I heard this murderous conversation. I immediately repeated it to Bill, who seemed much perplexed about it. At length he said—

"I'll tell you what I'll do, Ralph. I'll swim ashore after dark and fix a musket to a tree not far from the place where we'll have to land, and I'll tie a long string to the trigger, so that when our fellows cross it they'll let it off, and so alarm the village in time to prevent an attack, but not in time to prevent us gettin' back to the boat. So, Master Captain," added Bill, with a smile that for the first time seemed to me to be mingled with good-natured cheerfulness, "you'll be balked at least for once in your life by Bloody Bill."

After it grew dark, Bill put this resolve in practice. He slipped over the side with a musket in his left hand, while with his right he swam ashore and entered the woods. He soon returned, having accomplished his purpose, and got on board without being seen, I being the only one on deck.

When the hour of midnight approached the men were mustered on deck, the cable was cut and the muffled sweeps got out. These sweeps were immensely large oars, each requiring a couple of men to work it. In a few minutes we entered the mouth of the creek, which was indeed the mouth of a small river, and took about half an hour to ascend it, although the spot where we intended to land was not more than six hundred yards from the mouth, because there was a slight current against us, and the mangroves which narrowed the creek impeded the rowers in some places. Having reached the spot, which was so darkened by overhanging trees that we could see with difficulty, a small kedge anchor attached to a thin line was let softly down over the stern.

"Now, lads," whispered the captain, as he walked along the line of men, who were all armed to the teeth, "don't be in a hurry, aim low, and don't waste your first shots."

He then pointed to the boat, into which the men crowded in silence. There was no room to row; but oars were not needed, as a slight push against the side of the schooner sent the boat gliding to the shore.

"There's no need of leaving two in the boat," whispered the mate, as the men stepped out; "we shall want all our hands. Let Ralph stay."

The captain assented, and ordered me to stand in readiness with the boat-hook, to shove ashore at a moment's notice if they should return, or to shove off if any of the savages should happen to approach. He then threw his carbine into the hollow of his arm and glided through the bushes, followed by his men. With a throbbing heart I awaited the result of our plan. I knew the exact locality where the musket was placed, for Bill had described it to me, and I kept my straining eyes fixed upon the spot. But no sound came and I began to fear that either they had gone in another direction or that Bill had not fixed the string properly. Suddenly I heard a faint click and observed one or two bright sparks among the bushes. My heart immediately sank within me, for I knew at once that the trigger had indeed been pulled, but that the priming had not caught. The plan, therefore, had utterly failed. A feeling of dread now began to creep over me as I stood in the boat, in that dark, silent spot, awaiting the issue of this murderous expedition. I shuddered as I glanced at the water that glided past like a dark reptile. I looked back at the schooner, but her hull was just barely visible, while her tapering masts were lost among the trees which overshadowed her. Her lower sails were set, but so thick was the gloom that they were quite invisible.

Suddenly I heard a shot. In a moment a thousand voices raised a yell in the village; again the cry rose on the night air, and was followed by broken shouts as of scattered parties of men bounding into the woods. Then I heard another shout loud and close at hand. It was the voice of the captain cursing the man who had fled the premature shot. Then came the order, "Forward!" followed by the wild hurrah of our men as they charged the savages. Shots now rang in quick succession, and at last a loud volley startled the echoes of the woods. It was followed by a multitude of wild shrieks, which were immediately drowned in another hurrah from the men; the distance of the sound proving that they were driving their enemies before them towards the sea.

While I was listening intently to these sounds, which were now mingled in confusion, I was startled by the rustling of the leaves not far from me. At first I thought it was a party of savages who had observed the schooner, but I was speedily undeceived by observing a body of natives—apparently several hundreds, as far as I could guess in the uncertain light—bounding through the woods towards the scene of battle. I saw at once that this was a party who had outflanked our men, and would speedily attack them in the rear. And so it turned out; for in a short time the shouts increased tenfold, and among them I thought I heard a death-cry uttered by voices familiar to my ear.

At length the tumult of battle ceased, and from the cries of exultation that now arose from the savages, I felt assured that our men had been conquered. I was immediately thrown into dreadful consternation. What was I now to do? To be taken by the savages was too horrible to be thought of; to flee to the mountains was hopeless, as I should soon be discovered; and to take the schooner out of the creek without assistance was impossible. I resolved, however, to make the attempt, as being my only hope, and was on the point of pushing off, when my hand was stayed, and my blood chilled by an appalling shriek, in which I recognized the voice of one of the crew. It was succeeded by a shout from the savages. Then came another and another shriek of agony, making my ears to tingle, as I felt convinced they were murdering the pirate crew in cold blood. With a bursting heart and my brain whirling as if on fire, I seized the boat-hook to push from shore, when a man sprang from the bushes.

"Stop! Ralph, stop!—there, now, push off," he cried, and bounded into the boat so violently as nearly to upset her. It was Bill's voice! In another moment we were on board—the boat made fast, the line of the anchor cut, and the sweeps run out. At the first stroke of Bill's giant arm the schooner was nearly pulled ashore, for in his haste he forgot that I could scarcely move the unwieldy oar. Springing to the stern, he lashed the rudder in such a position as that, while it aided me, it acted against him, and so rendered the force of our strokes nearly equal. The schooner now began to glide quickly down the creek; but before we reached its mouth, a yell from a thousand voices on the bank told that we were discovered. Instantly a number of the savages plunged into the water and swam towards us: but we were making so much way that they could not overtake us. One, however, an immensely powerful man, succeeded in laying hold of the cut rope that hung from the stern, and clambered quickly upon deck. Bill caught sight of him the instant his head appeared above the taffrail. But he did not cease to row, and did not appear even to notice the savage until he was within a yard of him; then dropping the sweep, he struck him a blow on the forehead with his clenched fist that felled him to the deck. Lifting him up he hurled him overboard and resumed the oar. But now a greater danger awaited us, for the savages had outrun us on the bank, and were about to plunge into the water ahead of the schooner. If they succeeded in doing so our fate was sealed. For one moment Bill stood irresolute. Then drawing a pistol from his belt, he sprang to the brass gun, held the pan of his pistol over the touch-hole and fired. The shot was succeeded by the hiss of the cannon's priming, then the blaze and the crashing thunder of the monstrous gun burst upon the savages with such a deafening roar that it seemed as if their very mountains had been rent asunder.

This was enough. The moment of surprise and hesitation caused by the unwonted sound gave us time to pass the point; a gentle breeze, which the dense foliage had hitherto prevented us from feeling, bulged out our sails; the schooner bent before it, and the shouts of the disappointed savages grew fainter and fainter in the distance as we were slowly wafted out to sea.

Chapter 25

There is a power of endurance in human beings both in their bodies and in their minds, which, I have often thought, seems to be wonderfully adapted and exactly proportioned to the circumstances in which individuals may happen to be placed—a power which, in most cases, is sufficient to carry a man through and over every obstacle that may happen to be thrown in his path through life, no matter how high or how steep the mountain may be, but which often forsakes him the moment the summit is gained, the point of difficulty passed, and leaves him prostrated, with energies gone, nerves, unstrung, and a feeling of incapacity pervading the entire frame that renders the most trifling effort almost impossible.

During the greater part of that day I had been subjected to severe mental and much physical excitement, which had almost crushed me down by the time I was relieved from duty in the course of the evening. But when the expedition whose failure has just been narrated was planned, my anxieties and energies had been so powerfully aroused that I went through the protracted scenes of that terrible night without a feeling of the slightest fatigue. My mind and body were alike active and full of energy. No sooner was the last thrilling fear of danger past than my faculties were utterly relaxed; and when I felt the cool breezes of the Pacific playing around my fevered brow, and heard the free waves rippling at the schooner's prow, as we left the hated island behind us, my senses forsook me, and I fell in a swoon upon the deck.

From this state I was quickly aroused by Bill, who shook me by the arm, saying—

"Hallo, Ralph boy! rouse up, lad; we're safe now. Poor thing! I believe he's fainted." And raising me in his arms he laid me on the folds of the gaff-top-sail, which lay upon the deck near the tiller. "Here, take a drop o' this; it'll do you good, my boy," he added, in a voice of tenderness which I had never heard him use before, while he held a brandy-flask to my lips.

I raised my eyes gratefully as I swallowed a mouthful; next moment my head sank heavily upon my arm, and I fell fast asleep. I slept long, for when I awoke the sun was a good way above the horizon. I did not move on first opening my eyes, as I felt a

135

delightful sensation of rest pervading me, and my eyes were riveted on and charmed with the gorgeous splendour of the mighty ocean, that burst upon my sight. It was a dead calm; the sea seemed a sheet of undulating crystal, tipped and streaked with the saffron hues of sunrise, which had not yet merged into the glowing heat of noon; and there was a deep calm in the blue dome above that was not broken even by the usual flutter of the sea-fowl. How long I would have lain in contemplation of this peaceful scene I know not, but my mind was recalled suddenly and painfully to the past and the present by the sight of Bill, who was seated on the deck at my feet with his head reclining, as if in sleep, on his right arm, which rested on the tiller. As he seemed to rest peacefully, I did not mean to disturb him, but the slight noise I made in raising myself on my elbow caused him to start and look round.

"Well, Ralph, awake at last, my boy; you have slept long and soundly," he said, turning towards me.

On beholding his countenance I sprang up in anxiety. He was deadly pale, and his hair was clotted with blood. Blood also stained his hollow cheeks and covered the front of his shirt, which, with the greater part of his dress, was torn and soiled with mud.

"Oh Bill!" said I, with deep anxiety, "what is the matter with you? You are ill. You must have been wounded."

"Even so, lad," said Bill in a deep soft voice, while he extended his huge frame on the couch from which I had just risen. "I've got an ugly wound, I fear; and I've been waiting for you to waken, to ask you to get me a drop o' brandy and a mouthful o' bread from the cabin lockers. You seemed to sleep so sweetly, Ralph, that I didn't like to disturb you. But I don't feel up to much just now."

I did not wait till he had done talking, but ran below immediately and returned in a few seconds with a bottle of brandy and some broken biscuit. He seemed much refreshed after eating a few morsels and drinking a long draught of water mingled with a little of the spirits. Immediately afterwards he fell asleep, and I watched him anxiously until he awoke, being desirous of knowing the nature and extent of his wound.

"Ha!" he exclaimed, on awakening suddenly, after a slumber of an hour, "I'm the better of that nap, Ralph; I feel twice the man I was;" and he attempted to rise, but sank back again with a groan.

"Nay, Bill, you must not move, but lie still while I look at your wound. I'll make a bed for you here on deck, and get you some breakfast. After that, you shall tell me how you got it. Cheer up, Bill," I added, seeing that he turned his head away; "you'll be all right, and I'll be a capital nurse to you though I'm no doctor."

I then left him, and lighted a fire in the caboose. While it was kindling, I went to the steward's pantry and procured the materials for a good breakfast, with which, in little more than half an hour, I returned to my companion. He seemed much better, and smiled kindly on me as I set before him a cup of coffee and a tray with several eggs and some bread on it.

"Now then, Bill," said I cheerfully, sitting down beside him on the deck, "Let's fall to. I'm very hungry myself, I can tell you; but—I forgot—your wound," I added rising; "let me look at it."

I found that the wound was caused by a pistol shot in the chest. It did not bleed much, and as it was on the right side, I was in hopes that it might not be very serious. But Bill shook his head. "However," said he, "sit down, Ralph, and I'll tell you all about it."

"You see, after we left the boat an' began to push through the bushes, we went straight for the line of my musket, as I had expected; but by some unlucky chance it didn't explode, for I saw the line torn away by the men's legs, and heard the click o' the lock; so I fancy the priming had got damp and didn't catch, I was in a great quandary now what to do, for I couldn't concoct in my mind, in the hurry, any good reason for firin' off my piece. But they say necessity's the mother of invention; so just as I was givin' it up and clinchin' my teeth to bide the worse o't and take what should come, a sudden thought came into my head. I stepped out before the rest, seemin' to be awful anxious to be at the savages, tripped my foot on a fallen tree, plunged head foremost into a bush, an', ov coorse, my carbine exploded! Then came such a screechin' from the camp as I never heard in all my life. I rose at once, and was rushing on with the rest, when the captain called a halt.

"'You did that a-purpose, you villain!' he said, with a tremendous oath, and drawin' a pistol from his belt, let fly right into my breast. I fell at once, and remembered no more till I was startled and brought round by the most awful yell I ever heard in my life—except, maybe, the shrieks o' them poor critters that were crushed to death under yon big canoe. Jumpin' up, I looked round, and through the trees saw a fire gleamin' not far off, the light o' which showed me the captain and men tied hand and foot, each to a post, and the savages dancin' round them like demons. I had scarce looked for a second, when I saw one o' them go up to the captain flourishing a knife, and before I could wink he plunged it into his breast, while another yell, like the one that roused me, rang upon my ear. I didn't wait for more, but bounding up, went crashing through the bushes into the woods. The black fellows caught sight of me, however, but not in time to prevent me jumpin' into the boat, as you know."

Bill seemed to be much exhausted after this recital, and shuddered frequently during the narrative, so I refrained from continuing the subject at that time, and endeavoured to draw his mind to other things.

"But now, Bill," said I, "it behoves us to think about the future, and what course of action we shall pursue. Here we are, on the wide Pacific, in a well-appointed schooner, which is our own—at least no one has a better claim to it then we have—and the world lies before us. More over, here comes a breeze, so we must make up our minds which way to steer."

"Ralph boy," said my companion, "it matters not to me which way we go. I fear that my time is short now. Go where you will; I'm content."

"Well, then, Bill, I think we had better steer to the Coral Island, and see what has become of my dear old comrades, Jack and Peterkin. I believe the island has no name, but the captain once pointed it out to me on the chart, and I marked it afterwards; so, as we know pretty well our position just now, I think I can steer to it. Then, as to working the vessel, it is true I cannot hoist the sails singlehanded, but luckily we have enough sail set already; and if it should come on to blow a squall, I could at least drop the peaks of the main and fore-sails, and clew them up partially without help, and throw her head close into the wind, so as to keep her all shaking till the violence of the squall is past. And if we have continued light breezes, I'll rig up a complication of blocks and fix them to the top-sail halyards, so that I shall be able to hoist the sails without help. 'Tis true I'll require half a day to hoist them, but we don't need to mind that. Then I'll make a sort of erection on deck to screen you from the sun, Bill; and if you can only manage to sit beside the tiller and steer for two hours every day, so as to let me get a nap, I'll engage to let you off duty all the rest of the twenty-four hours. And if you don't feel able for steering, I'll lash the helm and heave to, while I get your breakfasts and dinners; and so we'll manage famously, and soon reach the Coral Island."

Bill smiled faintly as I ran on in this strain.

"And what will you do," said he, "if it comes on to blow a storm?"

This question silenced me, while I considered what I should do in such a case. At length I laid my hand on his arm, and said, "Bill, when a man has done all that he *can* do, he ought to leave the rest to God."

"Oh, Ralph," said my companion, in a faint voice, looking anxiously into my face, "I wish that I had the feelin's about God that you seem to have, at this hour. I'm dyin', Ralph; yet I, who have braved death a hundred times, am afraid to die. I'm afraid to enter the next world. Something within tells me there will be a reckoning when I go there. But it's all over with me, Ralph."

"Don't say that, Bill," said I, in deep compassion; "don't say that. I'm quite sure there's hope even for you, but I can't remember the words of the Bible that make me think so. Is there not a Bible on board, Bill?"

"No; the last that was in the ship belonged to a poor boy that was taken aboard against his will. He died, poor lad—I think through ill-treatment and fear. After he was gone the captain found his Bible and flung it overboard."

After a short pause, Bill raised his eyes to mine and said, "Ralph, I've led a terrible life. I've been a sailor since I was a boy, and I've gone from bad to worse ever since I left my father's roof. I've been a pirate three years now. It is true I did not choose the trade, but I was inveigled aboard this schooner and kept here by force till I became reckless and at last joined them. Since that time my hand has been steeped in human blood again and again. Your young heart would grow cold if I—— But why should I go on? 'Tis of no use, Ralph."

"Bill," said I, " 'Though your sins be red like crimson, they shall be white as snow.' 'Only believe.' "

"Only believe!" cried Bill, starting up on his elbow. "I've heard men talk o' believing as if it was easy. Ha! 'tis easy enough for a man to point to a rope and say, 'I believe that would bear my weight,' but 'tis another thing for a man to catch hold o' that rope and swing himself by it over the edge of a precipice!"

The energy with which he said this, and the action with which it was accompanied, were too much for Bill. He sank back with a deep groan. As if the very elements sympathized with this man's sufferings, a low moan came sweeping over the sea.

"Hist, Ralph!" said Bill, opening his eyes; "there's a squall coming, lad. Look alive, boy! Clew up the fore-sail. Drop the main-sail peak. Them squalls come quick sometimes."

I had already started to my feet, and saw that a heavy squall was indeed bearing down on us. It had hitherto escaped my notice, owing to my being so much engrossed by our conversation. I instantly did as Bill desired, for the schooner was still lying motionless on the glassy sea. I observed with some satisfaction that the squall was bearing down on the larboard bow, so that it would strike the vessel in the position in which she would be best able to stand the shock. Having done my best to shorten sail, I returned aft, and took my stand at the helm.

"Now, boy," said Bill, in a faint voice, "keep her close to the wind."

A few seconds afterwards he said, "Ralph, let me hear those two texts again."

I repeated them.

"Are you sure, lad, ye saw them in the Bible?"

"Quite sure," I replied.

Almost before the words had left my lips the wind burst upon us, and the spray dashed over our decks. For a time the schooner stood it bravely, and sprang forward against the rising sea like a war-horse. Meanwhile clouds darkened the sky, and the sea began to rise in huge billows. There was still too much sail on the schooner, and as the gale increased, I feared that the masts would be torn out of her or carried away, while the wind whistled and shrieked through the strained rigging. Suddenly the wind shifted a point, a heavy sea struck us on the bow, and the schooner was almost laid on her beam-ends, so that I could scarcely keep my legs. At the same moment Bill lost his hold of the belaying-pin which had served to steady him, and he slid with stunning violence against the skylight. As he lay on the deck close beside me, I could see that the shock had rendered him insensible, but I did not dare to quit the tiller for an instant, as it required all my faculties, bodily and mental, to manage the schooner. For an hour the blast drove us along, while, owing to the sharpness of the vessel's bow and the press of canvas, she dashed through the waves instead of breasting over them, thereby drenching the decks with water fore and aft. At the end of that time the squall passed away, and left us rocking on the bosom of the agitated sea.

My first care, the instant I could quit the helm, was to raise Bill from the deck and place him on the couch. I then ran below for the brandy-bottle and rubbed his face and hands with it, and endeavoured to pour a little down his throat. But my efforts, although I continued them long and assiduously, were of no avail; as I let go the hand which I had been chaffing, it fell heavily on the deck. I laid my hand over his heart, and sat for some time quite motionless; but there was no flutter there—the pirate was dead!

Chapter 26

It was with feelings of awe, not unmingled with fear, that I now
seated myself on the cabin skylight and gazed upon the rigid
features of my late comrade, while my mind wandered over his past
history and contemplated with anxiety my present position. Alone,
in the midst of the wide Pacific, having a most imperfect knowledge
of navigation, and in a schooner requiring at least eight men as her
proper crew! But I will not tax the reader's patience with a minute
detail of my feelings and doings during the first few days that
followed the death of my companion. I will merely mention that I
tied a cannon-ball to his feet, and with feelings of the deepest sorrow
consigned him to the deep.

For fully a week after that a steady breeze blew from the east, and
as my course lay west and by north, I made rapid progress towards
my destination. I could not take an observation, which I very much
regretted, as the captain's quadrant was in the cabin; but from the
day of setting sail from the island of the savages I had kept a dead
reckoning, and as I knew pretty well now how much leeway the
schooner made, I hoped to hit the Coral Island without much
difficulty. In this I was the more confident that I knew its position on
the chart (which I understood was a very good one), and so had its
correct bearings by compass.

As the weather seemed now quite settled and fine, and as I had got
into the trade winds, I set about preparations for hoisting the
top-sails. This was a most arduous task, and my first attempts were
complete failures, owing, in a great degree, to my reprehensible
ignorance of mechanical forces. The first error I made was in
applying my apparatus of blocks and pulleys to a rope which was too
weak, so that the very first heave I made broke it in two, and sent me
staggering against the after-hatch, over which I tripped, and striking
against the main-boom, tumbled down the companion-ladder into
the cabin. I was much bruised and somewhat stunned by this
untoward accident. However, I considered it fortunate that I was not
killed. In my next attempt I made sure of not coming by a similar
accident, so I unreeved the tackling and fitted up larger blocks and
ropes. But although the principal on which I acted was quite correct,
the machinery was now so massive and heavy that the mere friction
and stiffness of the thick cordage prevented me from moving it at all.
Afterwards, however, I came to proportion things more correctly;
but I could not avoid reflecting at the time how much better it would

have been had I learned all this from observation and study, instead of waiting till I was forced to acquire it through the painful and tedious lessons of experience.

After the tackling was prepared and in good working order, it took me the greater part of the day to hoist the main-top-sail. As I could not steer and work at this at the same time, I lashed the helm in such a position that, with a little watching now and then, it kept the schooner in her proper course. By this means I was enabled also to go about the deck and down below for things that I wanted, as occasion required; also to cook and eat my victuals. But I did not dare to trust to this plan during the three hours of rest that I allowed myself at night, as the wind might have shifted, in which case I should have been blown far out of my course ere I awoke. I was, therefore, in the habit of *heaving to* during those three hours—that is, fixing the rudder and the sails in such a position as that by acting against each other they would keep the ship stationary. After my night's rest, therefore, I had only to make allowance for the leeway she had made, and so resume my course.

Of course I was to some extent anxious lest another squall should come, but I made the best provision I could in the circumstances, and concluded that by letting go the weather-braces of the top-sails and the top-sail halyards at the same time, I should thereby render these sails almost powerless. Besides this, I proposed to myself to keep a sharp look-out on the barometer in the cabin, and if I observed at any time a sudden fall in it, I resolved that I would instantly set about my multiform appliances for reducing sail, so as to avoid being taken at unawares. Thus I sailed prosperously for two weeks, with a fair wind, so that I calculated I must be drawing near to the Coral Island; at the thought of which my heart bounded with joyful expectation.

On the evening of my fourteenth day I was awakened out of a nap into which I had fallen by a loud cry, and starting up I gazed around me. I was surprised and delighted to see a large albatross soaring majestically over the ship. I immediately took it into my head that this was the albatross I had seen at Penguin Island. I had, of course, no good reason for supposing this, but the idea occurred to me, I know not why, and I cherished it, and regarded the bird with as much affection as if he had been an old friend. He kept me company all that day, and left me as night fell.

Next morning, as I stood motionless and with heavy eyes at the helm—for I had not slept well—I began to weary anxiously for daylight, and peered towards the horizon, where I thought I observed something like a black cloud against the dark sky. Being always on the alert for squalls, I ran to the bow. There could be no doubt it was a squall, and as I listened I thought I heard the murmur of the coming gale. Instantly I began to work might and main at my cumbrous tackle for shortening sail, and in the course of an hour and a half had the most of it reduced—the top-sail yards down on the caps, the top-sails clewed up, the sheets hauled in, the main and fore peaks lowered, and the flying-jib down. While thus engaged the dawn advanced and I cast an occasional furtive glance ahead in the midst of my labour. But now that things were prepared for the worst, I ran forward again and looked anxiously over the bow. I now heard the roar of the waves distinctly, and as a single ray of the rising sun gleamed over the ocean I saw—what! could it be that I was dreaming?—that magnificent breaker with its ceaseless roar!—that mountain-top!—yes, once more I beheld the Coral Island!

Chapter 27

I almost fell upon the deck with the tumult of mingled emotions that filled my heart as I gazed ardently towards my beautiful island. It was still many miles away, but sufficiently near to enable me to trace distinctly the well-remembered outlines of the two mountains. My first impulse was to utter an exclamation of gratitude for being carried to my former happy home in safety; my second, to jump up, clap my hands, shout, and run up and down the deck, with no other object in view than that of giving vent to my excited feelings.

After that I looked up impatiently at the sails, which I now regretted having lowered so hastily, and for a moment thought of hoisting the main-top-sail again; but recollecting that it would take me full half a day to accomplish, and that, at the present rate of sailing, two hours would bring me to the island, I immediately dismissed the idea.

The remainder of the time I spent in making feverish preparations for arriving and seeing my dear comrades. I remembered that they were not in the habit of rising before six, and as it was now only three, I hoped to arrive before they were awake. Moreover, I set about making ready to let go the anchor, resolving in my own mind that, as I knew the depth of water in the passage of the reef and within the lagoon, I would run the schooner in and bring up opposite the bower. Fortunately the anchor was hanging at the cathead, otherwise I should never have been able to use it. Now, I had only to cut the tackling, and it would drop of its own weight. After searching among the flags, I found the terrible black one, which I ran up to the peak. While I was doing this a thought struck me. I went to the powder-magazine, brought up a blank cartridge and loaded the big brass gun, which, it will be remembered, was unhoused when we set sail, and as I had no means of housing it, there it had stood, bristling alike at fair weather and foul all the voyage. I took care to grease its mouth well, and, before leaving the fore part of the ship, thrust the poker into the fire.

All was now ready. A steady five-knot breeze was blowing, so that I was now not more than a quarter of a mile from the reef. I was soon at the entrance, and as the schooner glided quickly through, I glanced affectionately at the huge breaker, as if it had been the same one I had seen there when I bade adieu, as I feared for ever, to the island. On coming opposite the Water Garden, I put the helm hard down. The schooner came round with a rapid, graceful bend, and lost way just opposite the bower. Running forward, I let go the anchor, caught up the redhot poker, applied it to the brass gun, and saluted the mountains with a *bang* such as had only once before broke their slumbering echoes!

Effective although it was, however, it was scarcely equal to the bang with which, instantly after, Peterkin bounded from the bower, in scanty costume, his eye-balls starting from his head with surprise and terror. One gaze he gave, one yell, and then fled into the bushes like a wild cat. The next moment Jack went through exactly the same performance, the only difference being that his movements were less like those of Jack-in-the-box, though not less vigorous and rapid than those of Peterkin.

"Hallo!" I shouted, almost mad with joy, "what ho! Peterkin! Jack! hallo! it's *me*!"

My shout was just in time to arrest them. They halted and turned round, and the instant I repeated the cry I saw that they recognized my voice, by both of them running at full speed towards the beach. I could no longer contain myself. Throwing off my jacket, I jumped overboard at the same moment that Jack bounded into the sea. In another moment we met in deep water, clasped each other round the neck, and sank, as a matter of course, to the bottom! We were well-nigh choked, and instantly struggled to the surface, where Peterkin was spluttering about like a wounded duck, laughing and crying by turns, and choking himself with salt water.

It would be impossible to convey to my reader, by description, an adequate conception of the scene that followed my landing on the beach, as we stood embracing each other indiscriminately in our dripping garments, and giving utterance to incoherent rhapsodies, mingled with wild shouts. It can be more easily imagined than described, so I will draw a curtain over this part of my history, and carry the reader forward over an interval of three days.

During the greater part of that period Peterkin did nothing but roast pigs, taro, and bread-fruit, and ply me with plantains, plums, potatoes, and coco-nuts, while I related to him and Jack the terrible and wonderful adventures I had gone through since we last met. After I had finished the account, they made me go all over it again; and when I had concluded the second recital, I had to go over it again, while they commented upon it piecemeal. They were much affected by what I told them of the probable fate of Avatea, and Peterkin could by no means brook the idea of the poor girl being converted into a *long pig*. As for Jack, he clenched his teeth, and shook his fist towards the sea, saying at the same time that he was sorry he had not broken Tararo's head, and he only hoped that one day he should be able to plant his knuckles on the bridge of that chief's nose! After they had "pumped me dry", as Peterkin said, I begged to be informed of what had happened to them during my long absence, and particularly as to how they got out of the Diamond Cave.

"Well, you must know," began Jack, "after you had dived out of the cave, on the day you were taken away from us, we waited very patiently for half an hour, not expecting you to return before the end of that time. Then we began to upbraid you for staying so long, when you knew we would be anxious; but when an hour passed, we became alarmed, and I resolved at all hazards to dive out, and see what had become of you, although I felt for poor Peterkin, because, as he truly said, 'If you never come back I'm shut up here for life.' However, I promised not to run any risk, and he let me go; which, to say truth, I thought very courageous of him!"

"I should just think it was," interrupted Peterkin, looking at Jack over the edge of a monstrous potato which he happened to be devouring at the time.

"Well," continued Jack, "you may guess my consternation when you did not answer to my hallo. At first I imagined that the pirates must have killed you, and left you in the bush or thrown you into the sea; then it occurred to me that this would have served no end of theirs, so I came to the conclusion that they must have carried you away with them. As this thought struck me, I observed the pirate schooner standing away to the nor'ard, almost hull down on the horizon, and I sat down on the rocks to watch her as she slowly sank from my sight. And I tell you, Ralph, my boy, that I shed more tears that time at losing you than I have done, I verily believe, all my life before——"

"Pardon me, Jack, for interrupting," said Peterkin; "surely you must be mistaken in that; you've often told me that when you were a baby you used to howl and roar from morning to——"

"Hold your tongue, Peterkin," cried Jack. "Well, after the schooner had disappeared, I dived back into the cave, much to Peterkin's relief, and told him what I had seen. We sat down and had a long talk over this matter, and then we agreed to make a regular, systematic search through the woods, so as to make sure at least that you had not been killed. But now we thought of the difficulty of getting out of the cave without your help. Peterkin became dreadfully nervous when he thought of this; and I must confess that I felt some alarm, for, of course, I could not hope alone to take him out so quickly as we two together had brought him in; and he himself vowed that, if we had been a moment longer with him that time, he would have had to take a breath of salt water. However, there was no help for it, and I endeavoured to calm his fears as well as I could: 'for,' said I, 'you can't live here, Peterkin;' to which he replied, 'Of course not, Jack; I can only die here, and as that's not at all desirable, you had better propose something.' So I suggested that he should take a good long breath, and trust himself to me.

"'Might we not make a large bag of coco-nut cloth, into which I could shove my head, and tie it tight round my neck?' he asked, with a haggard smile. 'It might let me get one breath under water?'

"'No use,' said I; 'it would fill in a moment and suffocate you. I see nothing for it, Peterkin, if you really can't keep your breath so long, but to let me knock you down, and carry you out while in a state of insensibility.'

"But Peterkin didn't relish this idea. He seemed to fear that I could not be able to measure the exact force of the blow, and might, on the one hand, hit him so softly as to render a second or third blow necessary, which would be very uncomfortable; or, on the other hand, give him such a smash as would entirely spoil his figure-head, or mayhap knock the life out of him altogether! At last I got him persuaded to try to hold his breath, and commit himself to me; so he agreed, and down we went. But I had not got him half-way through, when he began to struggle and kick like a wild bull, burst from my grasp, and hit against the roof of the tunnel. I was, therefore, obliged to force him violently back into the cave again, where he rose panting to the surface. In short, he had lost his presence of mind, and——"

"Nothing of the sort," cried Peterkin indignantly, "I had only lost my wind; and if I had not had presence of mind enough to kick as I did, I should have burst in your arms!"

"Well, well, so be it," resumed Jack, with a smile; "but the upshot of it was, that we had to hold another consultation on the point, and I really believe that, had it not been for a happy thought of mine, we should have been consulting there yet."

"I wish we had," interrupted Peterkin, with a sigh. "I'm sure, Ralph, if I had thought that you were coming back again, I would willingly have awaited your return for months, rather than have endured the mental agony which I went through! But proceed."

"The thought was this," continued Jack, "that I should tie Peterkin's hands and feet with cords, and then lash him firmly to a stout pole about five feet long, in order to render him quite powerless, and keep him straight and stiff. You should have seen his face of horror, Ralph, when I suggested this; but he came to see that it was his only chance, and told me to set about it as fast as I could; 'for,' said he, 'this is no jokin', Jack, I can tell you, and the sooner it's done the better.' I soon procured the cordage and a suitable pole, with which I returned to the cave, and lashed him as stiff and straight as an Egyptian mummy; and, to say truth, he was no bad representation of what an English mummy would be, if there were such things, for he was as white as a dead man.

"'Now,' said Peterkin, in a tremulous voice, 'swim with me as near to the edge of the hole as you can before you dive, then let me take a long breath, and as I shan't be able to speak after I've taken it, you'll watch my face, and the moment you see me wink—dive! And oh,' he added earnestly, 'pray don't be long!'

"I promised to pay the strictest attention to his wishes, and swam with him to the outlet of the cave. Here I paused. 'Now then,' said I, 'pull away at the wind, lad.'

"Peterkin drew in a breath so long that I could not help thinking of the frog in the fable, that wanted to swell itself as big as the ox. Then I looked into his face earnestly. Slap went the lid of his right eye, down went my head, and up went my heels. We shot through the passage like an arrow, and rose to the surface of the open sea before you could count twenty.

"Peterkin had taken in such an awful load of wind that, on reaching the free air, he let out with a yell loud enough to have been heard a mile off, and then the change in his feelings was so sudden and great, that he did not wait till we landed, but began, tied up as he was, to shout and sing for joy as I supported him with my left arm to the shore. However, in the middle of a laugh that a hyena might have envied, I let him accidentally slip, which extinguished him in a moment.

"After this happy deliverance, we immediately began our search for your dead body, Ralph; and you have no idea how low our hearts sank as we set off, day after day, to examine the valleys and mountain sides with the utmost care. In about three weeks we completed the survey of the whole island, and had at least the satisfaction of knowing that you had not been killed. But it occurred to us that you might have been thrown into the sea, so we examined the sands and the lagoon carefully, and afterwards went all round the outer reef. One day, while we were upon the reef, Peterkin espied a small dark object lying among the rocks, which seemed to be quite different from the surrounding stones. We hastened towards the spot, and found it to be a small keg. On knocking out the head we discovered that it was gunpowder."

"It was I who sent you that, Jack," said I, with a smile.

"Fork out!" cried Peterkin energetically, starting to his feet and extending his open hand to Jack. "Down with the money, sir, else I'll have you shut up for life in a debtor's prison the moment we return to England!"

"I'll give you an IOU in the meantime," returned Jack, laughing, "so sit down and be quiet. The fact is, Ralph, when we discovered this keg of powder, Peterkin immediately took me a bet of a thousand pounds that you had something to do with it, and I took him a bet of ten thousand that you had not."

"Peterkin was right then," said I, explaining how the thing had occurred.

"Well, we found it very useful," continued Jack, "although some of it had got a little damp; and we furbished up the old pistol, with which Peterkin is a crack shot now. But to continue: We did not find any other vestige of you on the reef, and finally gave up all hope of ever seeing you again. After this the island became a dreary place to us, and we began to long for a ship to heave in sight and take us off. But now that you're back again, my dear fellow, it looks as bright and cheerful as it used to do, and I love it as much as ever.

"And now," continued Jack, "I have a great desire to visit some of the other islands of the South Seas. Here we have a first-rate schooner at our disposal, so I don't see what should hinder us."

"Just the very thing I was going to propose," cried Peterkin. "I vote for starting at once."

"Well, then," said Jack, "it seems to me that we could not do better than shape our course for the island on which Avatea lives, and endeavour to persuade Tararo to let her marry the black fellow to whom she is engaged, instead of making a long pig of her. If he has a spark of gratitude in him he'll do it. Besides, having become champions for this girl once before, it behoves us, as true knights, not to rest until we set her free; at least, all the heroes in all the story-books I have ever read would count it foul disgrace to leave such a work unfinished."

"I'm sure I don't know or care what your knights in story-books would do," said Peterkin; "but I'm certain that it would be capital fun, so I'm your man whenever you want me."

This plan of Jack's was quite in accordance with his romantic, impulsive nature; and, having made up his mind to save this black girl, he could not rest until the thing was commenced.

"But there may be great danger in this attempt," he said, at the end of a long consultation on the subject. "Will you, lads, go with me in spite of this?"

"Go with you?" we repeated in the same breath.

"Can you doubt it?" said I.

"For a moment?" added Peterkin.

I need scarcely say that having made up our minds to go on this enterprise we lost no time in making preparations to quit the island; and as the schooner was well laden with stores of every kind for a

long cruise we had little to do except to add to our abundant supply a
quantity of coco-nuts, bread-fruit, taro, yams, plums, and potatoes,
chiefly with the view of carrying the fragrance of our dear island
along with us as long as we could.

When all was ready, we paid a farewell visit to the different
familiar spots where most of our time had been spent. We ascended
the mountain-top, and gazed for the last time at the rich green
foliage in the valleys, the white sandy beach, the placid lagoon, and
the barrier coral reef with its crested breakers. Then we descended
to Spouting Cliff, and looked down at the pale-green monster which
we had made such fruitless efforts to spear in days gone by. From
this we hurried to the Water Garden, and took a last dive into its
clear waters, and a last gambol amongst its coral groves. I hurried
out before my companions, and dressed in haste, in order to have a
long examination of my tank, which Peterkin, in the fullness of his
heart, had tended with the utmost care, as being a vivid remembr-
ance of me rather than out of love for natural history. It was in
superb condition—the water as clear and pellucid as crystal; the red
and green seaweed of the most brilliant hues; the red, purple,
yellow, green and striped anemones fully expanded, and stretching
out their arms as if to welcome and embrace their former master; the
star-fish, zoophytes, sea-pens, and other innumerable marine insects
looking fresh and beautiful; and the crabs, as Peterkin said, looking
as wide awake, impertinent, rampant, and pugnacious as ever. It was
indeed so lovely and so interesting that I would scarcely allow myself
to be torn away from it.

Last of all, we returned to the bower and collected the few articles
we possessed, such as the axe, the pencil-case, the broken telescope,
the penknife, the hook made from the brass ring, and the sailneedle, with which we had landed on the island; also the long boots
and the pistol, besides several curious articles of costume which we
had manufactured from time to time.

These we conveyed on board in our little boat, after having carved
our names on a chip of iron wood, thus:

JACK MARTIN, RALPH ROVER,
PETERKIN GAY,

which we fixed up inside of the bower. The boat was then hoisted on
board and the anchor weighed, which latter operation cost us great
labour and much time, as the anchor was so heavy that we could not
move it without the aid of my complex machinery of blocks and
pulleys. A steady breeze was blowing offshore when we set sail, at a
little before sunset. It swept us quickly past the reef and out to sea.

The shore grew rapidly more indistinct as the shades of evening fell, while our clipper bark bounded lightly over the waves. Slowly the mountain-top sank on the horizon, until it became a mere speck. In another moment the sun and the Coral Island sank together into the broad bosom of the Pacific.

Chapter 28

Our voyage during the next two weeks was most interesting and prosperous. The breeze continued generally fair, and at all times enabled us to lie our course; for being, as I have said before, clipper-built, the pirate schooner could lie very close to the wind and make little leeway. We had no difficulty now in managing our sails, for Jack was heavy and powerful, while Peterkin was active as a kitten. Still, however, we were a very insufficient crew for such a vessel, and if anyone had proposed to us to make such a voyage in it before we had been forced to go through so many hardships from necessity, we would have turned away with pity from the individual making such proposal as from a madman. I pondered this a good deal, and at last concluded that men do not know how much they are capable of doing till they try, and that we should never give way to despair in any undertaking, however difficult it may seem—always supposing, however, that our cause is a good one, and that we can ask the divine blessing on it.

Although, therefore, we could now manage our sails easily, we nevertheless found that my pulleys were of much service to us in some things; though Jack did laugh heartily at the uncouth arrangement of ropes and blocks, which had, to a sailor's eye, a very lumbering and clumsy appearance. But I will not drag my reader through the details of this voyage. Suffice it to say that, after an agreeable sail of about three weeks, we arrived off the island of Mango, which I recognized at once from the description that the pirate Bill had given me of it during one of our conversations.

As soon as we came within sight of it we hove the ship to and held a council of war.

"Now, boys," said Jack, as we seated ourselves beside him on the cabin skylight, "before we go further in this business, we must go over the pros and cons of it; for although you have so generously consented to stick by me through thick and thin, it would be unfair did I not see that you thoroughly understand the danger of what we are about to attempt."

"Oh, bother the danger!" cried Peterkin. "I wonder to hear *you*, Jack, talk of danger. When a fellow begins to talk about it, he'll soon come to magnify it to such a degree that he'll not be fit to face it when it comes, no more than a suckin' baby."

"Nay, Peterkin," replied Jack gravely, "I won't be jested out of it. I grant you that when we've once resolved to act, and have made up our minds what to do, we should think no more of danger. But before we have so resolved it behoves us to look at it straight in the face, and examine into it, and walk round it; for if we flinch at a distant view, we're sure to run away when the danger is near. Now, I understand from you, Ralph, that the island is inhabited by thorough-going, out-and-out cannibals, whose principal law is, 'Might is right, and the weakest goes to the wall'?"

"Yes," said I, "so Bill gave me to understand. He told me, however, that at the southern side of it the missionaries had obtained a footing amongst an insignificant tribe. A native teacher had been sent there by the Wesleyans, who had succeeded in persuading the chief at that part to embrace Christianity. But instead of that being of any advantage to our enterprise, it seems the very reverse; for the chief Tararo is a determined heathen, and persecutes the Christians —who are far too weak in numbers to offer any resistance—and looks with dislike upon all white men, whom he regards as propagators of the new faith."

"'Tis a pity," said Jack, "that the Christian tribe is so small, for we shall scarcely be safe under their protection, I fear. If Tararo takes it into his head to wish for our vessel, or to kill us, he could take us from them by force. You say the native missionary talks English?"

"So I believe."

"Then, what I propose is this," said Jack. "We will run round to the south side of the island, and cast anchor off the Christian village. We are too far away just now to have been descried by any of the savages, so we shall get there unobserved, and have time to arrange our plans before the heathen tribes know of our presence. But in doing this we run the risk of being captured by the ill-disposed tribes, and being very ill-used, if not-a——"

"Roasted alive and eaten," cried Peterkin. "Come, out with it, Jack. According to your own showing, it's well to look the danger straight in the face!"

"Well, that *is* the worst of it, certainly. Are you prepared then, to take your chance of that?"

"I've been prepared and had my mind made up long ago," cried Peterkin, swaggering about with his hands thrust into his pockets. "The fact is, Jack, I don't believe that Tararo will be so ungrateful as to eat us! and I'm quite sure that he'll be too happy to grant us whatever we ask; so the sooner we go in and win the better."

Peterkin was wrong, however, in his estimate of savage gratitude, as the sequel will show.

The schooner was now put before the wind, and after making a long run to the southward, we put about and beat up for the south side of Mango, where we arrived before sunset, and hove to off the coral reef. Here we awaited the arrival of a canoe, which immediately put off on our rounding to. When it arrived, a mild-looking native, of apparently forty years of age, came on board, and taking off his straw hat, made us a low bow. He was clad in a respectable suit of European clothes; and the first words he uttered, as he stepped up to Jack and shook hands with him were—

"Good day, gentlemen. We are happy to see you at Mango; you are heartily welcome."

After returning his salutation, Jack exclaimed, "You must be the native missionary teacher of whom I have heard; are you not?"

"I am. I have the joy to be a servant of the Lord Jesus at this station."

"You're the very man I want to see, then," replied Jack; "that's lucky. Come down to the cabin, friend, and have a glass of wine. I wish particularly to speak with you. My men there" (pointing to Peterkin and me) "will look after your people."

"Thank you," said the teacher, as he followed Jack to the cabin; "I do not drink wine or any strong drink."

"Oh! then there's lots of water, and you can have biscuit."

"Now, 'pon my word, that's cool," said Peterkin; "his *men*, forsooth! Well, since we are to be men, we may as well come it as strong over these black chaps as we can. Hallo, there!" he cried to the half-dozen of natives who stood upon the deck, gazing in wonder at all they saw, "here's for you;" and he handed them a tray of broken biscuit and a can of water. Then, thrusting his hands into his pockets, he walked up and down the deck with an enormous swagger, whistling vociferously.

In about half an hour Jack and the teacher came on deck, and the latter, bidding us a cheerful good-evening, entered his canoe and paddled to the shore. When he was gone, Peterkin stepped up to Jack, and touching his cap, said—

"Well, captain, have you any communications to make to your *men*?"

"Yes," cried Jack; "ready about, mind the helm and clew up your tongue, while I con the schooner through the passage in the reef. The teacher, who seems a first-rate fellow, says it's quite deep, and good anchorage within the lagoon close to the shore."

While the vessel was slowly advancing to her anchorage under a light breeze, Jack explained to us that Avatea was still on the island, living amongst the heathens; that she had expressed a strong desire to join the Christians, but Tararo would not let her, and kept her constantly in close confinement.

"Moreover," continued Jack, "I find that she belongs to one of the Samoan Islands, where Christianity had been introduced long before her capture by the heathens of a neighbouring island; and the very day after she was taken, she was to have joined the church which had been planted there by that excellent body the London Missionary Society. The teacher tells me, too, that the poor girl has fallen in love with a Christian chief, who lives on an island some fifty miles or so to the south of this one, and that she is meditating a desperate attempt at escape. So, you see, we have come in the nick of time. I fancy that this chief is the fellow whom you heard of, Ralph, at the island of Emo. Besides all this, the heathen savages are at war among themselves, and there's to be a battle fought the day after tomorrow, in which the principal leader is Tararo; so that we'll not be able to commence our negotiations with the rascally chief till the day after."

The village off which we anchored was beautifully situated at the head of a small bay, from the margin of which trees of every description peculiar to the tropics rose in the richest luxuriance to the summit of a hilly ridge, which was the line of demarcation between the possessions of the Christians and those of the neighbouring heathen chief.

The site of the settlement was an extensive plot of flat land, stretching in a gentle slope from the sea to the mountain. The cottages stood several hundred yards from the beach, and were protected from the glare of the sea by the rich foliage of rows of large Barringtonia and other trees which girt the shore. The village was about a mile in length, and perfectly straight, with a wide road down the middle, on either side of which were rows of the tufted-top ti tree, whose delicate and beautiful blossoms, hanging beneath their plume-crested tops, added richness to the scene. The cottages of the natives were built beneath these trees, and were kept in the most excellent order, each having a little garden in front, tastefully laid out and planted, while the walks were covered with black and white pebbles.

Every house had doors and Venetian windows, painted partly with lamp black made from the candle-nut, and partly with red ochre, which contrasted powerfully with the dazzling coral line that covered the walls. On a prominent position stood a handsome church, which was quite a curiosity in its way. It was a hundred feet long by fifty broad, and was seated throughout to accommodate upwards of two thousand persons. It had six large folding-doors, and twelve windows with Venetian blinds; and although a large and substantial edifice, it had been built, we were told by the teacher, in the space of two months! There was not a single iron nail in the fabric, and the natives had constructed it chiefly with their stone and bone axes and other tools, having only one or two axes or tools of European manufacture. Everything around this beautiful spot wore an aspect of peace and plenty; and as we dropped our anchor within a stone's-cast of the substantial coral wharf, I could not avoid contrasting it with the wretched village of Emo, where I had witnessed so many frightful scenes. When the teacher afterwards told me that the people of this tribe had become converts only a year previous to our arrival, and that they had been living before that in the practice of the most bloody system of idolatry, I could not refrain from exclaiming, "What a convincing proof that Christianity is of God!"

On landing from our little boat, we were received with a warm welcome by the teacher and his wife; the latter being also a native, clothed in a simple European gown and straw bonnet. The shore was lined with hundreds of natives, whose persons were all more or less clothed with native cloth. Some of the men had on a kind of poncho formed of this cloth, their legs being uncovered; others wore clumsily fashioned trousers, and no upper garment except hats made of straw and cloth. Many of the dresses both of women and men, were grotesque enough, being very bad imitations of the European garb; but all wore a dress of some sort or other. They seemed very glad to see us, and crowded round us as the teacher led the way to his dwelling, where we were entertained, in the most sumptuous manner, on baked pig and all the varieties of fruits and vegetables that the island produced. We were much annoyed, however, by the rats: they seemed to run about the house like domestic animals. As we sat at table, one of them peeped up at us over the edge of the cloth, close to Peterkin's elbow, who floored it with a blow on the snout from his knife, exclaiming as he did so—

"I say, Mister Teacher, why don't you set traps for these brutes? Surely you are not fond of them!"

"No," replied the teacher, with a smile! "we would be glad to get rid of them if we could; but if we were to trap all the rats on the island, it would occupy our whole time."

"Are they, then, so numerous?" inquired Jack.

"They swarm everywhere. The poor heathens on the north side eat them, and think them very sweet. So did my people formerly; but they do not eat so many now, because the missionary who was last here expressed disgust at it. The poor people asked if it was wrong to eat rats; and he told them that it was certainly not wrong, but that the people of England would be much disgusted were they asked to eat rats."

We had not been an hour in the house of this kindhearted man when we were convinced of the truth of his statement as to their numbers; for the rats ran about the floors in dozens, and during our meal two men were stationed at the table to keep them off!

"What a pity you have no cats!" said Peterkin, as he aimed a blow at another reckless intruder, and missed it.

"We would indeed be glad to have a few," rejoined the teacher, "but they are difficult to be got. The hogs, we find, are very good rat-killers, but they do not seem to be able to keep the numbers down. I have heard that they are better than cats."

As the teacher said this, his good-natured black face was wrinkled with a smile of merriment. Observing that I had noticed it, he said:

"I smiled just now when I remembered the fate of the first cat that was taken to Rarotonga. This is one of the stations of the London Missionary Society. It, like our own, is infested with rats, and a cat was brought at last to the island. It was a large black one. On being turned loose, instead of being content to stay among men, the cat took to the mountains, and lived in a wild state, sometimes paying visits during the night to the houses of the natives; some of whom, living at a distance from the settlement, had not heard of the cat's arrival, and were dreadfully frightened in consequence, calling it a 'monster of the deep', and flying in terror away from it. One night the cat—feeling a desire for company, I suppose—took its way to the house of a chief who had recently been converted to Christianity, and had begun to learn to read and pray. The chief's wife, who was sitting awake at his side while he slept, beheld with horror two fires glistening in the doorway, and heard with surprise a mysterious voice. Almost petrified with fear, she awoke her husband, and began to upbraid him for forsaking his old religion and burning his god, who, she declared was now come to be avenged on them. 'Get up and pray! get up and pray!' she cried. The chief arose, and on opening his eyes beheld the same glaring lights and heard the same ominous sound. Impelled by the extreme urgency of the case, he commenced, with all possible vehemence, to vociferate the alphabet, as a prayer to God to deliver them from the vengeance of Satan! On hearing this, the cat, as much alarmed as themselves, fled precipitately away, leaving the chief and his wife congratulating themselves on the efficacy of their prayer."

We were much diverted with this anecdote, which the teacher related in English so good that we certainly could not have supposed him a native but for the colour of his face and the foreign accent in his tone. Next day we walked out with this interesting man, and were much entertained and instructed by his conversations, as we rambled through the cool shady groves of bananas, citrons, limes, and other trees, or sauntered among the cottages of the natives, and watched them while they laboured diligently in the taro beds or manufactured the tapa or native cloth. To some of these Jack put questions through the medium of the missionary; and the replies were such as to surprise us at the extent of their knowledge. Indeed, Peterkin very truly remarked that "they seemed to know a considerable deal more than Jack himself"!

"Have the missionaries many stations in these seas?" inquired Jack.

"Oh yes. The London Missionary Society have a great many in the Tahiti group, and other islands in that quarter. Then the Wesleyans have the Feejee Islands all to themselves, and the Americans have many stations in other groups."

On returning towards the village, about noon, we remarked on the beautiful whiteness of the cottages.

"That is owing to the lime with which they are plastered," said the teacher. "I set the Christian natives to work to build cottages for themselves, and also this handsome church which you see. When the framework and other parts of the houses were up, I sent the people to fetch coral from the sea. They brought immense quantities. Then I made them cut wood, and piling the coral above it, set it on fire.

"'Look! look!' cried the poor people in amazement; 'what wonderful people the Christians are! He is roasting stones. We shall not need taro or bread-fruit any more; we may eat stones!'

"But their surprise was still greater when the coral was reduced to a fine soft white powder. They immediately set up a great shout, and mingling the lime with water, rubbed their faces and their bodies all over with it, and ran through the village screaming with delight. They were also much surprised at another thing they saw me do. I wished to make some household furniture, and constructed a turning-lathe to assist me. The first thing I turned was the leg of a sofa; which was no sooner finished than the chief seized it with wonder and delight and ran through the village exhibiting it to the people, who looked upon it with great admiration. The chief then, tying a string to it, hung it round his neck as an ornament! He afterwards told me that if he had seen it before he became a Christian, he would have made it his god!"

As the teacher concluded this anecdote we reached his door. Saying that he had business to attend to, he left us to amuse ourselves as we best could.

"Now, lads," said Jack, turning abruptly towards us, and buttoning up his jacket as he spoke, "I'm off to see the battle. I've no particular fondness for seein' bloodshed, but I must find out the nature o' these fellows and see their customs with my own eyes, so that I may be able to speak of it again, if need be, authoritatively. It's only six miles off, and we don't run much more risk than that of getting a rap with a stray stone or an overshot arrow. Will you go?"

"To be sure we will," said Peterkin.

"If they chance to see us we'll cut and run for it," added Jack.

"Dear me!" cried Peterkin—"*you* run! I thought you would scorn to run from anyone."

"So I would, if it were my duty to fight," returned Jack coolly; "but as I don't want to fight, and don't intend to fight, if they offer to attack us I'll run away like the veriest coward that ever went by the name of Peterkin. So come along."

Chapter 29

We had ascertained from the teacher the direction to the spot on which the battle was to be fought, and after a walk of two hours reached it. The summit of a bare hill was the place chosen; for, unlike most of the other islanders, who are addicted to bush-fighting, those of Mango are in the habit of meeting on open ground. We arrived before the two parties had commenced the deadly struggle, and creeping as close up as we dared among the rocks, we lay and watched them.

The combatants were drawn up face to face, each side ranged in rank four deep. Those in the first row were armed with long spears; the second with clubs to defend the spearmen; the third row was composed of young men with slings; and the fourth consisted of women, who carried baskets of stones for the slingers, and clubs and spears with which to supply the warriors. Soon after we arrived the attack was made with great fury. There was no science displayed. The two bodies of savages rushed headlong upon each other and engaged in a general mêlée, and a more dreadful set of men I have never seen. They wore grotesque war-caps made of various substances and decorated with feathers. Their faces and bodies were painted so as to make them look as frightful as possible; and as they brandished their massive clubs, leaped, shouted, yelled, and dashed each other to the ground, I thought I had never seen men look so like demons before.

We were much surprised at the conduct of the women, who seemed to be perfect furies, and hung about the heels of their husbands in order to defend them. One stout young woman we saw whose husband was hard pressed and about to be overcome: she lifted a large stone, and throwing it at his opponent's head, felled him to the earth. But the battle did not last long. The band most distant from us gave way and were routed, leaving eighteen of their comrades dead upon the field. These the victors brained as they lay; and putting some of their brains on leaves went off with them, we were afterwards informed, to their temples, to present them to their gods as an earnest of the human victims who were soon to be brought there.

We hastened back to the Christian village with feelings of the deepest sadness at the sanguinary conflict which we had just witnessed.

Next day, after breakfasting with our friend the teacher, we made preparations for carrying out our plan. At first the teacher endeavoured to dissuade us.

"You do not know," said he, turning to Jack, "the danger you run in venturing amongst these ferocious savages. I feel much pity for poor Avatea; but you are not likely to succeed in saving her, and you may die in the attempt."

"Well," said Jack quietly, "I am not afraid to die in a good cause."

The teacher smiled approvingly at him as he said this, and after a little further conversation agreed to accompany us as interpreter, saying that, although Tararo was unfriendly to him, he had hitherto treated him with respect.

We now went on board the schooner, having resolved to sail round the island and drop anchor opposite the heathen village. We manned her with natives, and hoped to overawe the savages by displaying our brass gun to advantage. The teacher soon after came on board, and setting our sails we put to sea. In two hours more we made the cliffs reverberate with the crash of the big gun, which we fired by way of salute, while we ran the British ensign up to the peak and cast anchor. The commotion on shore showed us that we had struck terror into the hearts of the natives, but seeing that we did not offer to molest them, a canoe at length put off and paddled cautiously towards us. The teacher showed himself, and explaining that we were friends and wished to palaver with the chief, desired the native to go and tell him to come on board.

We waited long and with much impatience for an answer. During this time the native teacher conversed with us again, and told us many things concerning the success of the gospel among those islands; and perceiving that we were by no means so much gratified as we ought to have been at the hearing of such good news, he pressed us more closely in regard to our personal interest in religion, and exhorted us to consider that our souls were certainly in as great danger as those of the wretched heathen whom we pitied so much, if we had not already found salvation in Jesus Christ. "Nay, further," he added, "if such be your unhappy case, you are in the sight of God, much worse than these savages (forgive me, my young friends, for saying so): for they have no knowledge, no light, and do not profess to believe; while you, on the contrary, have been brought up in the light of the blessed gospel, and call yourselves Christians. These poor savages are indeed the enemies of our Lord; but you, if ye be not true believers, are traitors!"

I must confess that my heart condemned me while the teacher spoke in this earnest manner, and I knew not what to reply. Peterkin, too, did not seem to like it, and I thought would willingly have escaped; but Jack seemed deeply impressed, and wore an anxious expression on his naturally grave countenance, while he assented to the teacher's remarks and put to him many earnest questions. Meanwhile the natives who composed our crew, having nothing particular to do, had squatted down on the deck and taken out their little books containing the translated portions of the New Testament, along with hymns and spelling-books, and were now busily engaged, some vociferating the alphabet, others learning prayers off by heart, while a few sang hymns—all of them being utterly unmindful of our presence. The teacher soon joined them, and soon afterwards they all engaged in a prayer which was afterwards translated to us, and proved to be a petition for the success of our undertaking and for the conversion of the heathen.

While we were thus engaged a canoe put off from shore and several savages leaped on deck, one of whom advanced to the teacher and informed him that Tararo could not come on board that day, being busy with some religious ceremonies before the gods, which could on no account be postponed. He was also engaged with a friendly chief who was about to take his departure from the island, and therefore begged that the teacher and his friends would land and pay a visit to him. To this the teacher returned answer that we would land immediately.

"Now, lads," said Jack, as we were about to step into our little boat, "I'm not going to take any weapons with me, and I recommend you to take none either. We are altogether in the power of these savages, and the utmost we could do, if they were to attack us, would be to kill a few of them before we were ourselves overpowered. I think that our only chance of success lies in mild measures; don't you think so?"

To this I assented gladly, and Peterkin replied by laying down a huge bell-mouthed blunderbuss, and divesting himself of a pair of enormous horse-pistols with which he had purposed to overawe the natives! We then jumped into our boat and rowed ashore.

On reaching the beach we were received by a crowd of naked savages, who shouted a rude welcome, and conducted us to a house or shed where a baked pig and a variety of vegetables were prepared for us. Having partaken of these, the teacher begged to be conducted to the chief; but there seemed some hesitation, and after some consultation among themselves one of the men stood forward and spoke to the teacher.

"What says he?" inquired Jack when the savage had concluded.

"He says that the chief is just going to the temple of his god and cannot see us yet; so we must be patient, my friend."

"Well," cried Jack, rising, "if he won't come to see me, I'll e'en go and see him. Besides, I have a great desire to witness their proceedings at this temple of theirs. Will you go with me, friend?"

"I cannot," said the teacher, shaking his head; "I must not go to the heathen temples and witness their inhuman rites, except for the purpose of condemning their wickedness and folly."

"Very good," returned Jack; "then I'll go alone, for I cannot condemn their doings till I have seen them."

Jack arose, and we, having determined to go also, followed him through the banana groves to a rising ground immediately behind the village, on the top of which stood the Bure, or temple, under the dark shade of a group of iron-wood trees. As we went through the village, I was again led to contrast the rude huts and sheds and their almost naked, savage-looking inhabitants with the natives of the Christian village, who, to use the teacher's scriptural expression, were now "clothed and in their right mind".

As we turned into a broad path leading towards the hill, we were arrested by the shouts of an approaching multitude in the rear. Drawing aside into the bushes, we awaited their coming up, and as they drew near we observed that it was a procession of the natives, many of whom were dancing and gesticulating in the most frantic manner. They had an exceedingly hideous aspect, owing to the black, red, and yellow paints with which their faces and naked bodies were bedaubed. In the midst of these came a band of men carrying three or four planks, on which were seated in rows upwards of a dozen men. I shuddered involuntarily as I recollected the sacrifice of human victims at the island of Emo, and turned with a look of fear to Jack as I said—

"Oh Jack! I have a terrible dread that they are going to commit some of their cruel practices on these wretched men. We had better not go to the temple. We shall only be horrified without being able to do any good, for I fear they are going to kill them."

Jack's face wore an expression of deep compassion as he said in a low voice, "No fear, Ralph; the sufferings of these poor fellows are over long ago."

I turned with a start as he spoke, and glancing at the men who were now quite near to the spot where we stood, saw that they were all dead. They were tied firmly with ropes in a sitting posture on the planks, and seemed, as they bent their sightless eyeballs and grinning mouths over the dancing crew below, as if they were laughing in ghastly mockery at the utter inability of their enemies to hurt them now. These, we discovered afterwards, were the men who had been slain in the battle of the previous day, and were now on their way to be first presented to the gods and then eaten. Behind these came two men leading between them a third, whose hands were pinioned behind his back. He walked with a firm step, and wore a look of utter indifference on his face as they led him along; so that we concluded he must be a criminal who was about to receive some slight punishment for his faults. The rear of the procession was brought up by a shouting crowd of women and children, with whom we mingled and followed to the temple.

Here we arrived in a few minutes. The temple was a tall circular building, open at one side. Around it were strewn heaps of human bones and skulls. At a table inside sat the priest, an elderly man with a long grey beard. He was seated on a stool, and before him lay several knives, made of wood, bone, and splinters of bamboo, with which he performed his office of dissecting dead bodies. Farther in lay a variety of articles that had been dedicated to the god, and among them were many spears and clubs. I observed among the latter some with human teeth sticking in them, where the victims had been clubbed in their mouths.

Before this temple the bodies, which were painted with vermilion and soot, were arranged in a sitting posture; and a man, called a "dan-vosa" (orator), advanced, and laying his hands on their heads, began to chide them, apparently, in a low bantering tone. What he said we knew not, but as he went on he waxed warm, and at last shouted to them at the top of his lungs, and finally finished by kicking the bodies over and running away, amid the shouts and laughter of the people, who now rushed forward. Seizing the bodies by a leg or an arm, or by the hair of the head, they dragged them over stumps and stones and through sloughs, until they were exhausted. The bodies were then brought back to the temple and dissected by the priest, after which they were taken out to be baked.

Close to the temple a large fire was kindled, in which stones were heated red hot. When ready these were spread out on the ground, and a thick coating of leaves strewn over them to slack the heat. On this "lovo", or oven, the bodies were then placed, covered over, and left to bake.

The crowd now ran with terrible yells towards a neighbouring hill or mound, on which we observed the framework of a house lying ready to be erected. Sick with horror, yet fascinated by curiosity, we staggered after them mechanically, scarce knowing where we were going or what we did, and feeling a sort of impression that all we saw was a dreadful dream.

Arrived at the place, we saw the multitude crowding round a certain spot. We pressed forward and obtained a sight of what they were doing. A large wooden beam or post lay on the ground, beside the other parts of the framework of the house, and close to the end of it was a hole about seven feet deep and upwards of two feet wide. While we looked, the man whom we had before observed with his hands pinioned was carried into the circle. His hands were now free, but his legs were tightly strapped together. The post of the house was then placed in the hole, and the man put in beside it. His head was a good way below the surface of the hole, and his arms were clasped round the post. Earth was now thrown in until all was covered over and stamped down; and this, we were afterwards told, was a *ceremony* usually performed at the dedication of a new temple or the erection of a chief's house!

"Come, come," cried Jack, on beholding this horrible tragedy; "we have seen enough, enough—far more than enough! Let us go."

Jack's face looked ghastly pale and haggard as we hurried back to rejoin the teacher, and I have no doubt that he felt terrible anxiety when he considered the number and ferocity of the savages, and the weakness of the few arms which were ready indeed to essay, but impotent to effect, Avatea's deliverance from these ruthless men.

Chapter 30

When we returned to the shore and related to our friend what had passed, he was greatly distressed, and groaned in spirit; but we had not sat long in conversation, when we were interrupted by the arrival of Tararo on the beach, accompanied by a number of followers bearing baskets of vegetables and fruits on their heads.

We advanced to meet him, and he expressed, through our interpreter, much pleasure in seeing us.

"And what is it that my friends wish to say to me?" he inquired.

The teacher explained that we came to beg that Avatea might be spared.

"Tell him," said Jack, "that I consider that I have a right to ask this of him, having not only saved the girl's life, but the lives of his own people also; and say that I wish her to be allowed to follow her own wishes, and join the Christians."

While this was being translated, the chief's brow lowered, and we could see plainly that our request met with no favourable reception. He replied with considerable energy, and at some length.

"What says he?" inquired Jack.

"I regret to say that he will not listen to the proposal. He says he has pledged his word to his friend that the girl shall be sent to him, and a deputy is even now on this island awaiting the fulfilment of the pledge."

Jack bit his lip in suppressed anger. "Tell Tararo," he exclaimed, with flashing eye, "that if he does not grant my demand it will be worse for him. Say I have a big gun on board my schooner that will blow his village into the sea, if he does not give up the girl."

"Nay, my friend," said the teacher gently, "I will not tell him that; we must 'overcome evil with good'."

"What does my friend say?" inquired the chief, who seemed nettled by Jack's look of defiance.

"He is displeased," replied the teacher.

Tararo turned away with a smile of contempt, and walked towards the men who carried the baskets of vegetables, and who had now emptied the whole on the beach in an enormous pile.

"What are they doing there?" I inquired.

"I think that they are laying out a gift which they intend to present to some one," said the teacher.

At this moment a couple of men appeared leading a young girl between them, and going towards the heap of fruits and vegetables, placed her on the top of it. We started with surprise and fear, for in the young female before us we recognized the Samoan girl Avatea.

We stood rooted to the earth with surprise and thick-coming fears.

"Oh my dear young friend," whispered the teacher, in a voice of deep emotion, while he seized Jack by the arm, "she is to be made a sacrifice even now!"

"Is she?" cried Jack, with a vehement shout, spurning the teacher aside, and dashing over two natives who stood in his way, while he rushed towards the heap, sprang up its side, and seized Avatea by the arm. In another moment he dragged her down, placed her back to a large tree, and wrenching a war-club from the hand of a native who seemed powerless and petrified with surprise, whirled it above his head, and yelled, rather than shouted, while his face blazed with fury, "Come on, the whole nation of you, an ye like it, and do your worst!"

It seemed as though the challenge had been literally accepted; for every savage on the ground ran precipitately at Jack with club and spear, and doubtless would speedily have poured out his brave blood on the sod, had not the teacher rushed in between them, and, raising his voice to its utmost, cried—

"Stay your hands, warriors. It is not your part to judge in this matter. It is for Tararo, the chief, to say whether or not the young man shall live or die."

The natives were arrested; and I know not whether it was the gratifying acknowledgement of his superiority thus made by the teacher, or some lingering feeling of gratitude for Jack's former aid in time of need, that influenced Tararo, but he stepped forward, and waving his hand, said to his people, "Desist. The young man's life is mine." Then turning to Jack, he said, "You have forfeited your liberty and life to me. Submit yourself, for we are more numerous than the sand upon the shore. You are but one; why should you die?"

"Villain!" exclaimed Jack passionately, "I may die, but assuredly I shall not perish alone. I will not submit until you promise that this girl shall not be injured."

"You are very bold," replied the chief haughtily, "but very foolish. Yet I will say that Avatea shall not be sent away, at least for three days."

"You had better accept these terms," whispered the teacher entreatingly. "If you persist in this mad defiance, you will be slain, and Avatea will be lost. Three days are worth having."

Jack hesitated a moment, then lowered his club, and throwing it moodily to the ground, crossed his arms on his breast and hung down his head in silence.

Tararo seemed pleased by his submission, and told the teacher to say that he did not forget his former services, and therefore would leave him free as to his person, but that the schooner would be detained till he had further considered the matter.

While the teacher translated this, he approached as near to where Avatea was standing as possible, without creating suspicion, and whispered to her a few words in the native language. Avatea, who during the whole of the foregoing scene had stood leaning against the tree perfectly passive, and seemingly quite uninterested in all that was going on, replied by a single rapid glance of her dark eye, which was instantly cast down again on the ground at her feet.

Tararo now advanced, and taking the girl by the hand, led her unresistingly away; while Jack, Peterkin, and I returned with the teacher on board the schooner.

On reaching the deck, we went down to the cabin, where Jack threw himself, in a state of great dejection, on a couch; but the teacher seated himself by his side, and laying his hand upon his shoulder, said—

"Do not give way to anger, my young friend. God has given us three days, and we must use the means that are in our power to free this poor girl from slavery. We must not sit in idle disappointment, we must act——"

"Act!" cried Jack, raising himself and tossing back his hair wildly; "it is mockery to talk of acting when one is bound hand and foot. How can I act? I cannot fight a whole nation of savages single-handed. Yes," he said, with a bitter smile, "I *can* fight them, but I cannot conquer them or save Avatea."

"Patience, my friend; your spirit is not a good one just now. You cannot expect that blessing which alone can insure success unless you are more submissive. I will tell you my plans if you will listen."

"Listen!" cried Jack eagerly; "of course I will, my good fellow. I did not know you had any plans. Out with them. I only hope you will show me how I can get the girl on board of this schooner, and I'd up anchor and away in no time. But proceed with your plans."

The teacher smiled sadly. "Ah, my friend! if one fathom of your anchor chain were to rattle as you drew it in, a thousand warriors would be standing on your deck. No, no, that could not be done. Even now your ship would be taken from you were it not that Tararo has some feeling of gratitude toward you. But I know Tararo well. He is a man of falsehood, as all the unconverted savages are. The chief to whom he has promised this girl is very powerful, and Tararo *must* fulfil his promise. He has told you that he would do nothing to the girl for three days; but that is because the party who are to take her away will not be ready to start for three days. Still, as he might have made you a prisoner during those three days, I say that God has given them to us."

"Well, but what do you propose to do?" said Jack impatiently.

"My plan involves much danger, but I see no other, and I think you have courage to brave it. It is this. There is an island about fifty miles to the south of this, the natives of which are Christians, and have been so for two years or more, and the principal chief is Avatea's lover. Once there, Avatea would be safe. Now, I suggest that you should abandon your schooner. Do you think that you can make so great a sacrifice?"

"Friend," replied Jack, "when I make up my mind to go through with a thing of importance, I can make any sacrifice."

The teacher smiled. "Well, then, the savages could not conceive it possible that for the sake of a girl you would voluntarily lose your fine vessel; therefore as long as she lies here they think they have you all safe: so I suggest that we get a quantity of stores conveyed to a sequestered part of the shore, provide a small canoe, put Avatea on board, and you three would paddle to the Christian island."

"Bravo!" cried Peterkin, springing up and seizing the teacher's hand. "Missionary, you're a regular brick. I didn't think you had so much in you."

"As for me," continued the teacher, "I will remain on board till they discover that you are gone. Then they will ask me where you are gone to, and I will refuse to tell."

"And what'll be the result of that?" inquired Jack.

"I know not. Perhaps they will kill me; but," he added, looking at Jack with a peculiar smile, "I, too, am not afraid to die in a good cause!"

"But how are we to get hold of Avatea?" inquired Jack.

"I have arranged with her to meet us at a particular spot, to which I will guide you tonight. We shall then arrange about it. She will easily manage to elude her keepers, who are not very strict in watching her, thinking it impossible that she could escape from the island. Indeed, I am sure such an idea will never enter their heads. But, as I said, you run great danger. Fifty miles in a small canoe, on the open sea, is a great voyage to make. You may miss the island, too, in which case there is no other in that direction for a hundred miles or more: and if you lose your way and fall among other heathens, you know the law of Feejee—a castaway who gains the shore is doomed to die. You must count the cost, my young friend."

"I have counted it," replied Jack. "If Avatea consents to run the risk, most certainly I will; and so will my comrades also. Besides," added Jack, looking seriously into the teacher's face, "your Bible— *our* Bible—tells of ONE who delivers those who call on Him in the time of trouble; who holds the winds in His fists, and the waters in the hollow of His hand."

We now set about active preparations for the intended voyage; collected together such things as we should require, and laid out on the deck provisions sufficient to maintain us for several weeks, purposing to load the canoe with as much as she could hold consistently with speed and safety. These we covered with a tarpaulin, intending to convey them to the canoe only a few hours before starting. When night spread her sable curtain over the scene, we prepared to land; but first kneeling along with the natives and the teacher, the latter implored a blessing on our enterprise. Then we rowed quietly to the shore and followed our sable guide, who led us by a long detour, in order to avoid the village, to the place of rendezvous. We had not stood more than five minutes under the gloomy shade of the thick foliage when a dark figure glided noiselessly up to us.

"Ah! here you are," said Jack, as Avatea approached. "Now, then, tell her what we've come about, and don't waste time."

"I understan' leetl English," said Avatea, in a low voice.

"Why, where did you pick up English?" exclaimed Jack, in amazement; "you were dumb as a stone when I saw you last."

"She has learned all she knows of it from me," said the teacher, "since she came to the island."

We now gave Avatea a full explanation of our plans, entering into all the details, and concealing none of the danger, so that she might be fully aware of the risk she ran. As we had anticipated, she was too glad of the opportunity thus afforded her to escape from her persecutors to think of the danger or risk.

"Then you're willing to go with us, are you!" said Jack.

"Yis, I willing to go."

"And you're not afraid to trust yourself on the deep sea so far?"

"No, I not 'fraid to go. Safe with Christian."

After some further consultation the teacher suggested that it was time to return, so we bade Avatea good night, and having appointed to meet at the cliff where the canoe lay on the following night, just after dark, we hastened away—we to row on board the schooner with muffled oars, Avatea to glide back to her prison-hut among the Mango savages.

Chapter 31

As the time for our meditated flight drew near, we became naturally very fearful lest our purpose should be discovered, and we spent the whole of the following day in a state of nervous anxiety. We resolved to go ashore and ramble about the village, as if to observe the habits and dwellings of the people, as we thought that an air of affected indifference to the events of the previous day would be more likely than any other course of conduct to avert suspicion as to our intentions. While we were thus occupied, the teacher remained on board with the Christian natives, whose powerful voices reached us ever and anon as they engaged in singing hymns or in prayer.

At last the long and tedious day came to a close, the sun sank into the sea, and the short-lived twilight of those regions, to which I have already referred, ended abruptly in a dark night. Hastily throwing a few blankets into our little boat, we stepped into it, and whispering farewell to the natives in the schooner, rowed gently over the lagoon, taking care to keep as near to the beach as possible. We rowed in the utmost silence and with muffled oars, so that had anyone observed us at the distance of a few yards, he might have almost taken us for a phantom-boat or a shadow on the dark water. Not a breath of air was stirring; but fortunately the gentle ripple of the sea upon the shore, mingled with the soft roar of the breaker on the distant reef, effectually drowned the slight plash that we unavoidably made in the water by the dipping of our oars.

Quarter of an hour sufficed to bring us to the overhanging cliff under whose black shadow our little canoe lay, with her bow in the water ready to be launched, and most of her cargo already stowed away. As the keel of our little boat grated on the sand, a hand was laid upon the bow, and a dim form was seen.

"Ha!" said Peterkin, in a whisper, as he stepped upon the beach, "is that you, Avatea?"

"Yis, it am me," was the reply.

"All right! Now, then, gently. Help me to shove off the canoe," whispered Jack to the teacher; "and, Peterkin, do you shove these blankets aboard—we may want them before long. Avatea, step into the middle;—that's right."

"Is all ready?" whispered the teacher.

"Not quite," replied Peterkin. "Here, Ralph, lay hold o' this pair of oars, and stow them away if you can. I don't like paddles. After we're safe away I'll try to rig up rollocks for them."

"Now, then, in with you and shove off."

One more earnest squeeze of the kind teacher's hand, and with his whispered blessing yet sounding in our ears, we shot like an arrow from the shore, sped over the still waters of the lagoon, and paddled as swiftly as strong arms and willing hearts could urge us over the long swell of the open sea.

All that night and the whole of the following day we plied our paddles in almost total silence and without halt, save twice to recruit our failing energies with a mouthful of food and a draught of water. Jack had taken the bearing of the island just after starting, and laying a small pocket-compass before him, kept the head of the canoe due south, for our chance of hitting the island depended very much on the faithfulness of our steersman in keeping our tiny bark exactly and constantly on its proper course. Peterkin and I paddled in the bow, and Avatea worked untiringly in the middle.

As the sun's lower limb dipped on the gilded edge of the sea Jack ceased working, threw down his paddle, and called a halt.

"There!" he cried, heaving a deep, long-drawn sigh, "we've put a considerable breadth of water between us and these black rascals, so now we'll have a hearty supper and a sound sleep."

"Hear, hear!" cried Peterkin. "Nobly spoken, Jack. Hand me a drop of water, Ralph. Why, girl, what's wrong with you? you look just like a black owl blinking in the sunshine."

Avatea smiled. "I sleepy," she said; and as if to prove the truth of this, she laid her head on the edge of the canoe and fell fast asleep.

"That's uncommon sharp practice," said Peterkin, with a broad grin. "Don't you think we should awake her to make her eat something first? or perhaps," he added, with a grave, meditative look, "perhaps we might put some food in her mouth, which is so elegantly open at the present moment, and see if she'd swallow it while asleep. If so, Ralph, you might come round to the front here and feed her quietly, while Jack and I are tucking into the victuals. It would be a monstrous economy of time."

I could not help smiling at Peterkin's idea, which indeed, when I pondered it, seemed remarkably good in theory; nevertheless I declined to put it in practice, being fearful of the result should the victual chance to go down the wrong throat. But on suggesting this to Peterkin, he exclaimed—

"Down the wrong throat, man! why, a fellow with half an eye might see that if it went down Avatea's throat it could not go down the wrong throat!—unless, indeed, you have all of a sudden become inordinately selfish, and think that all the throats in the world are wrong ones except your own. However, don't talk so much, and hand me the pork before Jack finishes it. I feel myself entitled to at least one minute morsel."

"Peterkin, you're a villain—a paltry little villain," said Jack quietly, as he tossed the hind legs (including the tail) of a cold roast pig to his comrade; "and I must again express my regret that unavoidable circumstances hae thrust your society upon me, and that necessity has compelled me to cultivate your acquaintance. Were it not that you are incapable of walking upon the water, I would order you, sir, out of the canoe."

"There! you've wakened Avatea with your long tongue," retorted Peterkin, with a frown, as the girl gave vent to a deep sigh. "No," he continued, "it was only a snore. Perchance she dreameth of her black Apollo. I say, Ralph, do leave just one little slice of that yam. Between you and Jack I run a chance of being put on short allowance, if not—yei—a—a—ow!"

Peterkin's concluding remark was a yawn of so great energy that Jack recommended him to postpone the conclusion of his meal till next morning—a piece of advice which he followed so quickly that I was forcibly reminded of his remark, a few minutes before, in regard to the sharp practice of Avatea.

My readers will have observed, probably, by this time that I am much given to meditation; they will not, therefore, be surprised to learn that I fell into a deep reverie on the subject of sleep, which was continued without intermission into the night, and prolonged without interruption into the following morning. But I cannot feel assured that I actually slept during that time, although I am tolerably certain that I was not awake.

Thus we lay like a shadow on the still bosom of the ocean, while the night closed in, and all around was calm, dark, and silent.

A thrilling cry of alarm from Peterkin startled us in the morning, just as the grey dawn began to glimmer in the east.

"What's wrong?" cried Jack, starting up.

Peterkin replied by pointing with a look of anxious dread towards the horizon; and a glance sufficed to show us that one of the largest sized war-canoes was approaching us!

With a groan of mingled despair and anger Jack seized his paddle, glanced at the compass, and in a suppressed voice commanded us to "give way". But we did not require to be urged. Already our four paddles were glancing in the water, and the canoe bounded over the glassy sea like a dolphin, while a shout from our pursuers told that they had observed our motions.

"I see something like land ahead," said Jack, in a hopeful tone. "It seems impossible that we could have made the island yet; still, if it is so, we may reach it before these fellows can catch us, for our canoe is light and our muscles are fresh."

No one replied; for, to say truth, we felt that in a long chase we had no chance whatever with a canoe which held nearly a hundred warriors. Nevertheless, we resolved to do our utmost to escape, and paddled with a degree of vigour that kept us well in advance of our pursuers. The war-canoe was so far behind us that it seemed but a little speck on the sea, and the shouts, to which the crew occasionally gave vent, came faintly towards us on the morning breeze. We therefore hoped that we should be able to keep in advance for an hour or two, when we might perhaps reach the land ahead. But this hope was suddenly crushed by the supposed land not long after rising up into the sky, thus proving itself to be a fog-bank.

A bitter feeling of disappointment filled each heart, and was expressed on each countenance, as we beheld this termination to our hopes. But we had little time to think of regret. Our danger was too great and imminent to permit of a moment's relaxation from our exertions. No hope now animated our bosoms; but a feeling of despair, strange to say, lent us power to work, and nerved our arms with such energy that it was several hours ere the savages overtook us. When we saw that there was indeed no chance of escape, and that paddling any longer would only serve to exhaust our strength, without doing any good, we turned the side of our canoe towards the approaching enemy, and laid down our paddles.

Silently, and with a look of bitter determination on his face, Jack lifted one of the light boat-oars that we had brought with us, and resting it on his shoulder, stood up in an attitude of bold defiance. Peterkin took the other oar and also stood up, but there was no anger visible on his countenance. When not sparkling with fun, it usually wore a mild, sad expression, which was deepened on the present occasion, as he glanced at Avatea, who sat with her face resting in her hands upon her knees. Without knowing what I intended to do, I also arose and grasped my paddle with both hands.

On came the large canoe like a war-horse of the deep, with the foam curling from its sharp bow, and the spearheads of the savages glancing in the beams of the rising sun. Perfect silence was maintained on both sides, and we could hear the hissing water, and see the frowning eyes of the warriors, as they came rushing on. When about twenty yards distant, five or six of the savages in the bow rose, and, laying aside their paddles, took up their spears. Jack and Peterkin raised their oars, while, with a feeling of madness whirling in my brain, I grasped my paddle and prepared for the onset. But before any of us could strike a blow, the sharp prow of the war-canoe struck us like a thunder-bolt on the side, and hurled us into the sea!

What occurred after this I cannot tell, for I was nearly drowned; but when I recovered from the state of insensibility into which I had been thrown, I found myself stretched on my back, bound hand and foot between Jack and Peterkin, in the bottom of the large canoe.

In this condition we lay the whole day, during which time the savages only rested an hour. When night came, they rested again for another hour, and appeared to sleep just as they sat. But we were neither unbound nor allowed to speak to each other during the voyage, nor was a morsel of food or a draught of water given to us. For food, however, we cared little; but we would have given much for a drop of water to cool our parched lips, and we would have been glad, too, had they loosened the cords that bound us, for they were tightly fastened and occasioned us much pain. The air, also, was unusually hot, so much so that I felt convinced that a storm was brewing. This also added to our sufferings. However, they were at length relieved by our arrival at the island from which we had fled.

While we were being led ashore, we caught a glimpse of Avatea, who was seated in the hinder part of the canoe. She was not fettered in any way. Our captors now drove us before them towards the hut of Tararo, at which we speedily arrived, and found the chief seated with an expression on his face that boded us no good. Our friend the teacher stood beside him, with a look of anxiety on his mild features.

"How comes it," said Tararo, turning to the teacher, "that these youths have abused our hospitality?"

"Tell him," replied Jack, "that we have not abused his hospitality, for his hospitality has not been extended to us. I came to the island to deliver Avatea, and my only regret is that I have failed to do so. If I get another chance, I will try to save her yet."

The teacher shook his head. "Nay, my young friend, I had better not tell him that; it will only incense him."

"I care not," replied Jack. "If you don't tell him that, you'll tell him nothing, for I won't say anything softer."

On hearing Jack's speech, Tararo frowned and his eye flashed with anger.

"Go," he said, "presumptuous boy. My debt to you is cancelled. You and your companions shall die."

As he spoke he rose and signed to several of his attendants, who seized Jack and Peterkin and me violently by the collars, and dragging us from the hut of the chief, led us through the wood to the outskirts of the village. Here they thrust us into a species of natural cave in a cliff, and having barricaded the entrance, left us in total darkness.

After feeling about for some time—for our legs were unshackled, although our wrists were still bound with thongs—we found a low ledge of rock running along one side of the cavern. On this we seated ourselves, and for a long time maintained unbroken silence.

At last I could restrain my feelings no longer. "Alas! dear Jack and

Peterkin," said I, "what is to become of us? I fear that we are doomed to die."

"I know not," replied Jack, in a tremulous voice, "I know not. Ralph, I regret deeply the hastiness of my violent temper, which, I must confess, has been the chief cause of our being brought to this sad condition. Perhaps the teacher may do something for us. But I have little hope."

"Ah no!" said Peterkin, with a heavy sigh; "I am sure he can't help us. Tararo doesn't care more for him than for one of his dogs."

"Truly," said I, "there seems no chance of deliverance, unless the Almighty puts forth His arm to save us. Yet I must say that I have great hope, my comrades; for we have come to this dark place by no fault of ours—unless it be a fault to try to succour a woman in distress."

I was interrupted in my remarks by a noise at the entrance to the cavern, which was caused by the removal of the barricade. Immediately after, three men entered, and taking us by the collars of our coats, led us away through the forest. As we advanced, we heard much shouting and beating of native drums in the village, and at first we thought that our guards were conducting us to the hut of Tararo again. But in this we were mistaken. The beating of drums gradually increased, and soon after we observed a procession of the natives coming towards us. At the head of this procession we were placed, and then we all advanced together towards the temple where human victims were wont to be sacrificed!

A thrill of horror ran through my heart as I recalled to mind the awful scenes that I had before witnessed at that dreadful spot. But deliverance came suddenly from a quarter whence we little expected it. During the whole of that day there had been an unusual degree of heat in the atmosphere, and the sky assumed that lurid aspect which portends a thunderstorm. Just as we were approaching the horrid temple, a growl of thunder burst overhead and heavy drops of rain began to fall.

Those who have not witnessed gales and storms in tropical regions can form but a faint conception of the fearful hurricane that burst upon the island of Mango at this time. Before we reached the temple, the storm burst upon us with a deafening roar, and the natives, who knew too well the devastation that was to follow, fled right and left through the woods in order to save their property, leaving us alone in the midst of the howling storm. The trees around us bent before the blast like willows, and we were about to flee in order to seek shelter, when the teacher ran towards us with a knife in his hand.

"Thank the Lord," he said, cutting our bonds, "I am in time! Now, seek the shelter of the nearest rocks."

This we did without a moment's hesitation, for the whistling wind burst, ever and anon, like thunderclaps among the trees, and tearing them from their roots, hurled them with violence to the ground. Rain cut across the land in sheets, and lightning played like forked serpents in the air, while high above the roar of the hissing tempest the thunder crashed and burst and rolled in awful majesty.

In the village the scene was absolutely appalling. Roofs were blown completely off the houses in many cases; and in others the houses themselves were levelled with the ground. In the midst of this the natives were darting to and fro, in some instances saving their goods, but in many others seeking to save themselves from the storm of destruction that whirled around them. But terrific although the tempest was on land, it was still more tremendous on the mighty ocean. Billows sprang, as it were, from the great deep, and while their crests were absolutely scattered into white mist, they fell upon the beach with a crash that seemed to shake the solid land. But they did not end there. Each successive wave swept higher and higher on the beach, until the ocean lashed its angry waters among the trees and bushes, and at length, in a sheet of white curdled foam, swept into the village and upset and carried off, or dashed into wreck, whole rows of the native dwellings! It was a sublime, an awful scene, calculated, in some degree at least, to impress the mind of beholders with the might and the majesty of God.

We found shelter in a cave that night and all the next day, during which time the storm raged in fury; but on the night following it abated somewhat, and in the morning we went to the village to seek for food, being so famished with hunger that we lost all feeling of danger and all wish to escape in our desire to satisfy the cravings of nature. But no sooner had we obtained food than we began to wish that we had rather endeavoured to make our escape into the mountains. This we attempted to do soon afterwards; but the natives were now able to look after us, and on our showing a disposition to avoid observation and make towards the mountains, we were seized by three warriors, who once more bound our wrists and thrust us into our former prison.

It is true Jack made a vigorous resistance, and knocked down, with a well-directed blow of his fist, the first savage who seized him, but he was speedily overpowered by others. Thus we were again prisoners, with the prospect of torture and a violent death before us.

Chapter 32

For a long, long month we remained in our dark and dreary prison, during which dismal time we did not see the face of a human being, except that of the silent savage who brought us our daily food.

There have been one or two seasons in my life during which I have felt as if the darkness of sorrow and desolation that crushed my inmost heart could never pass away until death should make me cease to feel. The present was such a season.

During the first part of our confinement we felt a cold chill at our hearts every time we heard a footfall near the cave—dreading lest it should prove to be that of our executioner. But as time dragged heavily on we ceased to feel this alarm, and began to experience such a deep, irrepressible longing for freedom, that we chafed and fretted in our confinement like tigers. Then a feeling of despair came over us, and we actually longed for the time when the savages would take us forth to die! But these changes took place very gradually, and were mingled sometimes with brighter thoughts; for there were times when we sat in that dark cavern on our ledge of rock and conversed almost pleasantly about the past, until we wellnigh forgot the dreary present. But we seldom ventured to touch upon the future.

A few decayed leaves and boughs formed our bed, and a scanty supply of yams and taro, brought to us once a day, constituted our food.

"Well, Ralph, how have you slept?" said Jack, in a listless tone, on rising one morning from his humble couch. "Were you much disturbed by the wind last night?"

"No," said I; "I dreamed of home all night, and I thought that my mother smiled upon me, and beckoned me to go to her; but I could not, for I was chained."

"And I dreamed, too," said Peterkin, "but it was of our happy home on the Coral Island. I thought we were swimming in the Water Garden; then the savages gave a yell, and were immediately in the cave at Spouting Cliff, which, somehow or other, changed into this gloomy cavern; and I awoke to find it true."

Peterkin's tone was so much altered by the depressing influence of his long imprisonment, that, had I not known it was he who spoke, I should scarcely have recognized it, so sad was it, and so unlike to the merry, cheerful voice we had been accustomed to hear.

While I meditated thus, Peterkin again broke the silence of the cave, by saying, in a melancholy tone, "Oh, I wonder if we shall ever see our dear island more!"

His voice trembled, and covering his face with both hands he bent down his head and wept. It was an unusual sight for me to see our once joyous companion in tears, and I felt a burning desire to comfort him; but, alas! what could I say? I could hold out no hope; and although I essayed twice to speak, the words refused to pass my lips. While I hesitated, Jack sat down beside him, and whispered a few words in his ear; while Peterkin threw himself on his friend's breast, and rested his head on his shoulder.

Thus we sat for some time in deep silence. Soon after, we heard footsteps at the entrance of the cave, and immediately our jailer entered. We were so much accustomed to his regular visits, however, that we paid little attention to him, expecting that he would set down our meagre fare, as usual, and depart. But to our surprise, instead of doing so, he advanced towards us with a knife in his hand, and going up to Jack, he cut the thongs that bound his wrists, then he did the same to Peterkin and me! For fully five minutes we stood in speechless amazement, with our freed hands hanging idly by our sides. The first thought that rushed into my mind was, that the time had come to put us to death; and although, as I have said before, we actually wished for death in the strength of our despair, now that we thought it drew really near I felt all the natural love of life revive in my heart, mingled with a chill of horror at the suddenness of our call.

But I was mistaken. After cutting our bonds, the savage pointed to the cave's mouth, and we marched, almost mechanically, into the open air. Here, to our surprise, we found the teacher, standing under a tree, with his hands clasped before him, and the tears trickling down his dark cheeks. On seeing Jack, who came out first, he sprang towards him, and, clasping him in his arms, exclaimed—

"Oh my dear young friend, through the great goodness of God you are free!"

"Free!" cried Jack.

"Ay, free," repeated the teacher, shaking us warmly by the hands again and again—"free to go and come as you will. The Lord has unloosed the bands of the captive and set the prisoners free. A missionary has been sent to us, and Tararo has embraced the Christian religion! The people are even now burning their gods of wood! Come, my dear friends, and see the glorious sight."

We could scarcely credit our senses. So long had we been accustomed in our cavern to dream of deliverance, that we imagined for a moment this must surely be nothing more than another vivid dream. Our eyes and minds were dazzled, too, by the brilliant sunshine, which almost blinded us after our long confinement to the gloom of our prison, so that we felt giddy with the variety of conflicting emotions that filled our throbbing bosoms; but as we followed the footsteps of our sable friend, and beheld the bright foliage of the trees, and heard the cries of the paroquets, and smelt the rich perfume of the flowering shrubs, the truth that we were really delivered from prison and from death, rushed with overwhelming power into our souls, and with one accord, while tears sprang to our eyes, we uttered a loud long cheer of joy.

It was replied to by a shout from a number of the natives who chanced to be near. Running towards us, they shook us by the hand with every demonstration of kindly feeling. They then fell behind, and, forming a sort of procession, conducted us to the dwelling of Tararo.

The scene that met our eyes here was one that I shall never forget. On a rude bench in front of his house sat the chief. A native stood on his left hand who from his dress seemed to be a teacher. On his right stood an English gentleman, who I at once and rightly concluded was a missionary. He was tall, thin, and apparently past forty, with a bald forehead and thin grey hair. The expression of his countenance was the most winning I ever saw, and his clear grey eyes beamed with a look that was frank, fearless, loving, and truthful. In front of the chief was an open space, in the centre of which lay a pile of wooden idols, ready to be set on fire; and around these were assembled thousands of natives, who had come to join in or to witness the unusual sight. A bright smile overspread the missionary's face as he advanced quickly to meet us, and he shook us warmly by the hand.

"I am overjoyed to meet you, my dear young friends," he said. "My friend and *your* friend, the teacher, has told me your history; and I thank our Father in heaven, with all my heart, that He has guided me to this island, and made me the instrument of saving you."

We thanked the missionary most heartily, and asked him in some surprise how he had succeeded in turning the heart of Tararo in our favour.

"I will tell you that at a more convenient time," he answered; "meanwhile we must not forget the respect due to the chief. He waits to receive you."

In the conversation that immediately followed between us and Tararo, the latter said that the light of the gospel of Jesus Christ had been sent to the island, and that to it we were indebted for our freedom. Moreover, he told us that we were at liberty to depart in our schooner whenever we pleased, and that we should be supplied with as much provisions as we required. He concluded by shaking hands with us warmly, and performing the ceremony of rubbing noses.

This was indeed good news to us, and we could hardly find words to express our gratitude to the chief and to the missionary.

"And what of Avatea?" inquired Jack.

The missionary replied by pointing to a group of natives in the midst of whom the girl stood. Beside her was a tall, strapping fellow, whose noble mien and air of superiority bespoke him a chief of no ordinary kind.

"That youth is her lover. He came this very morning in his war-canoe to treat with Tararo for Avatea. He is to be married in a few days, and afterwards returns to his island home with his bride."

"That's capital," said Jack, as he stepped up to the savage and gave him a hearty shake of the hand. "I wish you joy, my lad; and you too, Avatea."

As Jack spoke, Avatea's lover took him by the hand and led him to the spot where Tararo and the missionary stood, surrounded by most of the chief men of the tribe. The girl herself followed, and stood on his left hand while her lover stood on his right, and, commanding silence, made the following speech, which was translated by the missionary:

"Young friend, you have seen few years, but your head is old. Your heart also is large and very brave. I and Avatea are your debtors, and we wish, in the midst of this assembly to acknowledge our debt, and to say that it is one which we can never repay. You have risked your life for one who was known to you only for a few days. But she was a woman in distress, and that was enough to secure to her the aid of a Christian man. We, who live in these islands of the sea, know that the true Christians always act thus. Their religion is one of love and kindness. We thank God that so many Christians have been sent here; we hope many more will come. Remember that I and Avatea will think of you and pray for you and your brave comrades when you are far away."

To this kind speech Jack returned a short, sailor-like reply, in which he insisted that he had only done for Avatea what he would have done for any woman under the sun. But Jack's forte did not lie in speech-making, so he terminated rather abruptly by seizing the chief's hand and shaking it violently, after which he made a hasty retreat.

"Now, then, Ralph and Peterkin," said Jack, as we mingled with the crowd, "it seems to me that the object we came here for having been satisfactorily accomplished, we have nothing more to do but get ready for sea as fast as we can, and hurrah for dear old England!"

"That's my idea precisely," said Peterkin, endeavouring to wink;

but he had wept so much of late, poor fellow, that he found it difficult. "However, I'm not going away till I've seen these fellows burn their gods."

Peterkin had his wish, for in a few minutes afterwards fire was put to the pile, the roaring flames ascended, and amid the acclamations of the assembled thousands the false gods of Mango were reduced to ashes!

Chapter 33

To part is the lot of all mankind. The world is a scene of constant leave-taking, and the hands that grasp in cordial greeting today are doomed ere long to unite for the last time, when the quivering lips pronounce the word—"Farewell". It is a sad thought, but should we on that account exclude it from our minds? May not a lesson worth learning be gathered in the contemplation of it? May it not, perchance, teach us to devote our thoughts more frequently and attentively to that land where we meet but part no more?

How many do we part from in this world with a light "Good-bye" whom we never see again! Often do I think, in my meditations on this subject, that if we realized more fully the shortness of the fleeting intercourse that we have in this world with many of our fellow men, we would try more earnestly to do them good, to give them a friendly smile, as it were, in passing (for the longest intercourse on earth is little more than a passing word and glance), and show that we have sympathy with them in the short, quick struggle of life, by our kindly words and looks and actions.

The time soon drew near when we were to quit the islands of the South Seas; and strange though it may appear, we felt deep regret at parting with the natives of the island of Mango: for after they embraced the Christian faith, they sought, by showing us the utmost kindness, to compensate for the harsh treatment we had experienced at their hands; and we felt a growing affection for the native teachers and the missionary, and especially for Avatea and her husband.

Before leaving we had many long and interesting conversations with the missionary, in one of which he told us that he had been making for the island of Rarotonga, when his native-built sloop was blown out of its course, during a violent gale, and driven to this island. At first the natives refused to listen to what he had to say; but after a week's residence among them, Tararo came to him and said that he wished to become a Christian, and would burn his idols. He proved himself to be sincere, for, as we have seen, he persuaded all his people to do likewise. I use the word persuaded advisedly; for, like all the other Feejee chiefs, Tararo was a despot, and might have commanded obedience to his wishes; but he entered so readily into the spirit of the new faith, that he perceived at once the impropriety of using constraint in the propagation of it. He set the example, therefore; and that example was followed by almost every man of the tribe.

During the short time that we remained at the island, repairing our vessel and getting her ready for sea, the natives had commenced building a large and commodious church, under the superintendence of the missionary, and several rows of new cottages were marked out; so that the place bid fair to become, in a few months, as prosperous and beautiful as the Christian village at the other end of the island.

After Avatea was married, she and her husband were sent away loaded with presents, chiefly of an edible nature. One of the native teachers went with them, for the purpose of visiting still more distant islands of the sea and spreading, if possible, the light of the glorious gospel there.

As the missionary intended to remain for several weeks longer, in order to encourage and confirm his new converts, Jack and Peterkin and I held a consultation in the cabin of our schooner—which we found just as we had left her, for everything that had been taken out of her was restored. We now resolved to delay our departure no longer. The desire to see our beloved native land was strong upon us, and we could not wait.

Three natives volunteered to go with us to Tahiti, where we thought it likely that we should be able to procure a sufficient crew of sailors to man our vessel; so we accepted their offer gladly.

It was a bright clear morning when we hoisted the snow-white sails of the pirate schooner and left the shores of Mango. The missionary and thousands of the natives came down to bid us God-speed, and to see us sail away. As the vessel bent before a light fair wind, we glided quickly over the lagoon under a cloud of canvas.

Just as we passed through the channel in the reef the natives gave us a loud cheer; and as the missionary waved his hat, while he stood on a coral rock with his grey hairs floating in the wind, we heard the single word "Farewell" borne faintly over the sea.

That night, as we sat on the taffrail gazing out upon the wide sea and up into the starry firmament, a thrill of joy, strangely mixed with sadness, passed through our hearts; for we were at length "homeward bound", and were gradually leaving far behind us the beautiful, bright green coral islands of the Pacific Ocean.